Copyright ©

Resurrection from T
Copyright (c) 2023 by Ian Britten-Hull

All rights reserved. This book or any portion thereof may not be reproduced or used in any manner whatsoever without the express written permission of the author Ian Britten-Hull, except for the use of brief quotations in a book review.

Cover Art - Annie Albici as Anne Bonny

# RESURRECTION

*The Buccaneers Legend
Trilogy - Book 1*

Ian Britten-Hull

*To Annie Albici who assisted with the editing
and by brining Anne Bonny to life on stage.
This book is also dedicated to Moneer Elmasseek
and Pippa Lea who created Jock McTavish and
Mary Read in the original stage production.*

## *About the Author*

Ian Britten-Hull was born in London in the early sixties but grew up in the north of England. Ian returned to London to study dramatic art at Middlesex University in the early 1980's. Whilst there, he trained to become an actor as well as studying stage management and theatre history. Upon graduating Ian worked as an actor for many theatre and TV companies, playing a wide range of parts from Shakespeare to Pantomime.

Throughout his career Ian has also directed many theatre shows; and devised shows of his own. During the pandemic lockdown, Ian along with his partner Annie Albici, conceived the idea of a show about pirates but, because of the restrictions, they made the original show as a one-hour video which they then streamed over the internet.

It was whilst making the video production that Ian became fascinated by the history of Anne Bonny, Mary Read and John Rackham. Researching the history and backgrounds of the three famous pirates, it became clear that the reasons people became pirates was more complex than one would imagine. A question that came to mind was, what if these three characters were alive today, how would their lives turn out with different opportunities, and would they be so different from the lives they led three-hundred years ago?

Having written so many plays for his own shows, Ian was compelled to try his hand at writing this trilogy, and thus the idea of The Buccaneers Legend novels.

## *Chapters*

Introduction – The Legend of the Pirates

Chapter 1 – Night of the Dead

Chapter 2 – Anne Bonny

Chapter 3 – Angus Jock McTavish

Chapter 4 – Calico Jack

Chapter 5 – Who Are We?

Chapter 6 – Mary Read

Chapter 7 – The Isle of Skye

Chapter 8 – The Battle of Culloden

Chapter 9 – Fare Thee Well

Chapter 10 – Prepare for Battle

Chapter 11 – Shore Leave

Chapter 12 – The Devil's Child

Chapter 13 – James Bonny

Chapter 14 – A New Dawn

Chapter 15 – When the Bough Breaks

Chapter 16 – Davy Jones

Chapter 17 – The Buccaneers

## Introduction

## **The Legends of the Pirates**

Mike Logan was a big fan of pirates. He had seen all the modern pirate movies, and his house was full of memorabilia that he had amassed from pirate fairs and conventions. When he wasn't attending pirate festivals, he spent his free time reading about them. It was on a bleak winter's evening, that Mike was sat in his favourite comfy chair reading a book about the legends of pirates. He was fascinated by the chapter on the legend of the Selkies or sea people, who were said to emerge from the sea, and after removing their cloaks, would take on human form. They would then hide their cloaks because if they were lost or stolen, the Selkies could never return to their home in the sea and would remain in human form forever. Then another chapter described the legend of Davy Jones' Locker. Mike was totally absorbed in the information given, as it described several beliefs among sailors relating to Davy Jones. Some believed only those sailors who drowned went there, while others believed the souls of all sailors travelled there after death.

The account also suggested that pirates believed that they would descend to the fiery pit of Davy Jones to atone for their sins in the afterlife. Being a big fan of pirates, like he was, Mike was not convinced by this assumption because he truly believed that although pirates were generally vicious murdering cutthroats, he also believed not all pirates were necessarily evil. He looked up from his book for a moment to reflect on what he thought pirates were really like. If they were nothing more than blood thirsty criminals, why had such a romantic vision of them been conjured up by so many people over the years? He understood that the idea of swashbuckling adventures and stories of treasure created a sense of excitement to anyone who considered them, but what were they really like? But of course, there was no way of ever finding out because the Golden Age of Piracy, when many of his heroes had lived, had been over, for nigh on three-hundred years. As his book rightly pointed out, the pirates of the 18th Century were now nothing more than legends. He fancied the idea of some pirates coming back to life so he could find out for himself just what they were really like. He smiled and then chuckled to himself at the idiocy of what he had just thought. Pirates returning from the dead was not something that was ever going to happen.

'I fancy a beer,' thought Mike.

He closed the book and placed it on the

table besides his chair and went to the fridge to get one. When he came back, he casually switched on the TV to catch up on news events of the day. As he sipped his beer, the troubles of the world spilled out of the screen on the wall and filled him with despair at all the reports of wars and innocent people, especially children, being killed. Then there were the reports about diseases and poverty and how people were taking out their troubles on minority groups; they would accuse foreigners of being responsible for lack of suitable housing, or lack of employment opportunities. It was certainly true that living standards had declined somewhat following the Covid's global pandemic. Everything in the world was a mess, thought Mike.

'If only we had something to celebrate; what we need,' he considered, 'is a hero; a hero like we used to have when I was a boy.'

He remembered how children of his generation idolised characters from TV programmes and films, pop stars and sport personalities.

'At least they all used to convey a sense of positivity in my day,' he thought, 'unlike these so-called modern celebrities who basically stood for the self-promotion, money, and greed.' Mike would get quite emotional about the way the global population seemed to be heading and he hurriedly switched off the TV in disgust.

For several minutes, Mike sat there in silence,

pondering on the problems of the world and wishing some of his pirate heroes would return.

'They would soon sort people out, he thought.' His mind returned back to thinking about pirates and he picked up his book again. He opened the volume nearer to the back and was drawn by a chapter named the prophecy. The title intrigued him as it didn't convey the usual idea of information about pirates. He eagerly began to read and was astounded at what he discovered. The text revealed that a hidden document had been discovered in a tin, buried behind the wainscoting of an old house in South Carolina in the USA, back in 1978. Apparently the house was due for demolition and the old container had been discovered by workmen as they stripped the interior of the house of salvage. The crumpled paper had evidently been buried there for a long time and consequently it was taken to the local museum as an item of possible interest. The book went on to describe that the document didn't get much media attention and so, not many people ever knew about it. The book then went on further, to describe; that upon analysis of the document, it was proved to have been written in about 1780. Naturally, the handwriting was unknown, but many historical researchers and pirate enthusiasts suggested the writer might have been Anne Cormac, otherwise known as Anne Bonny. This was extremely interesting to Mike, as the pirate Anne Bonny was one of his favourites. He knew very well the legend surrounding her and how it was believed she'd escaped execution and gone on to live out the rest of her natural life. The text suggested she may have lived into her eighties and that it was more than possible that she had remarried, and had several children. Apparently, the crumpled paper had a poem or nursery rhyme written on it, and it was supposed, it might have been written by Anne Bonny herself, for her grandchildren. It alleged, this hypothesis was reached by the last line of the poem; which stated, "My Bonny Girl."

Although intriguing, what interested Mike more, was the poem also seemed to suggest a prophecy of a time of great trouble, when good pirates would rise again. It was all nonsense, of course, and nothing more than a tale for children.

'But was it?' He thought. 'What if this poem had some truth in it?'

He stopped himself short, as he knew his imagination was running away with him again, and as he read the poem that had been printed in the book he decided it was, after all only a legend…..

*"When pirates ruled the oceans blue,*
*Many were bad, but just a few,*
*Were good in heart and spirit strong,*

*Forced to fight, to get along.*

*At night they came, on a sudden swell,*
*But the Crown dispatched them all to hell!*
*So, rest you now, your weary head,*
*And safely slumber, in your bed.*

*In times when evil casts his stain,*
*All good pirates shall rise again.*
*So never fear the pirate churl,*
*For now, you sleep, my bonny girl."*

# CHAPTER 1

## **Night of the Dead**

The early part of the twenty first century was a time of discord and turmoil. Many countries around the world suffered upheaval from the traditional comforts of life. Populism was rife, and a global pandemic hit causing mayhem and disruption. Wars broke out and thousands, if not millions were displaced from their homelands whilst others struggled to get by. Some became bitter, while others sought reasons for this downturn in living standards. Some blamed politicians, others blamed minority groups. The acceptance and understanding of others with different viewpoints broke down and people turned on each other. What the populace subconsciously required was a hero or heroes they could identify with, role models for example. Whatever the cause and whatever the solution, one thing was clear, some evil stain was creeping across the face of the earth and the storm clouds of doom were gathering. Even the one commodity that always remained abundant in times of trouble was diminishing. The commodity of hope. The time was ripe for a new legend, a legend that would provide hope and comfort but above all else, a legend that would create a burning beacon of light for mankind to follow.

As the oppressive metaphorical storm clouds gathered across the globe, actual storm clouds were accumulating twenty miles off the northwest coast of Scotland, late one September evening. Apart from the gentle rising and splashing of the sea, everything was dark and still. There were no ships in sight. No late-night fishermen making their weary way home with their catch. No cargo ships enroute with their freight to foreign shores, or pleasure cruises sailing to an exotic location while excited passengers slept. For miles, the surface of the ocean was completely devoid of life. Suddenly and without warning, a tremendous flash of lightning lit up the inky black ocean for miles. This was closely followed by a loud thunderclap that rang out like some kind of dire warning. Just as suddenly as it had struck, it stopped. No more lightning, and no more thunder. A storm late at night at sea is not uncommon, but there was a peculiarity with this specific weather front. It seemed to be over as soon as it had begun, and after about five minutes of the lightning flash, a peculiar fog began to rise from the surface of the ocean. The fog hung in the air like a damp heavy curtain. Then, without warning, the ferocious storm broke with a vengeance. Violent lightning flashes streaked across the night sky, and thunder bellowed like the voice of some terrible ogre, screaming in rage. The thunder and lightning was unrelenting as it came again and again with no pause in between. The onslaught of the storm was aggressive and destructive, and yet the strange fog hung motionless in the air while the storm raged around it. But then this strange storm abruptly stopped again, and everything suddenly plunged into a deathly black stillness once more. The unnerving quiet felt ominous, as if the monster was silently waiting for the optimum moment, to strike with its full force once again. The wait was brief, and with a heart stopping roar the storm resumed its attack, tearing its way through the night sky. Only this time, something else happened. As the lightning illuminated the fog and the surrounding ocean, out of the sagging heavy mist appeared, an eighteenth-century sailing ship. With each bolt of lightning, the outline of the ship became clearer and clearer, until finally, the entire ship sailed gently out of the mist. Its masts and yardarms were visible in the dull haze that now shadowed the ocean. The ship's tattered and torn black sails propelled it forward slowly through the water. A soft orange glow illuminated the deck, emanating from several old-fashioned oil lamps hanging around the walls. In the gloom, the ships wheel was prominent, set on a raised platform that had steps leading up to it on both sides. Behind the raised platform, were two doors leading to the Inner part of the ship, both of which were partially obscured by strands of torn rigging that dangled lifelessly from the yardarm above. Scattered about the deck, were remnants of discarded clothing, almost as if the owners had cast them off in a hurry. There were several crates and barrels lying around the deck, and a small brazier stood in the middle, wherein a fire had been lit. The fire must have been burning for some time, as the brazier now contained a heap of smouldering glowing embers and half burnt logs. Wisps of curling smoke drifted slowly upwards and mingled with the strange heavy fog. Where the smoke and the fog merged, a weird glowing halo seemed to emphasise the tattered remnants of an old black sail that hung from the uppermost yardarm, upon which was painted the distinctive symbol of the jolly roger. The emblem was of a slightly different design to the usually familiar icon. It had the familiar skull, but instead of two crossed bones, this flag had two cross swords beneath the grinning deathly cranium. There was no mistaking the fact that this ghostly vessel was a pirate ship! The lightning exploded once more across the heavens, and this time the brief illumination, gave witness to four creatures, if they could be called creatures, clambering up the sides of the strange vessel. As the beings climbed onto the deck and into the soft orange haze of the oil lamps, their true horrific appearance became apparent. They resembled corpses that had not been in the ground for that long. They were dressed in robes, apparently made from seaweed and other debris from the floor of the ocean. Their pungent rotting gowns consisted of a hood, beneath which, long dead faces stared out with dead eyes. The faces were skull like but with putrid bits of flesh, still weakly clinging to the discoloured bones of the skull. The creatures, or ghouls would be a better description, lurched backwards and forwards with seawater cascading from their decaying attire, and leaving pools of water on the deck as they moved about. They heaved themselves around as if searching for something. They seemed inquisitive as they explored the furniture on board as if trying to recall distant memories of their past. An old, battered chest stood in the middle of the deck, to which the ghouls appeared to be drawn. They swarmed over the chest as if it were some prized possessions that had been lost for many years. It was then they spoke. Or rather, they made a haunting chattering noise, like crickets in the fields on hot summer days. These sounds could not be described as chirpings though, but rather like moans of sorrow from a bygone age. But then the tone changed. Were they singing? More like wailing to a long-forgotten sea shanty. The noise they made was coarse and breathy, like the death throes of some tortured soul, desperately clinging to life even though death had the upper hand. The cacophony of despair rang out through the chill air of the night as they sang of betrayal and murder. To anyone who were to bear witness to this horrific spectacle, the one conclusion they would concede, would be that these ghouls were in pain. Their lumbering steps, the arching of their bodies, and the cold icy chanting they sang out, gave the distinct impression they were in agony. Although hellish and horrific in appearance, one could not help but feel a sense of sorrow for them. If the strange drama with the ghoulish protagonists singing their unworldly hymn, on a ship from the past, were not nightmarish enough, what occurred next would have driven any onlooker insane. The agony and torment the ghouls seemed to suffer from, appeared to increase dramatically. Three of them became more hunched and staggered more heavily. Their gnarled hands began clawing at their own faces, their bony fingers digging into their dark sunken eye sockets, as if trying to tear out from their very bodies, the thing that was causing them so much pain. Suddenly, with another burst of light and crashing of thunder from the storm, they wrenched hard at their own skull-like faces causing them to crack and split apart. As the shattered bone and rotting flesh fell away, three fresh faces replaced the hideous visages of death, as if emerging from some kind of grotesque chrysalis. Unnerving to say the least, the fourth ghoul stood motionless, looking on with its dark dead eyes, and taking in the sight of the other three. In one final act of ridding themselves of the torment they were suffering, they tore the hoods, together with the rotting flesh and bone, from their heads and dropped them to the floor, where they lay oozing in a deep dark green slime. For a moment, the three individuals stood there in shock, but then fell to their knees. Not so much in pain, but with the sheer overwhelming alarm they were undoubtedly experiencing. The first to drop to the floor, was a youngish man, who appeared to be in his late thirties, early forties. He had dark brown shoulder length hair that was matted and wet. Some strands clung to his face, while the rest of his lank hair, hung over his slumped and sagging shoulders. His face sported a short chin beard that was as dark as his hair, but with the odd fleck of grey that glinted in the pale light. The sight of the ship that greeted his newly formed eyes undoubtedly roused a distant memory within him. Was it possible he was remembering his last day on earth in a previous life? He seemed to be reliving in his mind, his own execution, for he lamented and wailed;

'Is this hell? Is my neck now stretched and I am condemned to an eternal existence in Davy Jones Locker?'

His accent, although hard to distinguish, appeared to be from the southern regions of Great Britain, possibly London. His face was twisted, not so much with pain, but with the struggle of trying to comprehend what was happening. The second individual sat hunched, and hugged his crossed legs, rocking backwards and forwards. He moaned incoherently, in a broad northern English brogue, about the whereabouts of some child. The young lad appeared to be in his late twenties and had a shock of light brown curly hair. On his upper lip, he had an odd-looking moustache, that looked as though it was his first attempt at growing facial hair since puberty. There was a look of dread in his eyes, and he too, seemed to be reliving some vague past memory of his execution in a previous life, as he began babbling about seeing the rope in front of his eyes. The third of the group to have suddenly taken on human form, was kneeling, and holding his stomach. His eyes were wild, and his long mane of red hair flailed about in the cool breeze. His thin pale lips, partially hidden beneath his long flowing red beard, parted, and he gasped in a huge amount of air, like someone who had just resurfaced from a long swim under water. As the cool clean air began circulating through his body, he seemed to grow in strength, and let forth at the top of his voice, a loud piercing howl. Flinging his arms wide, he shouted;

'I feel breath in my lungs!'

There was no doubting the strong Scottish twang in his words, and just like the other two, he spoke of a distant tragedy that he had suffered at the end of his previous existence. With his strong powerful Scottish voice, he boomed;

'I feel the cold steel of a claymore in my belly!'

At that moment, the heavens erupted once more with the storm, and in the glare of the lightning, the three newly formed beings caught sight of the fourth ghoul, who stood coolly watching them. The appearance of the hideous apparition, just standing there observing them, convinced them that they were indeed in hell. Calmly, the fourth ghoul reached up to its face, and just like the others, tore the hideous visage from its head. The contrasting transformation was both shocking and awe inspiring. Where a hideous demon corpse had been, there now stood a beautiful fresh faced young woman. Her eyes shone like diamonds, and her jet black long curly hair, hung down over her shoulder. There was no hint of surprise or shock in her eyes as she slowly surveyed the scene before her. There was only one word to describe the unruffled beauty that had appeared before them, and that word was formidable. The long-haired man, the young lad and the Scotsman wailed uncontrollably at the sight they had witnessed, only to be silenced by the strange alluring woman.

'Hold your tongues, you filthy dogs!' she yelled at them. 'Get yourselves cleaned up! I run a tidy ship!' she bellowed.

Her accent was strange, rather like the accents of those who have travelled throughout their lives, and their original accent had been superseded by the varying dialects they had amassed on their journeys. There was, however, a slight inflection of an Irish accent in some of the words she uttered. Surveying the remains of flesh and bone around the deck, she ordered them to clear up the mess. Instantly, the young lad and the Scotsman, leapt into action, and gathered up the gooey remains of the ghoulish headwear, and flung the revolting bundles over the side of the ship into the darkness of the water below. Before this strange woman could intimidate them further, they fled, still dressed in their putrid gowns, through one of the doors that led to the bowels of the ship.

One mystery at least seemed to be resolved, or at least conjecture implied a solution. That conclusion was that the ghouls, were in fact a type of chrysalis, or some kind of grotesque womb that the souls of the departed utilised, to transfer themselves from the realm of the dead, back to the land of the living. If this assumption was correct, these new-born creatures appeared to be unaware of what had just happened to them. They were confused and seemed to have no memory. Even the young woman seemed perplexed, even though she gave the impression she was in control. It was inconceivable that they themselves had planned their journey back from the underworld. This, being the case, they must have been conveyed from "Davy Jones' Locker" by some other unknown entity, but by who? And for what purpose? The hideously fantastical event that had just taken place was bewildering and fear-provoking, not just because of the spectacle of the ghouls, but because it meant, that three-hundred-year-old murderous cutthroat pirates, had returned. While all the cleaning activity was carried out, the long-haired male watched with an objective curiosity. He had no idea who he was, let alone what was going on. All he knew was, that whoever this strange woman was, he was not going to let her get the better of him. Some deep instinct within him, drove him to fight against whatever this hellish creature was that now stood before him. He summoned up the courage to challenge her.

'You! I know you!' he suddenly exclaimed.
She slowly turned to face him. Her steely pale blue eyes, bore into his very soul as if attempting to mentally manipulate him to her will. As she

slowly paced towards him, he crawled cautiously backward, his bravado diminished somewhat by this Siren's mere presence. Uncertain of his own surety, he asked if she were Davy Jones? As soon as he asked, he regretted it. It made him appear uncertain and appearing uncertain made one weak. Something inside his head warned him to be careful of this woman. It was as if something in his soul recognised her or knew her from somewhere, but his mind was blank. He was puzzled by her actions when she suddenly burst out laughing. He immediately went cold, as it seemed she had the power to read every thought his numb mind struggled to grasp.

'You poor wretched fool! You don't recognise me, do you?' She scorned.

Helpless as a young child who is questioned by its mother and has no answer to give, he responded with sarcasm.

'Recognise you? No, why should I? You see, I am new here in Hell and I'm not yet familiar with you fiendish apparitions!'

Even his clever use of sarcasm did nothing to diminish her relentless torture of his masculinity. She tossed her head back and laughed mockingly.

'Still as cynical and defiant as ever!' she sneered. 'The only fiendish apparition here, is you, John Rackham!'

This had the metaphorical effect of knocking the breath right out of his lungs. She obviously knew who he was, even though he didn't. She'd called him John Rackham, but the name was not familiar to him.

'Can't remember who you are? Now, there is justice!' she laughed, as she began pacing slowly towards him again, menacingly. 'In life you were known as John Rackham, and we were lovers. Can you believe that, you poor wretched fool, lovers!'

Her continued derision forced a spark of anger within him. With as much venom in his voice as he dared, he challenged her. Pulling himself upright, and with every muscle in his body as taught as the restraining ropes on a recently fired cannon, he snapped back.

'My memory might not be intact, but I know this!' His next words took him totally by surprise. 'I am a privateer!'

Where did that come from? Some long-lost memory suddenly shot to the front of his brain, and he remembered that he had been a privateer, a pirate!

'As a privateer, no one, but no one speaks to me like you do!'

Whether it was bravery or stupidity on his part, he then suddenly blurted out,

'And no one, especially a woman, tells me what to do!'

He dared to insult her; how would she react? Would this devil woman toss him into a pit of fire for eternity for his insolence? He stood frozen to the spot, waiting to feel the full wrath of her anger as she casually looked him up and down. But she did nothing, except turn away from him dismissively and told him to go and get cleaned up. It seemed the tempest of her outburst was over. Whether it was because the tension suddenly subsided, or whether it was because something that lurked hidden within his mind that he currently had no control over, forced him to, but he found himself obeying her without question. He meekly walked towards one of the doors that led to the interior of the ship. Whatever the reason, he instantly obeyed her, and because she offered no further abuse, it instilled a certain amount of confidence in him, and he immediately leapt into the saddle of sarcasm once more.

'I suppose you're right.' He casually called across to her.

She turned looking puzzled.

'About what?' she scoffed.

'Well, by obeying you without question, means....?' He hesitated ready to maximise the effect of the full thrust of the final blow of his cynicism.

She was genuinely confused by his change of stance and for the first time, Rackham had the advantage, and he knew it as she questioned his meaning.

'Means what?' she asked slowly, trying to anticipate his reply, and to ready herself for her next strategy to regain control.

But Rackham simply told her, that by obeying her every word, meant they must have been lovers. Rackham was smug and elated with his win! He laughed, and dodged through the door, as she took a half-charred log out of the brazier, and hurled it at him. But he was too quick. He was gone, and the log crashed into the doorframe. It fell to the floor, and lay there smouldering, just as she herself, stood there, seething inside. How could she have lost control that quickly and especially to Rackham, the same John Rackham, who had at one time been her lover and powerful ally. There was no doubting it though, this John Rackham was nowhere near the man he had once been.

# CHAPTER 2

## Anne Bonny

Anne was not a bad person. Yes, she could be tough, and she had shed blood in her time, but that was merely a consequence of survival, especially in later years when she was a fully-fledged pirate. It was difficult to comprehend that she had only been a pirate for less than two years, yet it seemed like a lifetime. That was probably because she had crammed so much into those two short years of adventure and freedom. Anne had never been a person to live her life by others' expectations, or to submit to the demands others made on how a young woman should behave. She did not like being classed as a second-rate citizen just because she was a woman. If she'd have been born a man, she would have had far more opportunities available to her, to pursue her life goals as she wanted.

Unfortunately, she had been born a woman, and as such, she was expected to marry young, keep house, and bear children. Not only that, but she would be expected to be under her husband's command and obey every wish that he desired. She would not be allowed to come and go as she pleased, nor would she be allowed any men friends, however platonic such a relationship might be. She certainly would not have been allowed to visit hostelries and Inns, to drink and dance to the lively music of the minstrels as she would have liked. That was it then, she was a woman and must accept the conditions of her sex, as laid down by the rules and guidelines, set out by society. Rules and guidelines made by men! This attitude angered Anne, why could she not do as men do? She didn't want to be an outlaw; she didn't want to harm anyone, and she certainly didn't want to rob and steal with violence. All she wanted, was to be respected as a human being, who could live her life as she wanted. What was so wrong with that? The short time she'd spent as a pirate had given her the life she had always craved. With Rackham and the others, she had been the person she was deep inside, she didn't have to pretend to be someone she wasn't. She had Rackham to thank for this, because it was he, who had introduced her to his crew, and told them she was joining their happy band. Not a normal course of action for a ship's captain constantly striving to control the acceptance of his men. The unfair expectations of women even stretched to the sailing fraternity, and women were deemed to be a sign of bad luck on a ship. Many crews had revolted and mutinied for less, so Anne was privileged to be accepted by Rackham and his men. The crew respected him as he was a good captain and looked out for them. There weren't many captains, pirate or otherwise, that treated their crew with respect and understanding. At first, the men accepted her on the ship begrudgingly, because their captain asked them to accept her. But their admiration and acceptance of her, only really became cemented, when they undertook their first raid together.

It was early one morning, and the sun was barely up when Rackham gave the order to advance. Many days of thought and planning had gone into the raid. Word had gone round in Nassau, that a supply ship was chartered to restock several of the Royal Navy ships that were patrolling around the north coast of Cuba. Rackham and his crew's food and water rations were low, and they needed provisions, the supply ship was the perfect target. What was expected to be an easy raid, turned out to be quite different. They expected a normal supply ship with a basic crew, that would not offer up much resistance. They could be in and out within thirty minutes and be dining back on their own ship by noon. What they actually met when they sailed up alongside the small supply ship, was a vessel full of redcoats, British Marines. Because of the increasing threat of pirate raids along the coast of Cuba, the British governors had drafted in extra troops to protect the interests of the Navy. The first Rackham and his men knew of the imminent danger, was when the cry came from the lookout above, alerting the ships company to the presence of "lobsters aboard!" the term used by pirates for soldiers. Rackham acted swiftly, and ordered the cannons be loaded, while he himself unlocked the weapons chest in his cabin. It was unwise for a captain to allow crew members easy access to weaponry, as that was a sure-fire way to encourage a mutiny. Indeed, that was exactly how Rackham himself had become captain. He had held a pistol to the temple of the previous skipper, Captain Vane, and called for a vote. The crew opted for him, and Vane had been deposed. From that moment, Rackham vowed to always keep the ships armaments safely locked away, and only issued in times of battle. Those skilled in muskets and flintlock pistols were the first to be armed, together with small bags of gunpowder and shot. After the musketeers took their firearms, the rest of the crew were issued with swords, daggers and any other implements designed to cause harm, that they had collected from other ships they had raided. As they sailed ever closer to the supply ship, they readied themselves for the inevitable battle. Rackham warned them not to fire the cannons until the last possible moment, so they could maintain an element of surprise. He then gave the order that was so out of place with any attacking leader, be they army or pirate. He ordered them not to cause harm or death to any man on the supply ship, unless it was absolutely necessary. This attitude was his strength, thought Anne, and she loved him for it. Many pirates were nothing more than outlaws, rebelling and fighting for their own selfish ends. It has to be remembered though, that all pirates at one time, had been mercenaries for the English crown, fighting against the Spanish. Privateers, they called themselves, and they were revered then, even regarded as heroes. But finally, the war was over, and the privateers were abandoned by the crown, forcing them to fend for themselves, just to survive. Many people's businesses had been lost when they turned to contribute to the war effort, and it was nigh impossible to re start old trades after the war. Taxes were high, and marketable goods, especially those good for profit, were scarce. The only option was to carry on plundering as they had done through the Spanish war, but now they were regarded as criminals and outlaws. They were given a new name - pirates. Rackham had a least a modicum of honour about him. Yes, they had to survive, and they had to take the necessary steps to ensure that survival, but it was wrong to cause unjust harm and suffering in that pursuit. Rackham never went after the big prizes to enrich himself and his men. He was not driven by greed and power. So long as they had a reasonably comfortable life, as comfortable as one could have on a pirate ship, that was all that mattered. That and the exciting sense of adventure such a life offered. After the anxious wait by the men for the action to begin, they were finally close enough and Rackham gave the order to attack. Cannons fired, pistols were discharged and the battle cries from both ships added to the chaos that followed. Suddenly, out of nowhere, sprang a young man, dressed in a brown knee length jacket and black boots with a scarf tied around his nose and mouth. He sported a ridiculously large brown leather tricorn hat on his head. The hat was large enough to obscure his eyes in shadow and he looked like some masked avenger ready to be their champion. With a pistol and cutlass in one hand, he ran forward, grabbed a boarding rope, and swung himself straight onto the deck of the supply ship and into the melee of British Marines, who were rushing about in the confusion, trying to make sense of what was happening. Rackhams' men gasped at the bravery, or as some muttered, "stupidity!" of the young man. Funny thing was, no one knew who he was. Where had he come from? Who was he? Although the men hadn't time to take him in properly as they were too busy engaged in battle, some did notice that Rackham completely ignored the actions of the lad, almost as if he had expected it. The young man sought out the captain of the vessel and immediately took him hostage, and held him at gunpoint. With his flintlock touching the captain's temple, and brandishing his sword in front of him, he dared any of the Marines, in a low, gravelly whisper to make a move. Rackham then appeared, standing on the taffrail of the supply ship, and holding onto the rigging. He fired a pistol in the air, and ordered everyone to be quiet. He informed the marines and the crew of the supply ship, that no harm would befall them, if they handed over provisions. The whole manoeuvre was completed within the hour, and after crate loads of food and drink, with the odd little trinkets here and there, had been stowed aboard, all the pirates returned to their ship. As a precaution, they made sure their cannons were fully loaded, and pointing at the supply ship, as Rackham and his men sailed off with a well-stocked pantry, well out of harm's way. There was a good wind and they headed for Crooked Island, about one hundred and thirty nautical miles from the coast of Cuba. The plan was to tack around the outer islands of the Caribbean, before heading back to Nassau, to ensure they were not followed. When Rackham was sure the danger had past, he mustered the crew together and relieved them of their weapons. The first mate locked them all back up in several crates ready for stowing back in the captain's cabin. The ships cook had taken some of the provisions back to the galley to prepare a celebratory feast, while the rest were stowed in the lower storerooms, that had heavy iron gates on them, to stop unnecessary pilfering. Everyone was in a good mood, and grog, a beverage consisting of rum diluted with water, was issued to every sailor. They drank heartily and looked forward to the delicious meal that awaited them later that day. As the crew revelled with their grog, one of them called out;

'Captin,' who were that new fella, that swung on 'em like a monkey?'

'Yeh, never seen anything of the like!' responded another.

Rackham smiled wryly.

'You'd all like to meet yer new crewmate would yer?'

'Aye!' everyone shouted.

'Very well,' he said, and opened the door that led into his cabin.

He beckoned into the gloom for an unseen person to come out. Rackham turned to the crew and announced;

'Gentlemen, please welcome Andy Cormack!'

The young lad stepped out of the cabin, dressed as before, in the long coat and hat, that was obviously too large for him. The men began to cheer and clap, but stopped abruptly as the boy pulled down the scarf covering his face, and removed his ever so large hat. As he did so, a cascade of jet-black curly hair sprang loose, and fell down over his shoulders. A gasp went up, and cries of;

'Whaaaat?' and

'I don't believe it!' came from around the deck. Andy Cormack the brave young lad that had won the day, was Anne!

Anne had a kind soul and would fiercely protect those she loved and befriended. There was no harm in the way she had reacted to the others, she thought, as she stood there gazing around their old familiar ship. After all, that's how they always used to bark at each other in the past. Her gaze settled on the tatty jolly roger, hanging high above the deck, and she smiled faintly as she remembered when they had made the famous black flag. Rackham had insisted that they paint two crossed bones on the standard.

'It will show we are as fierce as all the other pirates,' he pleaded. Anne considered his point for a moment, but then dismissed his suggestion, and asserted that they paint two crossed swords.

'This will be our mark,' she proclaimed. 'This will be the emblem that will become known as Rackhams' pennant, a more fearsome badge than other pirates. The swords will show we mean business!'

But that had been a long time ago, and Anne was no longer the impetuous girl she had once been.

She had soon calmed down after the run in with the newly reborn Rackham, and she stood there, alone on the deck, bathed in the pale flickering glow of the lanterns and the glowing coals on the fire in the brazier. She clasped the fetid cloak around her. It was cold. The gown felt clammy and damp between her fingers. It was disgusting, but it was warm. Her eyes stared into the distance as her mind reeled with images, one after the other, as she tried to make sense of what was happening. She was puzzled. Why did Rackham and the others not recognise or remember her, when she knew all of them? Was it the trauma of what had just happened that robbed them of their memories? If that was so, why could she remember them and much more besides? Although Anne could remember many things, she could not bring into focus recent events. How had they mysteriously appeared here on their ship? How did they get here, and what had happened just prior to their arrival? With too many questions to answer, her mind focused on Rackham and the incident that had just occurred. John Rackham seemed different to how she remembered him. He was pitiful and drained. It was as if the fight had been knocked out of him. At one time he was strong and forthright, a leader of men. But now he was just a pathetic shadow of his former self. It was curious that she could remember him, as if it were yesterday, but at the same time, it seemed so long ago. She smiled faintly as she recalled how he would always consult with her before issuing orders, and how, although he was the captain in name, it was she who actually manipulated and guided the daily activity on the ship. Anne felt a twinge of disappointment. In the past, she and Rackham had enjoyed their verbal sparring with each other. The cut and thrust of their wordplay, was one of the most enjoyable parts of their relationship. But now, he appeared meek and obliging, that spark that had once existed between them was gone. Yes, they had been lovers, and she began to think about those happier times so long ago. She stopped herself short as the memories that flooded into her mind were agonising, like a sharp dagger tearing painfully at her soul. Instead, she questioned herself again about the way she had yelled at them. Was it fair, to have acted like she did, shouting and ordering them about like that? After all, they had no memories. They were weak and frightened, but Anne couldn't help it. She had learned as a child that it was better to exert one's authority right from the start, dominate and manipulate, thereby keeping others at bay until the situation became clearer. Let others be wary of you, let them fear you until you know their intentions. That way it was easier to survive for longer. It was her natural survival instinct kicking in. Ever since she was a girl back in Cork in Ireland, she had built up a defence mechanism where she would attack first and ask questions later. The anguish of the time she was attacked as a child, rushed into her mind, and she could see again the brute in the marketplace advancing menacingly toward her. She had been cutting reeds at the edge of the small stream that flowed through the town. Squatting by the waterside with her skirts up around her thighs, she busied herself on cutting the bundles to strew across the floor of her father's cottage. As she worked, her mind drifted back several weeks to when the gypsies had been around for market day. As a child, Anne loved seeing the gypsies come into town on their annual visit to the markets, selling their wares and telling stories of adventure to the children. Many treated the gypsies as outcasts and vagabonds. Even her mother told her they were not to be trusted, but Anne could not see this. In her eyes, the gypsies were fun and entertaining. They brought a gaiety to the area with their brightly painted caravans and their colourful clothing. She loved it when they would sing and dance around the settlement, creating a wonderful carnival atmosphere, an atmosphere that was a great improvement on life in the otherwise drab, normal little urban town. She didn't care what others had to say about them, Anne loved them and their carefree ways, and that was all that mattered. One of the gypsies had given her a little carved wooden doll, and told her it would bring her luck, and would hasten the man she would eventually marry to her side. Anne wasn't gullible, she didn't take the fantastic tales as fact, but more as tales to amuse and ponder on. She would carry the little wooden doll with her virtually all the time, keeping it safe in the small pocket of her skirt. There was something about the gypsies that Anne admired greatly. Although she loved their tales and comical songs, the one thing she admired most about them was the way they lived their lives as they wanted. They didn't conform to how the governors or the priests, told them to live their lives, they lived their lives to please themselves, they were free, and Anne loved that. Suddenly, sensing danger behind her, and jolting her from her daydream, she quickly sprang to her feet, but in turning to face the unseen threat, she inadvertently stepped into the water and the mud beneath. The squelching mud held her feet fast as the scrawny cove approached her.

'You got fine calves me lovely.' He leered at her with his broken teeth.

'You keep back from me, Thomas Finlayson! I know what yer about!'

But his ardour was inflamed at the sight of her bare thighs, and he wanted satisfaction. He made a grab for her, but she somehow ducked out of the way, even though her feet were sinking ever further into the mud. She felt herself toppling, but as she regained her balance, he was on her. For such a scraggy individual, he had a surprisingly strong grip. He grabbed her round the waist, trapping one of her arms, and forced his hand up her skirt that had now fallen back to its full length, and sagged limply in the water. She felt his filthy hands reaching for her womanhood, and with one free hand, she scratched at his cheek. But he only laughed and continued his assault, panting in her face with breath that stunk of poteen. Something within her stirred, a part of her that had laid dormant within her for all of her life. It was difficult to discern which was the more frightening, Thomas Finlayson attacking her, or this unknown part of her own personality, that suddenly sprung from nowhere. Her newfound spirit immediately summoned up the strength to pull one of her legs out of the slimy mud, and to force her knee directly into Finlayson's groin. He yelped in pain and surprise, but it was enough for him to slacken his grip around her waist, and for her to free her right arm, the arm that still held the knife she had been using to cut the reeds. With a powerful swing, she slashed the knife across his face, cutting it deeply. As the red stain of his blood flowed out across his cheek, she plunged the dagger towards his chest. Somehow, he managed to deflect the blow and the tip thrust into his upper arm. He fell backwards clutching his face with one hand, while the other hung limply at his side. He staggered and regained his balance and without a second glance at her, he ran as fast as he could, shrieking about that "Devil Woman." With all the furore the incident caused, many of the townsfolk turned to watch the spectacle. Anne now sensing all eyes upon her, and fearful of the constable, she fled, leaving her basket of freshly cut reeds on the bank of the stream, that was now tinged red from the blood of Finlayson. With tears flowing down her cheeks, she ran as fast as she could, back to her father's cottage, trembling and agitated at the experience. Nasty and horrific as it had been, it served enough as a warning to Anne, and from that moment onward, she vowed she would always aggress first, until other people's intentions were clearer. It was after this incident with Thomas Finlayson, that her father decided to move to America with her and her mother. It wasn't just because of what had happened. Finlayson wasn't badly injured, and there were many townsfolk who'd back-up her story. She was only a young girl anyway, not much older than thirteen, and not deserving of the treatment she got from the old drunkard. America would give them a new start, and they could put all the animosity that existed in Cork behind them. William, her father, had taken up with her mother when his wife was ill. Her mother was a maid, and although it was commonplace in gentle society for maids to become pregnant by their employers, the difference here though, was her father fell in love with her mother, and didn't abandon her. Soon after Anne had been born, his wife died, and he took up with her mother full time. He looked after her and Anne, and stood by them, regardless of the gossip and finger pointing that went on. A clean break from the past and adventures anew were called for. It was a pity though, thought Anne, as she had just met up with this young English lad called Johnny. Even though she was only a child, her father had been furious with her over the affair with the watch, that had got the young boy into trouble, and how she took it upon herself to help him get out of gaol. She liked him, but as her father kept repeating, 'she was too young for boys!' There will be time enough for all that later!' So, it was on 5th April 1710, Annie McCormack, and her father William, together with her mother, Mary Brennan, took a ship from Dublin to the new world of the Americas. Her life would never be the same again.

As she stood in the gloom of the early hours of the morning, reminiscing about times long ago, other images of her past life started to come into her head. Images she did not like. But they came none the less, faster, and faster. Her husband, James Bonny and how he mistreated her. How her father had disowned her because of him. Other memories, both pleasant and distressing, flashed before her eyes and lurched into her brain, but it was too painful. Anne was conscious and curious of the fact that some memories weren't painful, even those that weren't particularly nice, whilst others that could be deemed pleasant, sent a pain of anguish through her like a steel blade piercing her heart. Grabbing and squeezing her temples, she managed to distract her mind away from the past, and blocked out the phantoms. Instead, she focused on the gentle undulating waves in front of the ship, as it sailed slowly through the now calm waters of the North Sea. Her mind turned back to the extraordinary events that had happened less than an hour since.

'This is all very strange indeed...' she muttered to herself, trying to make sense of it all.

With all the ghosts of the past that had tried to invade her mind, she wondered if this is what her mother meant before she died, all those years ago. She had whispered to Anne in her final hours;

'When you die, Annie, your whole life will flash before you.'

Anne wondered if that was exactly what had happened. Had she just died, and this place on the ship was the hereafter? It didn't look much like hell, yet it didn't look much like heaven either. Anne reasoned that whatever had happened to them, it must be for a reason.

'There must be a purpose for all this.' she whispered slowly to herself.

Anne felt cold, and wandered over to the smouldering brazier, with its dying embers, to warm herself, but the putrid gown was beginning to stink of rotting fish and rancid flesh, as it dried in the early morning breeze. The rancid gown had to go, but she was naked underneath. Looking around the deck, she casually examined the discarded clothing that was strewn about, but there was nothing suitable for her to clothe herself with. It was then she noticed a piece of cloth protruding from under the lid of the treasure chest. Opening the lid, she found an assortment of clothes that seemed more suitable. Anne was never prudish or embarrassed by her body, but she had always acted with respect for the men on the ship in the past. It was one thing to be accepted by a crew of men who deemed women unlucky on board, but to allow them to see her naked would have been overwhelmingly stupid and totally improper. She dragged the chest nearer to the low wall in front of the raised platform and crouched down in the gap. Reaching into the chest, she pulled out a pair of black breeches and a sail cloth shirt. Awkwardly, she managed to put them on in the cramped space, whilst at the same time, removing the rank and fetid cloak. Dressed in the breeches and shirt, she was now decent enough to stand up and completely remove the gown, and she could search for additional clothes inside the chest more easily.

'It can't be?' she spluttered to herself as she pulled out a pair of knee length black boots.

She examined them carefully, and was amazed when she realised they were her favourite ones from a bygone age! Anne had loved those boots as they had helped her escape unsavoury situations on many occasions. Not just because they gripped her feet snuggly and enabled her to run faster, but also because they were sturdy enough to cause nasty bruises on the shins of those she had kicked out at. Sitting on the edge of the platform, she tugged them on enthusiastically, then stood up and tested them by pacing up and down. Perfect! Turning back to the trunk, she next pulled out a finely embroidered maroon coloured waistcoat and slipped it on over the sail cloth shirt. Finally, she bundled up the foul-smelling robe and went to the side of the ship with it, and hurled it into the water below. It frazzled and dissolved, as she watched it from the deck. It then sank beneath the water, into the inky darkness. She wiped her sticky hands on an old canon wadding rag that was hanging from the rigging, and then noticed something familiar on the damaged stair post, next to the steps that led up to the ships wheel. On the newel, hung her old familiar coat. She hadn't noticed it before as this part of the ship was hidden in shadow. She'd loved that coat in the past as it had made her look important. It was dark red with a sort of black sheen to it, that glistened in the light. It hung down to her ankles, and she loved the way it would billow and float behind her as she walked along, making her look incredibly powerful. Anne took the coat off the post and slipped it on. It made her feel good to be wearing it again. Looking down, she saw her old dark red leather tricorn hat lying next to where her coat had been hanging, as if it had been placed there for her. Picking it up and plonking it on the back of her head, she felt she could face anything. She looked up and yelled at the sky.

'What does this all mean?'

Not really being overly religious, her father being a lawyer, had taught her to reason things through.

'Analyse and observe,' he would often say to her. So, not being devout and preferring to live by the laws of logic, she wasn't really speaking to anyone. She certainly didn't expect anyone to reply! The explosion of the thunderclap, together with the searing flash of the lightning, gave the impression that the storm had one last burst of energy left within it, and was eager to go out in a blaze of glory. The noise and the flare caused her to immediately leap for cover behind the trunk. For a moment, she feared it was another ship attacking, sending its fiery cannon ball hurtling onto the deck, with the aim of ripping their vessel apart. She dispelled this thought from her mind almost at once because a howling gale suddenly sprung up around the ship. Anne could hear and see the wind ripping through the sails, but the odd thing was, the sea remained calm. The ship continued its steady pace gently rocking to and fro as it glided through the water, and she felt not the slightest draught on deck. Then the voice came…! The voice was hardly discernible from the wind, but it was there, nonetheless.

'Anne Bonny…!' the wind called out.

Anne was scared but she didn't show it. She cautiously stood up from behind the old chest as if to acknowledge the voice calling to her. Her fear soon subsided, as her logic told her this was yet just another bizarre occurrence in this latest peculiar adventure. Her father had always insisted on a good education for Anne, and the words of Shakespeare came into her head, "O brave new world, that has such people in it." Anne listened out for the voice in the wind, and soon it came again.

'Anne Bonny, a new destiny awaits you and your companions. A destiny that went unfulfilled in your past life three-hundred years ago….!'

'Three-hundred years…?'

The enormity of what the wind had said, stunned Anne, and she sat on the trunk to steady herself.

'We've been dead for three-hundred years?' she gasped.

'Three-hundred years have passed since you died, but this night you live again,' The strange voice whispered. 'In life you were a good person, but unforeseen circumstances forced you into a life of lawlessness, necessary for your own survival.' The voice in the wind was calm and reassuring, even though the words it spoke were unnerving. 'The same is true of your companions.' the voice went on. 'The ancient prophecy foretells that in times when evil casts his stain, all good pirates shall rise again. Now is that time. And you, Anne Bonny, you must lead them to their ultimate destiny.' Annes' defence mechanism kicked in as she became more confident, and she began to argue back with the unnatural voice that echoed around her.

'Lead them. What do you mean, lead them?'
She thought now was the right time to get answers, and she launched into a forthright verbal interrogation of the unknown voice.

'What do you mean, lead them? Lead them as a ghost of spectres or as pirates?'
Anne was pleased with the way she phrased her question. The voice should now confirm, that either they were all indeed dead and nothing more than ghosts, or that they were truly alive again and should resume their old pirate existence. Unfortunately, Annes' probing didn't have the effect she had wished for. The voice

answered dismissively and ambiguously.

'That is yet to be determined.'

Although her question had not been answered, Anne did glean a tiny fact from the reply. From the answer the voice gave, Anne reasoned that they did still have some kind of free will! She and the others could still follow their own path towards their own destinies. This small victory was soon overshadowed by the voice, as it continued its address, and sent a chill right through her bones.

'For now, all of you must face your past and confront your personal haunting memories.'

Anne didn't want to face her past, it was too painful, but she knew if answers were to be found, that was precisely what she was going to have to do. The voice continued.

'This will drive you to become nobler people. Only then will your purpose be discovered. Be the wise and compassionate being you truly are within your soul.'

Anne listened intently as the voice spilled out what was expected of them, but it wasn't clear and raised more questions than answers.

'Be strong, Anne Bonny…!'

Anne knew that the lecture was over, and that whoever or whatever the voice belonged to, was going. Anne was determined to know more from this haunting inhuman voice, that echoed all around her before it departed. This was her chance to gain that precious commodity she had always valued over and above wealth, the commodity of knowledge. Anne yelled into the wind;

'Hold I say! I have questions! Are we dead? Are we ghosts? I say it again, what must I do? Answer me!'

But the voice simply replied;

'You will find your way.'

Anne desperately shouted back with as much authority in her voice as she could muster.

'Answer me!'

But the voice was gone and so had the wind. Everything was calm and silent once more. Anne leaned on the taffrail of the ship scanning the horizon, looking for any evidence as to where the voice had come from, or where it had gone to. But there was nothing there. Anne was alone again, with just the gentle lapping of the sea against the bow of the ship, and the dark sky meeting the black ocean in the far distance. She placed her hand casually into the pocket of her coat, and her fingers touched something small and hard. As she gripped it, she knew what it was. It was the little wooden doll the gypsies had given her all those years ago. She smiled, because she now knew that whatever all this was about, everything was going to be alright.

# CHAPTER 3

## Angus McTavish

Angus "Jock" McTavish had no memory! But that didn't bother him, he was used to it! He'd often awoken after a raucous night of revelry, alcohol, and exotic tobacco with absolutely no recollection of the past twenty-four hours! The only difference being that on those occasions, he would have the mother of hang overs. This time it was different, he felt more alive than he had ever done. He had no idea what had happened, but Jock, as everyone affectionately called him, never looked back, only forward and would let facts come to light only when they were good and ready. The here and now was all that mattered to Jock. He was always on the alert for danger, and then clearing up after that "hideous lassie," as he called her, he took one of the oil lamps from the wall, and ushered the young lad through the doorway, and into the bowels of the ship. He couldn't recall where the passages would lead, as the ship was not familiar to him, but all ships were of a similar design, and it was better to be out of sight for the present. Withdraw and consider your next move, was Jocks' way of thinking. He was a big, brawny man, standing well over six feet tall with calves as big as tree trunks. It would only be a drunken fool or a complete idiot that would take on McTavish. Unlike Anne, Jock needn't strike first and ask questions later, as he knew anyone who tried to put one over on him, must be some kind of simpleton, and he could knock them into the middle of next week if he felt they were attempting to exploit him. The young lad that had helped him clear up the mess on the deck was frightened and trembling, as Jock led him down the rickety dark stairs to the lower decks of the vessel.

'Yer be fine with me, laddie,' he assured him, as they entered a small dark cabin below.

'All a wee bit strange, don't yer think?' he said. The lad just stood there petrified and nodded.

'Och, there's no need to let the wee demons get yer laddie. Yer safe with me. I'll protect yer!'
Jock had always been fiercely loyal to his companions, and although he was strong and powerful, and had the look of a man mountain about him, underneath he was an honourable

and fair-minded man.

'Angus McTavish,' he boomed, offering out an enormous hand to the boy, 'but everyone calls me Jock,' he said.

The young lad who was no taller than five feet, was dwarfed by the Highlander. If the situation they were currently in, weren't so serious, it would have been quite comical to see the pair of them standing together.

'Mark,' the young lad said, as he grasped the giant's hand.

'Mark what?' Jock asked.

'Mark Read.' The boy responded.

'Well, nice to meet yer lad,' Jock answered.

For a brief moment there was a flicker of recognition in both of them, but as soon as it came, it was gone again. Each of them put the feeling down to the fact they felt safe in each other's company, given what had happened on the deck some minutes before. Jock broke the awkward silence that followed.

'Yer ken what we could do with right now, don't yer Mark lad?'

Mark just stood there and shook his head, his pale skin was clammy in the darkness, and the dampness under his eyes gave the impression he was crying, but he wasn't.

'What we could do with, right now,' thundered Jock, 'is a good noggin of rum! What says you, Mark Read?'

'Where we goin' to find rum down here?' Mark

asked. 'It don't look like anythin's been down here for quite some time.'

Mark spoke with a gentle northern dialect from somewhere between Liverpool and Manchester, in northern England no doubt. He was gaining his confidence and becoming surer of himself. More than likely, due to Jocks' influence and calming nature.

'Och, there's bound to be somethin' down here, lad,' McTavish suggested.

'How do you know?' said Mark.

McTavish scratched his head. It suddenly dawned on him that he had no idea where he was and what he was doing there. He could remember his name and that he had some connection with ships, but that was about it. The more he tried to focus his mind on his situation, the more his mind seemed to shut him out.

'I don't,' he suddenly retorted. 'But there must always be stuff, on an old ship like this.'

They wandered on through more dark narrow passages and Mark began to think about what was going on. Sheepishly, and with a slight fear in his voice, he whispered;

'Do you think we're dead, Mr McTavish?'

Jock instantly turned on him.

'Never say that to me again, laddie, yer hear me?'

Mark jumped, and felt awful that he might have said something to upset the Scotsman.

'I'm sorry, I didn't mean to offend you by

suggesting we might be dead.'

'I was nay referring to that, yer wee Sassenach,' answered Jock. 'I was meanin', yer never calls me Mister! Yer understands?'

A faint smile crossed his lips and Mark was sure he saw a twinkle in his eyes.

'And regarding yer other question, laddie, Nae! I dinnae think we're dead.'

'Well, what is happening? I don't understand it,' pleaded Mark.

'Never fear, laddie, the truth will out in due course, and until then, we just remain calm and wait. Nothin' will happen to us until then.!'

And with that, he plonked himself down on a small wooden bench that happened to be standing by the wall in the narrow corridor. He folded his arms and closed his eyes, and prepared to wait for what fate had in store for them. Mark observed that as the big man relaxed, it seemed that his wild mane of red hair and beard, also relaxed and became still. Up until that point, Mark was sure Jocks' hair and beard had a life of their own. Several times he had noticed the hair on the big man's head had bristled and stood on end as they explored the dark corridors of the ship, like some dowsing rod that would shake uncontrollably, when near to water. He smiled to himself at the prospect of Jocks' hair being a separate entity to the great man, like some long-haired fox or rabbit that lived constantly on his head. The thought cheered him and helped him become a little more confident, although he was still somewhat tentative, he decided to let the Scotsman rest, while he delved deeper into the ship, to see what he could find.

'Who knows,' thought Mark, 'I might even find him some rum!'

With that thought, he picked up the oil lamp that Jock had set on the bench next to himself, and set off to explore on his own.

It was the beginning of the "seachd bliadhna gorta," or the seven lean years, in Scottish Gaelic, which occurred throughout most of the 1690's. James and Mary McTavish were celebrating the birth of their son, Angus. It was a cold October night in Tulloch, a small village twenty miles northwest of Aberdeen. James rummaged in an old wooden box that didn't seem to contain anything but straw, but James had a treasure hidden in that box. Within a moment, his fingers curled around the neck of the bottle, and he pulled out a small flask.

'Oh, no!' Mary gasped, 'not Whisky?'

'Och, just a wee dram to whet the bairns head, yer ken.'

James had been saving the flask of whisky for Christmas, but the baby arriving in October was a God send, for it gave him the excuse to indulge in the fine malt early. He was not a heavy drinker, but like many of his clan, he enjoyed a tot now and then. He felt he deserved it as things had been hard for some time now. For the past year a severe shortage had gripped Scotland tightly, and things were scarce. Cold weather had caused the harvests to fail, and the wars with France didn't help. James considered himself fortunate though. He had a nice warm cottage and a loving and caring wife in Mary, even though she did nag him from time to time. Many of the inhabitants locally, didn't fare too well though, but James would do what he could to help. He could only do so much, especially with a new mouth to feed. Turning to look at his wife cradling the tiny baby in her arms, he smiled and remembered their wedding day. Mary was a bonny lass, with her flaming red hair and ivory white skin that glowed with such a delicate hue. Her eyes would shine like tiny emerald orbs, that seemed to radiate a caring and sympathetic air to all around her. James was grateful, God had smiled on him, and provided him with so much, especially in these bleak times. Although they would not describe themselves as overly religious, they believed in God, and followed the ten commandments, as any good Christian would. Every Sunday, they would go to the tiny stone church and listen to the Presbyterian minister, Angus McBain, read the lesson. Angus was a good friend to James and Mary, so much so, that they had decided to name their new bairn after him. James would often undertake jobs for the minister, like ensuring his small flock of sheep were safely secure in the barn through the winter months. Whenever McBains' cottage was damaged in bad weather, it was always James McTavish that was there, up the rickety ladder, replacing the thatch. Maybe, it was because of the kindness James had always shown towards him, that one Sunday afternoon, Angus McBain asked James to meet him at his cottage, to discuss something of high importance. Ensuring Mary and the bairn were comfortable, and a large fire was blazing in the hearth, James McTavish set off for the cottage of the minister. As he traipsed along the muddy footpath through the back meadow, and past the little stone church, he wondered what Angus wanted to see him about. It was probably just some job that needed doing, he thought to himself. Finally, James reached the ministers small cottage. He stepped up and knocked loudly on the small wooden door, because McBain was slightly hard of hearing. Perhaps that's why he would bellow at you in conversation, thought James, even when you stood right next to him. A crack at the side of the door appeared, and the door swung open to reveal the little man who stood no taller than five feet. He had a balding head with salt and pepper hair encircling his bare pate. His face was sombre and stern and for a moment, James wondered if he had done something to offend him.

'Come in, James.' The minister mumbled.
This was highly unusual, as he would normally boom out a welcome with an almost exaggerated

grinning visage. James did not say anything, but meekly walked into the cottage as the minister beckoned him in.

'Sit yer self doon, James,' he commanded, still in that worrying tone that was so out of place.

'What's wrong, Angus?' Asked James in an urgent yet concerned manner. 'Yer don't seem your usual sunny self today.'

'Aye, well, neither would you be James me lad, if you ken what I do.'

'What is it?' queried James, who was now beginning to worry, as there was obviously something troubling the minister greatly.

'It's like this, James me lad,' he began. 'I have received news from various outlying villages round about, and they predict a famine is on the way. There are several who have already starved to death because of a lack of food, and there are others who are on the brink of death. I'm worried that at the rate things are deteriorating, within a year or so, at most, it is going to affect a very large area. The church and civic dignitaries predict a severe famine will soon be upon us, from Forres in the west, to Boddem in the east. From Alvah in the north, to Cothal in the south. In other words, most of Aberdeenshire.'

At this revelation, James did nothing except stare hard into McBains' sorrowful eyes.

'But it cannae be,' James spoke slowly and softly. He thought about Mary and the baby, and tears welled up in his eyes just thinking, that within less than two years they could all be dead. A smouldering knot of anger began forming in the pit of his stomach. He was incensed at the thought that God had blessed him with a beautiful baby, and within less than two weeks, that same God was going to snatch the poor wee thing back again, out of their loving arms. McBain, saw the torture in James' eyes, and although he knew there was not much he could do for many of the hundreds of people that lived in the northeast corner of Scotland, he knew he could do something for James and his new family.

'Listen James,' the minister uttered, 'there is a way you, Mary and the bairn can be saved from all this.'

James' eyes widened.

'Saved? How?'

'By going to the Americas,' The old minister announced.

'Going to the Americas?' James mouthed. 'How in Gods...,' he pulled himself up sharply, remembering where he was. 'How are we gonna get to America?'

Many Scots had emigrated to the Americas over the past several years, but as the cost of passage was well beyond the means of ordinary people, many had taken advantage of indenture servitude. The scheme had allowed those without financial support, to volunteer as servants, in exchange for their passage and keep, whilst they made the transition. With all the turmoil of late, including troubles with the monarchy, and England becoming a republic under Oliver Cromwell, this might have been the perfect solution for those wishing to start a better life in the Americas. But it also had its disadvantages. Indentured servitude was no more than slavery under contract for at least three years. Those that volunteered under the scheme, found themselves at the mercy of their employers, who would often find faults so they could increase the length of their servants' contracts. Many found themselves open to abuse by their employers, who treated their workers like slaves. Many women were raped, and many men beaten to such an extent, that some were killed.

'I'm no goin' under indenture!' James responded sharply. 'I'll have no o' that!'

'Calm yer' self, lad,' the minister breathed, and laid his hand on James' knee. 'There's no way in this world I'd see you and yer family put in those conditions,' Angus responded. 'Nae,' he continued. 'Let me explain. Many of us in the church, together with ex-soldiers, merchants and aided by many of the nobility, are setting up a colony base in a town called Darien, in Panama. We believe the position will be good for trade and we have a strong and realistic opportunity to build a very successful trading colony.'

'Och, no!' said James.

'Why not?' Angus asked.

'I have nae money to invest in such a venture,' James sighed. 'I'd be better off takin' me chances here.'

'Look,' McBain retorted. 'I'm nae askin' yer to invest! I'm goin' meself and I'm inviting yer to come with me. I'm getting' on in years, and I could do with young blood around the place, to help with maintenance and the general running of my house. You see, I will be busy sitting on the committee of the new colony, and seeing to my ministerial duties.'

James was humbled and regretted his thoughts of anger towards God. He pondered on the fact, that in a matter of a few days, the almighty had given him a son, appeared to want to take him away again, and was now handing him the opportunity of a lifetime. James began nodding. His nods got faster and faster, as a broad grin crept across his face. He stood up and clasped the old ministers' hands, which in turn led to a firm embrace. It was agreed. James and Mary McTavish, together with their little boy Angus, would leave their homeland of Scotland to take on new adventures in America. The transition wouldn't be straight away, as there were many official arrangements to be made. McBain estimated all the planning and organising could take up to, two to three years, and they should prepare as best they could, for the lean years ahead. It would be a tough few years, but McBain insisted James keep a strong focus on the light at the end of a very long dark tunnel.

Just under three years after James McTavish and Angus McBain had discussed the move to the Americas, the first boat load of colonists arrived in Darien, excited and eager to build the "New Caledonia." Amongst the new arrivals were the minister, McBain and his entourage of James and Mary McTavish with their now three-year-old son, Angus. James could hardly believe it was happening and that they were finally in the Americas. They had bided their time and saved as much as they could from two years harvests, so they could survive the winter months. They had scrimped and saved arduously, just so they could endure the challenging times before the move. It had been tough, but they never shied away from the sight of the adventures and a new prosperous life that was waiting for them. James could not stop beaming with pleasure at the mere thought that finally, his little family was now safe, and there was much to look forward to. In the three short years that they had strived and battled against the onset of the famine, whilst the arrangements were made for the trip, baby Angus had grown considerably. James marvelled at the fact his little offspring was now three years old and was growing up to be just like his father in stature. James and Mary would often argue over which of them Angus took after.

'He has my nose!' Mary would exclaim.

'Nae, he has my nose,' James would retort. 'He has yer mouth, Mary!'

'Nae, he has yer mouth,' Mary would claim.

One thing was certain however, little Angus certainly had his mother's fiery red hair. James was not alone in his feelings of pure joy and hope at being in this new land, everyone in the colony felt the same. Everyone had plans and goals for the future. They talked about how they were going to do this, and how to do that. There was an air of general hope and excitement among the newly arrived Scottish brethren. That excitement was short lived however, as the entire project was doomed to failure from the outset. Within a year, things began to deteriorate badly. Beset by insufficient supplies, poor trading stock, and the outbreak of tropical disease, the newly arrived colonists were devastated. Angus McBain blamed himself, as he felt he should have researched the situation thoroughly before bringing the McTavish family to this new world with disasters abound. Even James McTavish, although he didn't blame McBain, regretted the decision to come. They would have stood more of a chance at home with the famine, than they would here. With all the regrets and guilt felt about the move, nothing could change the fact that they were there, and they would have to manage as best they could. Unfortunately, the odds of survival were unsurmountable and within a matter of months, following the anniversary of their arrival, when everyone was filled with hope for the future, death visited with a fury. Half their number had succumbed to disease, whilst the other half struggled against hunger, due to lack of resources. The colony felt totally isolated and betrayed, for none of the other settlements in the area gave any assistance, not even the English colonies. They were on their own, but another threat was breathing down their necks. If the disease and shortages weren't enough to cope with, they now had the threat of a Spanish invasion to contend with. McBain was furious and disappointed at the same time

'Why weren't we warned about this!' he would moan. 'They must've known these lands were subject to Spanish occupancy.'

It transpired the principality of Darien, was in close proximity to territories claimed and owned by the Spanish, and the Spanish military had laid claim to the exact area where the Scottish colonials had settled. To begin with, it seemed the Spanish were not too concerned about the Scottish settlers, but as things went from bad to worse, the Spanish made it clear that they intended to take over the colony with force if necessary. As the Scottish colonists fought to survive, they were mindful of the broken promises made to them, before undertaking the migration to the new world and especially, the promise of assistance by the crown. In 1695, the act of promise of assistance, proposed by William II, had come into force, but even this so-called guarantee of help, fell by the wayside. This festered a feeling of resentment by the colonists and in a funny sort of way, made them more determined to fight back. They were on their own, and so must fight on their own. It was agreed by the committee, that they should employ someone to help the fight against the threat of the Spanish take over, but who? And with what money? With half the original settlers now dead and with all the overshadowing threat from the Spanish, the colony of Scots fought with an iron will of determination. They had managed to survive the three years before the migration with the famine, back in Scotland, so they reasoned they could fight against the odds here. Their resolve was strong, they had to make it work, they just had to! It was three years to the day, after they had arrived, that Mary McTavish felt unwell. James was worried and tried as best as he could to nurse her, but she would have none of it.

'It's just a cold.' She would protest. 'I feel fine, now stop fussing James and look after Angus.' Although James was as concerned for the boy as much as he was for his wife, he knew Angus was strong and resilient and that at nearly six-years-old, didn't need his father's constant attention.

The boy would often be out and about, foraging for berries and fruit in the wooded areas, and sometimes he would be down by the water, trying to catch fish with his bare hands. He would wade in the sea with his arms outstretched, his hands together, just under the water, waiting for an unsuspecting fish to swim past. As quick as lightning, he would fling his arms upwards in an attempt to toss the fish right out of the water, but invariably the fish would be too quick for him, and the results of his efforts would be nothing more than a handful of seawater gushing all over him. Everyone would laugh at the boy's antics, but at the same time, they'd admire his pluck and patience. It was late one afternoon, after one of his many failed fishing attempts, that Angus decided to call it a day and head back to their little cottage. It was a ramshackle place, but it had the basics, such as a fireplace with a little stove to cook with, and room for straw palliasses to be laid out for sleeping. Angus was proud that he had helped his father build their home, even though all he had actually done was play with the mud that James had made to smear over the wooden framework of the cottage. There are events in everyone's life that one never forgets, and for little Angus MacTavish, this was one of them. As he approached their little cottage, he called out to his parents, but no one replied. No one came to the wooden door to greet him. This was not entirely unusual, for often his father, would be off fetching water for the evening meal, and his mother might be at the stream, in the small, wooded area behind the cottage, skinning a rabbit. Angus reached the wooden door of the cottage and pushed it open.

'Ma,? are yer there, ma?' he called.

As he stepped into the cottage, he froze at the sight that greeted him. His mother wasn't out, she was inside laying on her mattress, but she wasn't asleep, she was dead.

A small crowd stood around the hole in the ground, as Marys' body was lowered into it. Minister McBain said a few words and then it was all over. Mary had died of Malaria, so too had many of the colonists. Their number was now about a quarter of the original number that had arrived three years ago, and as their situation grew more desperate by the day, the very least they could do, would be to engage someone to help them.

'We can't afford it!' many would say at the meetings, that were called daily, to discuss their dire situation.

'I know someone who might help.' The voice came from McDougal, a tough looking man about forty years of age. 'I often meet with the local fishermen to barter for fish, and I ken one of them who might be just what we are lookin' for.'

It was agreed that McDougal should speak with

this local fisherman, after all, they had no other plans or ideas. The fisherman, a Jamaican, agreed to meet with the committee to listen to their proposals. At length it was agreed that the Jamaican would work for the colonists as a privateer, to protect them from the Spanish. The committee suggested his fee should be taken from any plunder he could seize from the Spanish ships, but the Jamaican wanted more. He wanted some insurance. There was no guarantee that he would manage to take much from the Spanish ships he attacked, and so he expected a small token from the Scots.

'We have nothing,' was the general response from the settlers.

The Jamaican gazed around the assembled clan, seemingly scanning each and every one of them. His eyes then settled on young Angus who was sitting on the ground, drawing in the dry soil with a stick.

'Him!' the Jamaican suddenly exclaimed, and pointed straight at Angus. 'I want him as my cabin boy!' he insisted, but James leapt to his feet and yelled

'NO! Yer nae takin' my wee lad!'

However much James protested, there was really no other solution to their situation. The Jamaican promised that as a cabin boy, Angus would be trained in all aspects of sea faring duties. It would be a kind of apprenticeship, and although he would face many dangers, his future would be much more secure than if he remained in the colony. And so it was, just before his seventh birthday, Angus stood on the deck of the Jamaicans' ship and waved back to his father, who stood on the shore, and who seemed to get smaller and smaller the further the ship cruised away. Finally, the figure of his father disappeared, and Angus McTavish would never see him again.

All Jocks' memories of those early days in Darien, with his mother and father, and how he became a cabin boy at the age of seven, had completely gone from his mind. So too had the memories of the rest of his previous life. All he knew, was waking up on this strange ship feeling a pain in his belly. Jocks' eyes suddenly shot open as the discomfort in his abdomen was throbbing. Shrugging the twinge off, he realised he was sitting in complete darkness. At first, he was alarmed as he had no idea where he was. He thought for a moment, but could only recall the recent events with the "Devil Woman." There was no flicker of any memory of his past, just the memory of the last hour or so. He did, however, remember talking with the young lad.

'What did he say his name was?.. ah, yes, Mark. Och, where's the silly young Sassenach gone? Shouldn't be wanderin' around down 'ere on his own.'

Jock stood up sharply in the darkness and

immediately banged his head on the low beam of the ceiling.

'Ow! Yer doaty bampot!' he cursed, as he lumbered off down the corridor into the darkness.

Mark had discovered a tiny cabin with two bunks, but the odd thing was, there were clothes laid out on the cots. It was as if the clothes had been left there for them on purpose. On one bunk, lay a full Scottish highland outfit, which was obviously meant for McTavish. On the other bunk, lay a pair of mustard yellow stockings and breeches, an off-white sailcloth shirt, and a brown leather tunic. There was also a red bandana, which Read picked up, and tied it around his unruly mop of curly hair. He quickly removed the now stinking gown and dressed in the clothes that had been laid out for him. Just as he was about to put on the leather tunic, he was suddenly paralysed by an excruciating pain in his head. He clutched his temple to try and alleviate the pain and although it only lasted an instant, it knocked the wind out of him. Gasping, he suddenly became aware of someone behind him. He spun round with one hand still clutching his temple to face his silent stalker. Mark breathed a sigh of relief and relaxed when he saw the giant form of McTavish standing in the doorway.

'Jock! You gave me a fright!'

'What you doin' 'ere, laddie?' Jock boomed. 'Should nae go off on yer own like that. Don't ken what might be lurkin' down 'ere!'

McTavish noticed that Mark had changed and commented on his new clothes.

'Lovely colours lad!' He laughed and winked, as he teased him about the somewhat garish attire.

Mark smiled. 'There's some clothes for you too, Jock,' he cried enthusiastically and pointed to the apparel laid out on the bunk.

'Well, bless me!' Jock declared excitedly, and immediately threw off his putrid gown and chucked it into the corner, on top of where Marks' gown had fallen.

Mark let out a stifled yelp.

'What's up, laddie?' Jock asked, fearing another threat had just presented itself.

'You!' spluttered Mark, turning round to face the door to hide his awkwardness.

'What's wrong with me, laddie?' Jock pleaded.

'Yer naked!' whispered Mark. Jock was dumbfounded at this apparent show of embarrassment from the young boy.

'Don't be so ridiculous, yer acting like a wee lassie!' Jock retorted, as he picked up the kilt and wound it around his waist. 'Hand me that yon belt,' Jock said, as he held the reams of tartan cloth to his waist.

Mark picked up a broad leather brown belt from the bunk, and handed it to Jock, who took it and secured the kilt with it. Having regained his composure, Mark said to Jock

'I could do with a belt like that to hold up these breeches, they're a little large for me.'

Jock eyed the boy with a puzzled curiosity, as he finished dressing. He sat on the bunk and pulled on a stout pair of boots, that had been placed neatly at the end of the bed. Why would he be embarrassed about his nakedness, he wondered. It then occurred to Jock, that Mark probably thought of him as an authoritative and higher-status person than himself, and that it was not respectable to view a superior without their clothes on. McTavish had the bearing of a man of authority, or certainly no one you should mess with, but Jock often forgot the impression he gave, because in his heart, he was nothing like that. Mark yawned and stretched.

'I feel tired,' he exclaimed. 'Must be all the excitement,' he said, but actually Marks' mind was racing. He couldn't remember anything except, like Jock, his name, but there was something else. That "something else" that he could remember, must remain safely locked away in his mind for his own survival. As he thought about his little personal secret, the pain in his head suddenly struck him again. He reeled backward and tore at his temples. He let out an agonising wail and a deep sense of guilt washed over him. Mark thought he was going to be sick, and at that moment he fainted. Luckily, Jock was alert, and caught the boy the moment he passed out. He picked the lad up in his arms, and laid him gently on the bunk where his clothes had been. The boy seemed to fall into a deep sleep and McTavish felt it best to let him rest. There were no outward signs that there was anything drastically wrong with him. He was breathing gently, and there was no movement beneath his eyelids, suggesting he was now peacefully asleep. Jock decided to let the lad slumber for a while, after all, the past couple of hours had been extraordinarily stressful for them both. It had been quite a shock to wake up on this unfamiliar ship, with no memory of anything, and to be confronted by a fiendish Siren. Jock could easily wait for the facts to reveal themselves, but he understood that others didn't always have the willpower he did. He had known people who would be constantly worrying about what the future might hold. He didn't understand that way of thinking, but he never dismissed anyone that did. He would often remark, we are all unique, and that's what makes life interesting. With that, he strode off back towards the steps that led to the upper deck. It was getting stuffy in the bowels of the ship, and he decided to go up on deck and breathe some fresh air once again.

Anne was gazing over the side of the ship at the horizon, thinking about what the voice in the wind had said, and was trying to make sense of it. It was then she heard a noise. She turned slowly in the direction of the sound, so as not to draw attention to herself by turning quickly. A broad smile crossed her face as she saw a familiar figure appear out of the other door. She thought he looked majestic, in his bluish-purplish tartan kilt and sash. He stood there with his long red hair floating in the breeze behind him. Anne was drawn to his masculine muscular legs, visible beneath the hem of his kilt. He wore dark grey knee length woollen stockings and protruding out of the top of one of them, was the distinctive shiny hilt of his Skean Dhu. On his feet, he wore a pair of toughened leather ankle boots, and around his waist, was a thick brown leather belt, from which hung several pouches of varying sizes. He did not see her standing there as he emerged out of the doorway; he was more attracted to the front of the ship, where he could breathe in the rich ozone of the breeze that flowed over the bow, as they sailed gently along. He took in a great gulp of air, and slowly let it escape from his lungs. It felt wonderful and cleared his head somewhat. Not enough to bring back his memories, but enough to make him feel alive and at peace. He pondered on the fact, that the clothes he now wore, had just been lying on the bunk.

'Ha!' he exclaimed, 'anyone would have thought this full highland dress had been placed down below, just for me. But that's ridiculous!' he laughed at the absurdity of it. Hearing a sudden noise behind him, instinct took over, and he whirled round ready to face the potential threat behind him. He straight away recognised the face of the "Devil Woman." This was it, he concluded. The showdown. The confrontation with the truth he had been waiting for, was now about to be realized. Using the full weight of his bearing and aggression, he bellowed;

'Yer talkin' to me?'

The strange woman didn't respond with any hostility, she simply stood there calm and composed, and she then gently whispered

'Jock!'

Anne observed that not even a flicker of recognition passed across his face, so she spoke again, hoping he might remember her.

'Jock, look it's me, Anne!'

She stood gently smiling at him, willing him to remember who she was. It seemed to work, as slowly an inkling of familiarity appeared to glint in his eyes. Slowly he sat down on one of the packing crates staring enquiringly at Anne. Softly and hesitantly, he muttered

'Anne? Anne Bonny? Is it really you?'

As her now familiar face swam into his memory, the brief joy of seeing his old crewmate again, suddenly dissipated, and was replaced with an overwhelming sense of despair. His mind raced to make sense of what was happening. His confused mind led to the obvious conclusion, and for clarification of his belief, he looked Anne straight in the eyes and asked

'Tell me lassie, am I slain?'

He believed that the Anne Bonny, who now stood before him, as clear as day, must be an angel, and that he had died and gone to Heaven. Annes' answer didn't make much sense to him, for she simply said

'I fear that was a long time ago.'

'Och, I dInnae ken of what yer speak, lassie,' Jock sighed. 'All I remember, is a battle and a claymore hurtlin' t'ward me.'

His memory was starting to return gradually, the more he concentrated on each fact that popped into his mind. There was still a long way to go before he remembered everything, but he had started to remember, and for now, that was good enough. Another spark of recollection shot through his mind like a thunder bolt. It was so quick, and he could barely contain the image. It was like a flash in the darkness, that briefly illuminated something, but had gone again before anyone could identify it. Although he didn't catch the meaning of the brief recollection, it did make him feel something. There was a feeling about the woman that stood before him now. He remembered who she was, but for the life of him, he couldn't recall anything about her. Jock gently spoke to her, saying

'I feel I should be grateful to yer lassie, but I ken nae why.'

Anne could see that he was struggling to

remember, and somehow she knew his efforts were pointless. In the grand scheme of things, she believed his full memories would only return when the time was right. Forcing his lost memories would not help, instead, the effort would only add to his anxiety. Jock opened his mouth to speak again, but Anne cut him off.

'Enough Jock, for now.'

She knew Jock, she had known him for a long time. She knew things about him that he could no longer remember, and she would have to mind what she said. Blurting out some fact from the past would only add to his confusion, or worse, it could be traumatic, and it might have a negative impact on him. Anne knew that Jock was not a violent man, but his passion could run away with him at times, which could give the impression he was deranged. It was the passion in his soul that had made him a successful pirate, and not the selfish greed and murderous thirst for blood, like so many others had been guilty of. In the past, they had found the best way to calm him down when he got overly enthusiastic about something, was to give him a tot, or invariably several tots, of rum. To this strategy she now turned and said

'Come, I think we could both do with a tot, bound to be some below.'

Her plan worked because Jock McTavish instantly perked up, and with excitement in his voice replied;

'Now that is music to my ears, lassie!'
He stood up and putting his arm around Annes' shoulder, just like two old pals who had met up for the first time in years, they cheerfully went back through the door, McTavish had recently emerged from, in search of that elixir to all pirates, a large ration of rum!

Mark awoke to find himself alone on the bunk, with the light from the oil lamp, casting ominous shadows around the small cabin. He sat up, rubbed his eyes, and tried to recall what had happened. Had he been dreaming? But, as his eyes focused on the shadows on the wall, cast by the lamp, recent events came rushing back into his mind, and he felt a wave of anxiety wash over him. Swinging his legs over the side of the bunk, he stood up ready to begin exploring again, and to try and find some answers. He was suddenly aware that his breeches were falling down, so he grabbed the waist band, and yanked them up. Lying on the bunk where Jocks' clothes had been, was a large thick brown leather belt that he'd left behind. Mark picked it up and tried to fasten his breeches with it, but the belt was a little large, and although they helped a bit with his problematic dress situation, his breeches were still loose and in danger of slipping down again.

'I need something to make an extra hole with,' he thought. And with that, he set off to look for a suitable tool for the job. Clutching the waistband of his breeches with one hand, and the lamp in the other, he traipsed off along a narrow corridor. He hadn't gone far when his attention was arrested by a glint of light shining through the crack in a door. Cautiously he peered in. He immediately withdrew, and as quiet as a mouse, quickly continued along the passage. Inside the cabin, Mark had seen the long dark-haired man preening himself, and holding up a tunic in front of his body, whilst examining himself in a tin handheld looking glass. Mark had too many questions on his mind as it was, without burdening himself with more anomalies. Besides, he wasn't ready to start making new acquaintances just yet. After his hasty retreat, from the door of the cabin with the man preening himself inside, Mark soon came to a flight of steps that seemed to lead to the upper deck. At the foot of the stairs was a small shelf fixed to the wall, with an assortment of rusty metal objects piled untidily in the middle. It wasn't clear what all the objects were, but some things were easily recognisable. There was a rusty old wrench, a broken mallet, and a pair of odd-looking tongs. 'Ah,' thought Mark. 'There might be something here to make a hole in this wretched belt.' Rummaging through the collection of discarded articles, he came across a rather rusty long ship's nail. 'Perfect,' he thought, as he took off the belt and laid it on the bottom wooden step. He picked up the nail and placed the tip on the belt, where it had scuffed slightly, as he'd tried to force it into the position, necessary to keep his breeches up. Taking what was left of the mallet in his left hand, he brought it down smoothly and firmly, and struck the head of the iron pin. Success! The nail pierced the leather like a hot knife through butter. He hurriedly threw the nail and the mallet back on the table and started refastening the belt. As he fiddled with it, he climbed the stairs to the upper deck. The leather was tough, and although the nail had made the perfect hole, it was proving difficult to fasten the buckle pin through it. He walked out of the opposite door to that, which Anne and Jock had taken moments earlier. To anyone watching, it might have looked farcical as one pair exited through one door, while someone else immediately entered through the opposite one, but Mark was not finding anything funny. The belt really was resisting all his efforts to secure it. Tugging as hard as he could at the leather, to give himself a little more purchase, he caught his thumb in the catch, causing him to wince. 'Stupid thing!' Mark whinged, as he sucked his thumb to ease the sting. Although he had nipped his skin in the process, the pin of the buckle finally found its home in the hole of the belt. 'That's better,' thought Mark, and contemplated his new outfit. It wasn't the sort of clothes he would usually wear; they were more like the clothes for a boy much younger than himself, but at least they were warm and comfortable. 'Mustn't grumble,' he said to himself, 'at least I found some, albeit a little flashy for my taste.' His safely guarded secret drifted into his mind, and he muttered under his breath, 'Don't want to draw attention to myself, do I? That will never do.' Whether it was a coincidence. or whether it was because he thought about his little secret, but the pain in his head struck without warning again, but this time it struck with much more force. Mark grasped his temples and squeezed as hard as he could, to try and alleviate the excruciating pain that seared through his brain like a red-hot poker, when it burns the flesh of an animal being branded. Along with the piercing awful pain, a very vivid mental image suddenly took over his mind, in absolute agony he looked skyward and screamed; 'GOD, NO!' Completely overcome with the physical and mental pain, Mark collapsed to the floor, holding his head in his hands.

Down below, Anne had unbelievably discovered a small flagon of rum, and she and Jock, were enjoying the smooth taste as they took a sip. The warm alcoholic drink slipped down their throats, and immediately radiated a warm tingling glow through their bodies. Jock wondered why he had not discovered the bottle earlier.

'Probably missed it whilst talking to the laddie,'

he thought.

Anne sat there in silence, because she thought it best to say as little as possible at this stage, and Jock hadn't got anything to say because he still didn't remember anything about Anne, and so they had no topic of conversation to chat about. So, they both sat there and relished their drink in silence. Their calm and peaceful moment was suddenly shattered by a piercing scream coming from the upper deck. Anne jumped to her feet and Jock made to follow, but she ordered him to sit down and wait for her to return. This was something only she could deal with at this moment. She hurried up the steps and out onto the upper deck. She stopped dead when she saw Mark writhing in agony on the floor. He was shouting something about it only being a child, and that God should have taken him instead. He pleaded with God to give him answers to the questions and visions he didn't understand.

'Oh, God, why? Why?' he howled. An enormous wave of guilt and remorse seemed to envelop him, for he beat himself about his own head and wailed, 'why was I so evil?'

Anne was mortified at the sight of the poor young lad suffering like that, but what was worse in her mind, was that although the boy had no idea what his visions and pain meant, she knew exactly what it was all about. What could she do? She couldn't say or do anything. In that split moment she realised this was going to be hard for her, knowing the reasons for everyone's pain, but not being able to do anything about it. All she could do was to be there, and offer as much comfort and guidance to them as she could. She sprinted over to the spot where the pitiful boy squirmed and writhed in mental torment on the floor, and scooped him up in her arms.

'Shh, now! Come dry your tears. Let me look at you.'

Anne turned the boy's face to meet hers. She gazed into his eyes with a ferocious urgency of concern and sympathy. It was almost as if she was willing her soul to climb into Marks' weak and battered body and somehow fix him from the inside. She held onto him firmly and tried to reassure him.

'Now why do you take on so?'

In that same instant the pain stopped, and Mark reverted to his normal self as if nothing had happened. It was as if the past few minutes of torture had simply never occurred. Mark disentangled himself from Annes' arms with a slight sense of embarrassment. He looked up and met Annes' gaze and tried to answer her question.

'I.. I.. I don't know,' he said, as he struggled to comprehend what was going on. 'I.. I had a terrible feeling come over me, oh, it was awful. There was a child Anne...,'

He abruptly stopped mid-sentence and was instantly puzzled by the strange recollection. He turned his gaze away from her and muttered to himself, 'Anne..? Anne..? How do I know that?' he questioned. This was a moment where Anne felt she could do something practical to help. It had worked with McTavish when she gently encouraged him to remember who she was, perhaps it will work with Mark.

'Look at me,' Anne said firmly. 'You know my name because you know me.'

'Do I?' Mark replied, 'I don't know how. I can't remember anything except flashing horrific thoughts, like waking nightmares.'

'It will be alright,' affirmed Anne, as she helped him to his feet, 'I promise you.'

Anne began to realize the enormity of the responsibility she was going to have to undertake with all of them. She was going to have to be there for each of them when the tragic realisation of their past would manifest itself within their minds. She also knew that of all of them, Mark was the one she was going to have to be extra vigilant with, and strong for. There was a deep bond between them, that had lasted a long time, a bond that could never be broken. Yes, she had a bond with both Jock as a good friend and with Rackham as a lover, but the bond she had with Mark was much deeper because, she believed, a bond is much stronger with those of your own kind.

'I will always look out for you, Mar...,'

Anne pulled herself up sharply, because she

nearly said something she shouldn't, especially as she was instantly aware that Jock had suddenly appeared. He got bored waiting for Anne to return and was curious to know what was going on. He also had the feeling that he should protect her if she were in any kind of danger, he didn't know why he felt that, but he did. As he got up from the stool in the cabin where they had found the rum, he noticed a little drawer on the side of a desk that had obviously been stored in there as it was so out of place with the other furniture. Curiously, he opened the drawer, as he was prone to do. Jock was a dreadful fiddler and would always reach out for things that didn't concern him. There had been a time when on a raid, he had gone to hide in a cabin on the target ship they were ransacking. He was supposed to lie in wait, and at a given signal, was to leap out and begin the attack with surprise. Whilst he loitered in the cabin, waiting for his cue, he noticed a loaded flintlock on the table. His irresistible urge to touch it overcame him, and he picked it up and turned it over and over in his hands. As he fiddled with the gun he inadvertently caught the trigger, and the gun went off with a loud bang, not only giving the game away, but endangering everyone on the raid. Of this incident, of course, he had no memory. When he opened the drawer in the small desk, he discovered an old hand carved pipe, and a small pouch of tobacco. What the pipe and tobacco were doing there was anyone's guess, but he quickly took the pipe and hastily filled it with some of the sweet-smelling tobacco from the pouch. He enjoyed a good smoke, did Jock, and after the noggin of rum, a good draw on the pipe would be blissful. The problem was, he didn't have any flint to light it with. He then remembered the smouldering brazier up on the deck, and hurried upstairs so he could light his pipe. He stepped out onto the upper deck and made straight for the brazier. He took a glowing twig from the fire and ignited the tobacco, drawing deeply on the fragrant smoke. Lost in his own thoughts, he sauntered towards Anne. She seemed alright and not in any need of his protection. She was just chatting with young Mark. As he drew close to them, a word, or a name perhaps, popped into his mind and he spoke aloud.

'Culloden!'

Anne was startled by this declaration.

'What?' she probed.

Was Jock starting to remember more of his past? she wondered, and if so, she'd better stand ready for the shocking consequences.

'Culloden, I remember Culloden!'

He WAS starting to remember; Anne assumed, and encouraged him to remember more. If there was going to be any pain when his memories returned, it would be better to get it over with as quickly as possible.

'What about Culloden?' Anne coaxed.

Jock inhaled deeply from his pipe and thought for a moment. He went to say something but stopped. His eyes seemed to glaze over, he exhaled a huge cloud of tobacco smoke, and then slowly whispered;

'I don't remember.'

# CHAPTER 4

## Calico Jack

John Rackham was feeling smug as he arrogantly swaggered down the steps into the bowels of the ship, after escaping from the fiendish Siren up on the deck.

'Who the hell was she?' he asked himself. More importantly, he wondered, 'who the hell am I?' The more he tried to remember what had happened, the more he became frustrated at not being able to remember anything. Something must have happened, he reasoned, to cause this temporary lack of memory. Rackham liked to think he was a methodical man and relied on facts and educated guesses to make decisions, but not being able to recall anything, hampered his strategic planning. 'Have I been hit over the head in a raid,?' He wondered. Or have I consumed some illicit substance in a night of revelry, which has yet to wear off? He could phrase the questions without any trouble, but finding the answers to those questions was proving to be nigh on impossible. He was temporarily distracted from his thoughts by a dim light emanating from a small cabin, just ahead in the dingy corridor, which was a welcome relief from the irritation of his memory loss. His curiosity took over, and he cautiously made his way to the cabin where the light was coming from, eager to find out what was going on and whether he could find any answers to his current predicament. Although his memory was blank, his instincts were as sharp as they had always been. The one thing he did know, was that he was a pirate, and to survive as a pirate, one had to have their wits about them at all times. If he had been hit over the head in a raid and had blacked out, it was very possible the ship had been taken over by some other band of outlaws, or worse, the British Marines. The ring leaders of the marauding enemy were more than likely in that cabin, planning their next move, and if he had any chance to overpower them, he needed the element of surprise on his side. He sidled up to the side of the door, keeping himself pressed hard against the wall, so he could remain as invisible as possible. It would be fatal to make even the slightest noise or even cast the faintest of shadows. As he stood motionless with his back against the wall, hardly daring to breathe, he desperately wished he had a weapon. A sword would have granted him more of a successful outcome in the imminent battle for the ship, but he didn't have one! There was no point in dwelling on the idea of a sword, as he knew very well there would not be one anywhere to be found down here. Any invading legion would not be stupid enough to leave their weapons lying about, and if his crew had been taken by surprise, he would not have had time to issue arms from the locked trunks in his cabin.

'Locked in his cabin?'

The thought startled him, as he realised he was the captain of this vessel, and by remembering this, meant his memory was starting to return. But he didn't have time to think about that now, he had these rogues who had taken over his ship to deal with. Surprise and brute force were going to have to suffice as his armoury in this skirmish. In a split second he leapt through the door ready to take on whoever was in the room, in the desperate fight to regain control. In the brief moment he was flying through the air into the cabin, out of the corner of his eye he noticed someone lying on the bunk to the left. As soon as his foot touched the ground, he immediately used it to propel himself into the air again, but this time in the direction of the bed. He landed on the hard mattress and immediately started grappling with the unknown occupant of the cot. The brawl was over in seconds, as he realised the person he had assumed was lying on the bunk, was nothing more than a pile of clothes that had been part laid out and part piled up on the bed. With a silk sash on his head, dangling down the side of his face, he sat up and laughed with relief at his own folly. The curious thing was though, why were all these clothes in this cabin and why was a lamp burning? Well, of course, it was obvious. The clothes were evidently part of some crazy antics they had got up to last night. He, along with the rest of his crew had been celebrating some victory and had downed far too much wine and rum, and probably some of that infamous "Jamaican Tobacco!" Mind you, he thought, there really could have been a take over last night and they would not have stood a chance, being under the influence as they so evidently were. He vowed there and then, to make sure that however much they indulged in future, some of the crew would have to remain sober and act as both look out and ships guardian. Rackham fell back onto the bunk and stared up at the ceiling, thinking about recent events. Who was that woman upstairs? The question had hardly entered his mind when he sat bolt upright.

'Anne!' he said.

That was who she was, it was Anne! He began laughing again. Must have been some powerful concoction they had consumed last night for him to totally forget Anne, he thought. Anne was the love of his life, well some of the time. The rest of the time she was a pain in the backside. He had known Anne on and off since he'd been a mere lad, and in later years, they had loved and raided in perfect harmony. He now had vague memories of her, but his mind resisted any attempt to recall other details of their past. His short-term memory was perfectly intact though, and he began to think about the scene with Anne up on the deck. He mulled over the recent events with her, and it all became clear. Must have been some intense revel rousing that caused them both to act like they did. He smiled as he thought of her, and how she had this knack of appearing to be in total control, when she hadn't got the slightest clue what was going on. It was a strength of hers, that had got them out of many a dangerous situation in the past, he thought. He froze abruptly. Another memory! He had remembered something about Anne before the episode up on the deck! That confirmed it, his mind was gradually healing, and his memories were starting to come back. He was suddenly aware that he was itching all over and he began inadvertently scratching himself vigorously.

'Not, bloody fleas!' He complained under his breath.

It wasn't fleas that caused the itching though, it was the fetid clothing he was wearing that had started to rot alarmingly. He wrenched the decaying robe over his head and slung it in the corner where it virtually disintegrated before him.

'Where the hell did we get those things from?' he wondered.

Probably one of Annes' brilliant ideas to put on some daft play whilst they were under the influence. He then remembered not being able to breathe, or so he thought, and he recalled pulling something off his head that had been covering his face.

'She does have some damn stupid ideas when she's plastered,' he reflected, and he could not help smiling because she made him laugh with her odd Irish ways, that endeared her to him. The curious thing was, that although he could remember pulling off the strange suffocating head covering, he couldn't remember a single thing before that. His mind raced trying desperately to remember exactly what had happened, not purely because he wanted his memory back, but partly because, to be in full knowledge of the facts, would help him maintain control of the crew and especially Anne. Methodically, he began piecing together the facts in the sequence of events, or at the very least, the facts he could remember. He remembered pulling off the head covering and there was a vague recollection that he had been executed. Well, that was ridiculous because here he was, still very much alive, and the only conclusion was that he must have been hallucinating. Everything became much clearer, and it was now obvious to him what had happened. They got drunk, took powerful narcotics, and played some stupid dressing up game with restrictive costumes which caused them to blackout. The lack of oxygen, together with the effects of the alcohol and drugs, caused the delusions and caused their temporary memory loss. Rackham was pleased he had pieced together the events from the previous night and knew exactly what had happened. He reasoned his memories would soon return once the stimulants had worn off, but for now he was confident of the facts. With everything now in place, his mind turned to getting dressed. He had always believed in dressing smartly and grandly, "clothes maketh man," he often exclaimed. A man's attire gave him a high status and radiated a sense of intellect, but above all, it conveyed the idea of success and not someone to be challenged. A man dressed slovenly, gave the impression he was lowly and easily crushed, Rackham believed. Realising he was standing as naked as the day he was born; he hastily closed the door of the cabin. There was only one situation worse than presenting yourself in poor clothing, and that was to parade oneself with nothing on! He rummaged through the clothes on the bunk, looking for something suitable to wear. He soon found a pair of white stockings, brown breeches, and a pale satin shirt, which he quickly put on. A pair of long brown leather boots stood in the corner, which he slipped on and turned the tops down, so they fitted snuggly just below his knees. Now all he needed was a tunic or coat that would be impressive, and would give him an air of importance. Unfortunately, there was nothing amongst the pile of clothes that came close to his satisfaction. He held up a variety of tops, and examined his look in a tin hand mirror that he found on a small shelf next to the bed, but he was disappointed with everything he found. There was only one thing for it, and that was to adapt some of the clothes into something more suitable. Rackhams' fingers explored the heap of fabric and came across something that felt velvety and smooth. Pulling it out of the heap, he found it was a short golden patterned tunic, evidently from some Eastern shores as the material was finely woven. As he held it up in the light, he noticed the maroon silk sash that had ended up on his head after the tussle with the clothes earlier, picking it up he compared the two.

'Hmm, maybe,' he whispered to himself, and within a moment, he put the tunic on, and wound the sash around his waist, tying it in a large knot on his right hip. As he disentangled the sash from the rest of the jumble, he noticed an identical one that was much shorter and narrower than the one he tied around his waist.

'This one I can tie my hair back with,' he thought, and holding the shorter sash to his forehead, he wrapped it around his temples and tied it at the back with the ends hanging down over his shoulders. Looking at himself in the tin mirror, he grinned broadly, 'Wonderful!' he thought, this looks perfect. The style of his outfit was not something he had sported before, but as he was always eager to try out new fashions, this was a look he rather liked. It was then, he noticed a long thin cupboard in the corner. Such cupboards were usually for storing muskets, and a powerful weapon would be very useful. Rackham opened the door but there was no firearm inside, instead, he found a rather ornate coat made from the finest velvet. The coat was jet black with red velvet cuffs and collar. The coat was the perfect addition to his costume, and he immediately put it on. On the floor of the cupboard was a black velvet tricorn hat, with an enormous white feather attached to the side, this he plonked on his head. Although he was pleased with his new look, he did resemble a modern caricature of a pirate that was slightly ridiculous and comical, but Rackham could not see past his own vanity. Armed with the facts of the past few hours, together with his impressive new look, John Rackham was ready to assert his authority with the crew, up on the deck. Heaven knows what inane yarns Anne had been telling everyone whilst he'd been down below, and so it was imperative he took control before further chaos ensued. Climbing the steps to the upper deck, Rackham felt the cool, salty sea breeze on his face as it wafted down the stairwell. As he stepped out onto the deck, he saw that Anne, a Scotsman and a young lad were in conversation. He did not recognise either the boy nor the highlander, presumably they had recently joined the crew, and he couldn't remember them due to the dwindling effects of the substances consumed the night before. More than likely,

'I'll remember them later,' he thought, but at this moment it wasn't important.

It was more important to remind them all that he was their captain and reaffirm his position.

Anne had been gently coaxing McTavishs' and Reads' memories, slowly but surely, things were falling back into place. Both of them remembered being on the ship, and their captain, John Rackham, although actual events remained scratchy. Whilst they were in deep conversation, Rackham stood in front of the door briefly watching them. Silently he climbed the steps up to the raised platform where the ships wheel was situated, as this would afford him a suitable stage from which he could command his authority. Taking a deep breath of sea air, he announced his presence by shouting to the three individuals gathered near the bow of the ship;

'Stand to, I am your captain!'

At that moment, a feeling of self-doubt shot

through his mind, and he murmured, 'I think.' Covering up this lapse of uncertainty, he continued hastily.

'I found these fashionable clothes below! Very fitting for a captain don't you think?'

Anne, McTavish and Read whirled round to face him, as his sudden outburst shook them from their quiet debate. The spectacle of him flaunting himself up on the platform, dressed in the outlandish clothes, caused them to fall into a fit of hysterical laughter. Rackham was deeply offended and retorted in a gruff offhand way;

'What the hell are you all laughing at?'

'You!' cried Anne, not even attempting to conceal her sniggers.

Rackham stormed down the steps onto the deck in a strop, as his well thought out plan to assert his authority came crashing down. Anne walked all round him, inspecting him like a disgruntled sergeant major examining an unkept soldier.

'Some things never change,' she mocked.

'What?' he mumbled sulkily.

Anne knew Rackham well, and at this moment she fully remembered their previous life together. She knew he didn't remember, and she was aware he had probably put two and two together to make five. This was an opportunity not to be missed, she thought, as she had to turn the situation to her advantage. Not because she had a thirst for power, but because she knew if Rackham continued on the path he had reasoned for himself, it would lead to chaos. Rackham had been a good and fair captain, and he knew how to sail a ship and to plan strategies for raids, but what he wasn't very good at, was managing a crew. Yes, he was always fair, and he respected every sailor on board, and in the main, they respected him back, but that was not enough. A strong captain would give respect, but also be slightly wary of everyone, and always think ahead of all possibilities that might occur in relation to the actions of each and every man.

'Make them fear you slightly,' she would often advise him. 'I don't mean scare them, but rather keep an air of mystery about yourself. Let them be slightly unsure of your next move, that way you will stay one step ahead.'

Anne had always been the brains behind his captaincy, and they had worked well together, except for those times when he would suddenly veer off on his own course, and she had to immediately rein him in again. This was one of those occasions, but this time, Anne had the disadvantage as Rackham had no memory. In the past he would resist at first, but soon gave in because he knew she was always right. This time though, he would not remember those past episodes and he might not be so easy to control. It was vital that she'd activate his memory, or at least some of it. Looking around the small group that had encircled Rackham, it occurred to her, that although each of them had memory loss, each of them could remember some things, that the others didn't. It was puzzling that McTavish and Read had both remembered their names, but Rackham hadn't. She noticed that with both of them, their memory seemed to improve somewhat when she coaxed them, but Rackham seemed to have an impenetrable barrier around his mind. Anne knew she had to be careful because there were certain memories each of them had locked deep in their heads, which could be traumatic when they finally broke through. Jock had a mental block around a battle and Mark around the memory of a child. Suddenly it occurred to Anne, that although she knew everything about Jock and Marks' past, especially the certain harrowing chapters they had both endured, she could not think of a single episode in Rackhams' life that would have a possible negative effect on him when his memories returned. She assumed the memory loss was a natural part of the rebirth process they had experienced, and was nature's way of protecting them from trauma. The shock of being alive again, coupled with all one's memories of tragic past events, including their own deaths would have a catastrophic effect on them. The only incident in Jacks' past; that might come as a shock, was his own execution. But even the memory of that, wouldn't be strong enough to damage his mental state too severely. Why then, had Rackhams' memory been totally suppressed? This question would have to go unanswered for now, as she had to do something to jog his memory. But what could she do? Shock him into remembering! she suddenly thought. Rackham had always responded well when she had forcefully introduced an undeniable fact into their arguments, for which he had no answer. This tactic always ensured he climbed down and thought more reasonably about the situation, rather than following his own flawed logic. Anne hastily thought what she could say that would shake him, and hopefully trigger his mind into remembering. Scanning his outlandish attire as she walked around him, she suddenly remembered Rackhams' nickname! Because he was well known for his passion of fine clothes, he had gained the epithet, "Calico Jack" from everyone who knew, or had heard of him, and it was a name that was partially endearing and partially derisive. Rackham had accepted the name begrudgingly, because although he hated it, he knew it swelled his fame and popularity. Even though this nickname was common when referring to John Rackham, none of the crew would ever call him that to his face for fear of retribution. Anne at once knew, this would be the perfect jolt he needed. With her best sardonic poise, she let him have it with both barrels!

'You used to have such a high opinion of yourself didn't you?' she venomously spat at him.

'Always pompously trying to dress grandly and failing miserably,' she continued. 'No wonder they used to call you Calico Jack!'

McTavish and Read tried desperately to stifle their laughter. They had both, of course, known the nickname, but no one, not even Anne, would have dared to use it on the ship in front of everyone. Anne was pleased they laughed, not only would it add to the shock aimed at Rackham, but it also meant more of their general memories were gradually returning. Rackham froze at the mention of that "dreadful name," and Anne saw the anger flash in his eyes, which made her convinced her plan was working! She continued with the insult, but with more of a casual air, and flippantly said;

'But this time, I think we'll just call you Jack Calico!'

The other two could contain their amusement no longer and exploded with hysterics, which in turn, caused Jack to be even more indignant. It was a delicious cutting thrust of cynicism from Anne, not only was she victorious in the rapport, but she had also succeeded in forcing his mind to start the process of regaining his memory, and not to rely on inaccurate facts, that he maddingly pieced together. By announcing that he would be hereto called Jack Calico, it meant that the nickname would be used generally, and no longer as a name whispered behind his back.

'Right, you lot, we've had our fun, now down to business,' Anne said, but Rackham was not going to be defeated that easily.

'Mock me if you will, woman,' he sneered as he menacingly advanced towards her, 'But if we were lovers as you claim, then I claim what is rightfully mine!'

With that, he grabbed Anne up in his arms, and sweeping her off the ground, he attempted to land a slobbering kiss, right on her partially open mouth as she started to protest. "Crack!" The sound rang out like a pistol shot in the early morning air, and shocked everyone into silence. Even Rackham, for a split second, was so taken aback he didn't feel the full force of Annes' hand as it struck him across the side of his face. Then the pain of the full impact of the slap hit him, and he dropped her instantly and grabbed his cheek, as the searing sting travelled up the side of his face and into his temple.

'What you do that for?' he grumbled.

'You're a fool, John Rackham, a fool!' she spat.

'What?' he replied exasperatedly.

Being fully confident that there were no major traumatic experiences in Rackhams' life during the time they had been pirates together, unlike McTavish and Read, Anne decided to go a lot further with her stimulation of his memories.

'You! With your stupid bravado! I told you, but you wouldn't listen, and we got taken!'

Anne took a huge risk in digging up their past at

the point they were captured as she had no idea how he would react. She felt sure though, that although this episode would be shocking, it would not have the same drastic effect on him as a similar tactic would have had with the other two. If she were to deploy this tactic on either Jock or Mark, she knew that could have devastating consequences, but then their situations were completely different to Rackhams'.

The authorities had allowed her to visit him before he was hanged, and Anne repeated the last thing she ever said to Rackham, whilst he languished in the condemned cell.

'Had you fought like a man, you need not have been hanged like a dog!'

If this didn't jolt him back into reality, nothing would. But it didn't work, though! He was so immersed in the facts as he saw them, and his irrationality only served to reinforce those beliefs. Was he deliberately shutting out the past or was he genuinely vacant in his mind, for he responded,

'Hanged? Ha! What you talkin' about?'

It did seem that he genuinely didn't remember his own execution, and he firmly believed that everything that was happening was due to the drunkenness of the previous evening. Anne had the awful realisation she had been wrong! There was a traumatic event in Rackhams' life that was stubbornly being blocked, and that was the memory of his own execution! She'd better pull back and change direction with her strategy, as she now realised she would have to be as cautious with Rackham over this situation, as she was with the other two. What Rackham said next was somewhat concerning, for not only did he obviously not remember his hanging, but he appeared to have invented a completely false narrative of his own history.

'Look,' he began. 'We've escaped, haven't we?'
He believed that he had actually escaped his execution and Anne realised she must advance with caution. Sympathetically and almost to the point of being patronising, she asked him;

'Escaped? Where exactly do you think we are?'

'Oh, look around you woman!' he responded, 'We're on the ship!'

For all his faults, Rackham was a fair man and would always give credit where credit was due.

'Yes, alright, I suppose we have you to thank for aiding our escape, and so I concede and, I thank you!'

If this was Rackhams' way of trying to exert his authority over her reasoning, it was a pathetic attempt. Thinking he could get round her by humbly offering his thanks was a stupid move, thought Anne, and she told him so.

'Ha! You see I was right; you are a fool!'

'Yeh, alright Anne Bonny,' He wearily replied, 'You've got guts and yer clever, I'll give you that,' and on the brink of losing control, he turned and barked at her, 'But, I'm yer captain, so don't call me a fool!'

Anne was not in the mood for his foolish attempts at trying to dominate her by shouting and pulling rank, and she cooly looked him in the eye and sneered.

'Captain? You lost that right when we were taken!'

It wasn't so much what was in his memory of Anne, but more what had developed into an instinct within him when dealing with her, that made him change tact. He'd tried playing the dominant role, now it was time to be subservient.

'Look, Annie, I am grateful you've somehow rescued us from the executioners' rope,' he said, in a rather unpalatable servile manor. 'How you done it?' he squawked, and then proffered his own suggestion in a sickly sycophantic way. 'Yer used one of your noxious potions that sent us all to sleep and wiped our memories, I'll wager! Yeh, that's it! Yer put us all to sleep, then you got us back here! Oh, very good!'

The distasteful grovelling tone, together with the ridiculous notion that Anne had managed to get three unconscious bodies back to the ship, was too much for Jock. He squared up to Rackham and growled;

'Potion or nay, the lassie's right, you are a fool Calico Jack!'

Jock had a lot of respect for Anne, and although he knew Rackham was technically their captain, he would not put up with anyone speaking to her like that, no matter who they were.

'Who asked you, yer dog!' Rackham snapped back, and before the situation rapidly deteriorated into physical violence, Anne cut in and yelled at him.

'Hold yer temper! Come-to, Jack Calico!'

'John Rackham!' he barked back, in an attempt to thwart her efforts to normalise the use of that derogatory name.

Anne, however, stubbornly stuck to her guns.

'Look at me, Jack Calico,' she demanded. 'There is no potion I know of that could have that effect. There is only one solution to this strange affair,' she said with an air of authority.

'And what's that?' he responded sarcastically.

Anne had tried several ways to steer him back into reality, but every tactic she employed had failed. There was only one course open to her and that was to resort to the truth. Turning to address everyone, she announced with confidence;

'We are back from the dead!'

# CHAPTER 5

## <u>Who Are We?</u>

To Anne, everything was starting to make sense, the tangible facts of reality before her, the memory loss of the others, and the words of the wind that echoed in her mind, were seemingly converging into a clearer image of what this was all about. Although she knew she had to be careful with Jack, Mark, and Jock in relation to those parts of their memories that were safely locked away, she also felt that because her tricks and games hadn't worked with Jack, the best course of action for now was to concentrate on the truth. After her startling declaration that they were back from the dead, a heavy silence hung around the deck, and as she looked at each of them, she saw a look of bewilderment in their eyes. Jack was the first to break the tension as he let forth a scornful laugh, but she cut him off.

'I think we all died a long time ago, but this night we have risen from Davy Jones Locker, and we live again.'

Jack was so firmly fixed in his version of the facts, that his mind could not accept any other account of the truth. In fact, the whole idea that they had returned from the dead was preposterous and frankly, he thought, downright impossible.

'And she calls me a fool! Back from the dead? That's ridiculous,' he scoffed.

'Hold fast there, Jack! I'm not so sure,' Mark piped up.

Mark had been sitting quietly on one of the packing crates, observing and listening to everything that had been going on. Watching Anne and Jack waging a war of words, and Jock standing up to Rackham, enabled many of his memories to return. He remembered how Anne and Jack had been in the past, and how different they seemed now. Anne seemed more mature and more confident in her manner as if she had developed with age. The Anne Bonny that was here with them now on the ship, came across as much older and wiser, but she still had that young girl charm about her that she'd had, when Mark knew her before. Jack or Rackham, as he had always referred to him, was different too. He appeared to be older than he remembered, yet, unlike with Anne, he came across as more childish and immature. Jock was just the same however, and as Marks' mind cleared, he remembered more about the giant Scotsman and some of the fun they used to have. Jock would often tease him, but in an endearing way, rather than with any hostility. Jack turned, and faced the young lad. Suddenly he remembered him, or at least, he thought he did. Mark Read seemed familiar. Glancing towards the Scotsman, he remembered him too. McTavish! That's who it was. Turning back to the boy Mark, he took several steps towards him. Mark remembered that look, in Jacks' eye, whenever anyone suggested or commented on a plan for a raid, or an order he had issued. It wasn't a look of reproach like so many other captains would have given, but a sort if inquisitive look, encouraging the questioner to speak more on their thoughts. This allowed the crew members to feel confident in offering their ideas, and was one of the main reasons they respected Rackham.

'Think about it. Think about what has just happened,' Said Mark. 'I for one, feel as if I've been asleep for a long time, and then suddenly, I remember a bright light, and I was here. My mind was full of images of a child, and the inside of a prison cell, and although I don't know what that means, I am sure something extraordinary has happened. What Anne says is the only thing that makes any sense.'

Before Jack could argue and dismiss what the boy had said, Jock, who had now taken a perch on the other packing crate, blurted out

'Aye! I felt the cold steel in my belly, and then I too saw a bright light, I felt my lungs fill with air and then I woke up here! I'm with the lassie on this one.'

Anne was fascinated by the three of them as they began to remember and interact with each other, like the times they used to do all those years ago when they were pirates. It felt like hardly any time had passed at all and that they were continuing with their lives from where they had left off, death having only been a minor interruption in the flow of their existence. Anne was more than convinced now, that the reason for the memory loss in her three companions, was precisely what she'd thought it was. It was a way of protecting them from the trauma of coming back to life, which was disturbing in itself, let alone being overwhelmed at the same time with catastrophic memories. She also observed that there was a pattern. The biggest hole in each of their memories was around the time of their deaths. Jack had been executed, but refused to face it, Jock was confused by the ache of a sword in his belly, and Mark was unable to remember the ordeal with a child in the prison cell. With all her focus on the three of them, Anne had hardly thought about her own part in the grand scheme of things. She pondered on the fact that her memories were intact, and even though there were things she would rather not remember, it was her choice to block them out. There was an odd thing however, the further she thought back, the clearer her memories became, but when she tried to remember her later life, the memories were somewhat hazy. As she thought about it, she couldn't actually remember her own death. Why was that? She can't have died in some tragic circumstances or else she would be suffering memory loss too. Her thoughts were suddenly interrupted by Mark.

'What about you Anne? What did you feel?'
Anne thought for a moment, and then answered
'Nothing.'
'What? nothing?' queried Jock.
'No, I just woke up, that's all.' she dismissively replied.
When Anne thought of the way they had returned, and those hideous cloaks and masks, coupled with the pain they had obviously suffered, she shuddered at the grotesqueness of it all. The fact they had been dead was equally repugnant, and she vowed there and then to refer to the episode as, "their awakening." Incredulously Mark asked:
'You saw no bright light?'
'No.' Anne confirmed.
Even Jock couldn't quite believe that she felt nothing, and he pressed her
'Yer had nae images in yer mind, lassie?'

'No, nothing,' Anne confirmed.

Trying to take it all in, Mark and Jock sat there in silence trying to make sense of what Anne had said. Jack had wandered off to the side of the ship, not wanting any part of this outrageous proposition that they had come back from the dead. As he gazed out across the horizon, he closed his mind to any suggestion that they had died, and refused to accept any other version of events, except those he had formed for himself. He was also starting to worry somewhat. There were many strange and dangerous substances abound in this part of the world, substances known to many of the indigenous savage tribes that lived on the islands around the Caribbean. The people of those tribes, along with their medicine men, were used to the powerful effects of those potions, but for Europeans, they could be deadly. Had they consumed some toxic sedative in their drunken revelry, that was affecting Anne and the others? He had seen people who had completely lost their sanity through such potions and were never the same again. Had their minds been altered by some hallucinogenic? And if so, what could he do about it? If they had taken any dangerous mixture, there was not much he could do pathologically, but he could, at the very least, try to engage them in a more normal situation and steer them away from their conversations about being risen from the dead. Jack crept up ominously to the centre of the deck, with Mark sitting to the left, Jock to the right, and Anne behind him, sitting on the chest. Anne wondered what the hell he was up to now, as he appeared to be in some sort of artificial trance. Flinging his arms wide and rolling his eyes, he whispered darkly

'I dreamed I was on the gallows,'

'Are you taking the piss?' Anne fumed.

'Yeh, and so what?' he flippantly responded. 'Look, it was just a dream,' Jack implored.

'Like as not, we had too much rum, laced with some narcotic, last eventide, which induced these strange visions!'

With that, he leapt upon the treasure chest that Anne had just vacated, and addressed his crew like some general commanding a large army, only thing was, there were only two people in his crew. Jack was on a roll, he had them, his idea was working. All he had to do, was rouse them like he had done so many times before when preparing for battle.

'All that matters is we are here now, on our ship and we are free,' he continued. 'So, I say, set too lads, and prepare for pillaging!'

'Aye!' Jock and Mark responded enthusiastically. Anne was enraged! This was pure stupidity on Jacks' part, and liable to turn everything in the wrong direction. By geeing them up, he was encouraging them to fall back into their old ways of piracy, instead of focusing on the new path they were expected to take. The words of the voice in the wind echoed in her mind;

'All of you must face your past and confront your personal haunting memories. This will drive you to become nobler people.'

This action of Jacks' was in direct conflict to what was expected of them, and she had to regain control and stop this outburst of rebel rousing, before it took any kind of hold. She dodged through the door on the right of the ship, and at the top of the stairs, was the door to the captain's cabin. She ducked inside, knowing exactly what she was going to do! The cabin looked as though it hadn't been touched for three-hundred years, it was exactly as she had remembered it. The image of the cabin that confronted her, brought back so many memories of the times she and Rackham had spent in there arguing and love making, but she stopped herself, as she had a mission to perform, and an urgent mission at that. In the small desk near the window, was a small drawer, which she pulled open, and rummaging inside, soon found what she was looking for. She pulled out a small key that looked so incongruous for the purpose it was intended. Bending down, she pulled a large wooden crate from under the bunk, inserted the key in the lock, and flung back the lid. Inside the crate was an assortment of weapons, including an array of pistols, shot and bags of gunpowder. Anne grabbed one of the pistols and rammed a large quantity of powder down the barrel, far too much for the normal purposes of pistol firing. She skipped on the ball of shot, for that was not necessary for her purpose. As the cabin was level with the upper deck, outside she could still hear Jack as he continued his rebel rousing.

'I say, set-to for debauchery, thievery and pillaging!' he was shouting, and the others were inspiringly cheering him on.

Anne stormed out of the cabin and back onto the deck just as Jack was encouraging them to set sail to seek treasure. Holding the gun high in the air, she pulled the trigger. Being overly packed with explosives, the pistol went off with a tremendous "bang," that caused Jack, Mark, and Jock to dive for cover.

'What the hell?' Jack shouted, as he emerged from behind the treasure chest and seeing Anne standing there motionless holding a flintlock aloft.

'What you do that for?' Mark cried.

'Bloody hell, lassie!' Jock yelled.

'Shut it! Just shut it; you dogs!' Anne screamed at the top of her voice. 'We will have a special kind of treasure soon enough, but now is not the time to be setting sail on a voyage of pillaging and debauchery!'

'Why not?' Jack barked back.

Anne was in no mood to pussy foot around any longer and she let everything out, regardless of the effect it might have on them.

'You poor wretched fools! You just don't get it, do you?'

'Get what?' spluttered Jack.

'We've been dead for over three-hundred years,' she continued

'Not that again,' he interrupted, but he soon backed down when she glared at him with that look of wrath in her eyes, that he knew only too well and knew this was not the time to challenge her. Cementing her authority, she continued on with her tirade.

'It stands to reason that at lot would have changed in three-hundred years, changes we know nothing about. We do not know what is out there! The people of this world have probably got more powerful weapons than us, large armies could roam the lands. There is only the four of us, and we are not yet fit to take on what this new world may throw at us!'

Everyone fell silent as they digested her words, and Anne just stood there, trembling with the rage she felt. She was furious with them for not thinking through the enormity of their situation. Mark was the first to speak.

'How do you know it's been three-hundred years?'

Anne was not ready to divulge the details of the voice in the wind just yet. She was fully aware that being reborn, after being dead for several centuries, was a fantastic revelation on her part, but to speak about hearing voices in the wind at this stage, might make them think she had totally lost the plot. Not referring directly to what the voice in the wind had actually said to her, she posed them a question instead, hoping that it might encourage them to consider their situation more rationally.

'Think about it,' she said calmly, 'rising from the dead is not something that occurs every day, so why has it happened to us? We have not risen again through choice, something has caused this to happen, and we have to ask the question, why?'

'Why what?' Jack asked slightly puzzled.

'Oh, you can be so dense at times Jack!' Anne chided. 'The question we must ask ourselves is why have we been resurrected?'

No one answered, because it was a question no one had ever had to think about before, and although it seemed absurd, especially to Jack, there was a ring of truth in Annes' words that sent a shiver through each of them. Anne then went on and asked them about their memory loss.

'You all say you had a vision, and you remember waking up here, but what about before that?'

Anne smiled as Mark was the first to speak again, and it showed that it was always her kind that actually had the intellect to ask the right questions, however difficult they might be.

'I remember we were close Anne, and that we were pirates of course, and I remember us all being together, but apart from that, my memory is very hazy.'

'Same here,' Jock interjected, 'I remember us being pirates, but that's about all I can remember.'

Anne let their thoughts dwell in their minds before speaking again. She then pressed them further by asking;

'But what about before we were pirates? What do you remember about those times?'

By interrogating them about their lives before they became pirates, stunned each of them into the stark reality, that at that very moment, their own past did not exist, well, not in their minds at least.

'You can't remember, can you? And Jack, don't you think that conflicts with your belief, that all this was caused by some potion we consumed?'

This statement worried Jack, as it created a doubt in his own mind, and Anne went further to push this point home.

'You see Jack, if we had been under the influence of some narcotic that numbed our memories, how come we can remember some things and not others? If we can remember being pirates, surely we should remember what happened to us last night?'

Whichever way they thought about it, they had to admit that what Anne spoke of, must be the truth, and it scared them. Jack still wasn't ready to totally concede to Anne, and although what she said made some kind of sense, he wanted to know what Anne herself knew. How come she knows all this, and they didn't? Was she up to something? Jack didn't like being kept in the dark and asked her outright.

'What about you Anne, what do you remember?'

Either Anne was lying or telling the truth, but either way, her answer metaphorically smacked him across the face, just as if she had done so physically.

'Everything.' she answered cooly.

She could see from the reaction on their faces that they were puzzled by her response. It was fair, she supposed, because they were all experiencing memory loss and they naturally would expect her to be suffering the same. But this was a chance to gently coax them nearer to the point of remembering those events that were currently locked from their consciousness.

'Look,' she explained, 'it seems to me, that you can't remember certain things about your past, such as when you died, because there is a certain amount of trauma associated with those events.'

Mark yet again supported Anne with his reaction.

'I see what you mean, Anne. My waking recollection was of a prison cell, and some child that filled me with terror.'

'Exactly; Mark,' Anne continued. 'You can see that there was some trauma connected with your deaths. As for me, I had no such visions, I felt I was waking from a deep restful sleep.'

'Yer mean, yer must have died a peaceful death?' Jock suggested.

'I believe so, yes,' continued Anne, 'and because of that, my memory was not affected, and so, I remember everything.'

Anne felt slightly uncomfortable as they were dangerously near the truth of her own demise. How would they react when they realised she escaped the hangman's noose, when they themselves succumbed to death through devastating ways? There was no fear of them questioning that aspect of history at the moment, because of their memory loss, and that was very convenient for Anne. After a short pause, Jack spoke with an air of despondency:

'Oh, that's just great, that is. You have your mind intact, but I don't! You know, I can't think of a more unpleasant situation than that!'

'Why?' Anne asked curiously, not fully comprehending what lay behind the reason for his comment.

'Well, because when yer woman can remember everything, and you can't, it puts a man at a very distinct disadvantage!'

Anne was unsure whether Jack meant it as some sort of joke or as an insult, but before she had chance to think of a witty response, Jock chimed in.

'Aye, rather like waking up after a night binging

on rum!'

Everyone laughed at the supposition, and it gave Anne the perfect riposte. She stood up and declared;

'Aye, except when Jack used to binge on rum, it wasn't just his mind that didn't work!'

And with that, she wiggled her little finger suggestively in the air, and moved her hand, still waggling her finger, in front of Jacks' nose, to the delight and amusement of the others.

'Oh, bad 'cess! To you Anne Bonny!' he spat and sulkily plonked himself on the treasure chest.

Anne was in her element as she was finally making progress with Jack, and she had him exactly where she wanted him. She was determined to break down the façade of his false mirage of the truth.

'And another thing; where is the rest of the crew, Jack?' she asked. 'If we have only awoken from a drinking binge, where is everyone else?'

There was no answer to this question, and Jack knew it, he knew the ship should be full of sailors, all going about their duties, but there was no one else on board, apart from the four of them.

'We have been chosen!' she concluded.

'Chosen?' Jock cut in, 'You make it sound like this has all been prearranged.'

'Precisely,' Anne added, 'and if we want to find out why we have been selected, we must examine what we do know, and not dwell on what we don't.'

No one said anything, and so Anne persisted with her narrative.

'We all agree we remember waking up here, back on our ship, and we agree that recollections of our past are vague, to say the least, especially in relation to the times before we became pirates and the nature of our own deaths. Until we open up the gateway to our past again, we will learn nothing. It is imperative therefore, that we focus our minds on regaining our long-lost memories, so we can start to find the answers to this strange and extraordinary situation we find ourselves in.'

It was a brilliant and well thought out speech she had delivered, she thought. The only problem was, the others hadn't a clue what she was talking about. They knew Anne would often reason through situations that were beyond their reach of comprehension, but as she was always proved to be right, they trusted her. That was a wonderful compliment to Anne, but the disadvantage was that everyone would just rely on her to solve difficult problems, rather than taking the time to reason things through for themselves. Jack, Mark, and Jock had some recollection of the time they were pirates but there were still patches of mist in their minds about those days. One thing Anne was sure of, was that by stimulating some of their memories, others would return naturally. It was just a matter of setting the process going. Of the three of them, she thought, Jack was the one least likely to suffer any long term upset by his hidden traumatic experiences, and so, was the best candidate to start with. The only problem with Jack, was being able to break down his stupid mental barrier that prevented him from rationalising the facts before him. What she needed to do, was to get him to remember things for himself, without any prompting from herself. She thought about Jacks' personality rather than his manner, as this was possibly where she would find the stimulant she needed. She recalled how he used to sing to himself when going about the ship, checking on what everyone was doing and ensuring duties were carried out correctly. There was a song he would sing to himself a lot, which told the story of a crew of pirates and their adventures, and Anne wondered if this might be the key she was looking for. Everyone was deep in thought as they considered what she had said, and while they contemplated, Anne made out she was preoccupied with something and casually wandered around the deck. She sauntered over to the brazier where the coals had virtually burnt away, but still gave off a warm glow. Absent-mindedly she warmed her hands over the dying embers, and softly began singing to herself.

'As we were sailing over, the blue Caribbean ocean….' The tune was soft and gentle, and her voice, although quiet, echoed around the deck. Something then remarkable happened! Upon hearing Anne singing, Jack sat bolt upright and began joining in.

'..On the sloop of Captain Vane, t'was then I had the notion...!'

'Captain Vane,' Jack then cried out, 'I remember captain Vane!'

'Aye, I remember him too!' Jock proclaimed, 'he were a right useless captain he was! Afraid to attack large ships!'

'Ha, that's true enough!' laughed Jack.

Anne was overjoyed at the progress she had made with Jack and encouraged him further.

'That's right! You overthrew him, remember?'

As one memory unlocked itself, so did the rest, like a line of toppling dominoes, Jacks' memories started falling back into place faster and faster. It was really quite fascinating to Anne, and she beamed all over her face.

'The Spanish man o'war!' he blurted out excitedly. 'We came on her one night just off the coast of Cuba!

'Aye, I remember that!' Mark yelled with glee, as he jumped up and down clapping his hands.

Even Jock started performing a type of highland fling, with both hands on his waist, and skipping on the spot whilst his kilt rose dangerously high, as it flapped in the breeze he was creating. Jack was certainly on a roll and heading straight for the memory of his execution, and Anne was ready. How would it affect him? She didn't know, but she was prepared and ready to comfort and care for him when the crashing realisation struck. She didn't have to wait too long, for the crazy merriment the three of them were indulging in, was rapidly reaching its climax.

'Ha!' laughed Jack, as he leapt on the treasure chest again. 'I can see that fool captain Barnet! It's early in the morning and he's upon us!'

Jack tailed off suddenly, and Jock and Mark froze as they both knew, to whom he was referring to. Captain Barnet was the one that had captured them and taken them to trial. This is it, thought Anne. It seemed like an eternity before Jack spoke again, and when he spoke, his tone was dark, and he whispered softly;

'John Rackham! You will be taken from this court and hanged for your wicked deeds.'

Anne smiled gently to herself as it was not a bad impression of the judge, she thought. Jack then leapt off the treasure chest laughing hysterically, and everyone was concerned for his sanity.

'Jack? Jack? Are you alright?' Anne pleaded sincerely; desperately hoping she had not gone too far.

Still laughing, although somewhat not quite as erratically, he turned to her and bellowed:

'They cheered Anne! They Cheered!'

Anne was taken aback by his joviality and couldn't understand his behaviour. She had expected him to be devastated by the memory of his execution, but he was happy, he was ecstatic.

'They cheered for me Anne! They cheered for me, Calico Jack!'

# CHAPTER 6

## Mary Read

Everyone was concerned for Jack, as the exuberance of his emotions was totally out of character. Mark and Jock moved over to him with a certain expression of puzzlement and concern on their faces. Mark took Jacks' hand, almost as if he was about to feel for a pulse, while Jock took Jacks' face in his enormous hands, turned his head towards himself, and gazed deeply into his eyes. Anne smiled dryly to herself at the peculiar scene before her, not because they all looked rather comical in their pose, but rather because she was pleased they were showing a certain amount of concern for each other. The question was why? Why were they suddenly concerned for Jack? Nothing like this had ever happened before, so why now? All she could surmise was that it was because they were alone, the four of them, on the ship once again and they needed each other for protection, especially as they didn't know what might happen next.

'So, Jack, the memory of your past life has returned then?

'Oh yes!' he dreamily replied, as he plonked himself down on the treasure chest.

Mark and Jock, being satisfied there was nothing wrong with Jack, apart from his odd behaviour, contented themselves and sat on the two packing crates.

'Yes, I can remember much now, about our pirating days. I remember Mark and Jock vividly, but I'm still not sure about you though,' Jack said to Anne.

For a moment she was puzzled, but when she saw the faint smile cross Jacks face, she knew he was teasing her, and she laughed.

'Something else has struck me too,' said Jack. We've all been so engrossed in our strange situation, that none of us have thought about the ship.

'What do you mean?' queried Anne.

Jack pointed out that nobody had realised they were adrift and could be smashed to pieces on unseen rocks at any moment. Anne gasped as she realised what Jack meant. Ever since they had returned, the ship had been sailing without anyone at the helm. Anne called to Mark and Jock to go and lower the anchor, but Jack cut in.

'No, leave this to me. I'll do it,' Jack said as he wandered off towards the stern of the ship. Mark and Jock sat back down on the crates and Anne turned to them and asked how much they could remember. After a moment, Mark piped up.

'Mostly. I remember much, but there are dark shadows in my mind.'

Memories of their adventures, of when they were all pirates in the past, swam back into his consciousness in a slow-motion dream like vision, and because his memories seemed to be returning fast, he attempted to remember, the one memory that had alluded him. The more he tried to think about the memory of the mysterious child, the more distant the memory became. After trying desperately to remember for several seconds, without success, he turned to Anne and asked;

'Anne, who was that child in my vision?'

Anne was pleased that their memories were starting to return, and she was relieved that Jack had not been affected by the sudden restoration of his memory, but the missing piece of the jigsaw in Marks' mind was of great concern. Although she knew Mark would eventually remember, it was vital that not only should he remember in his own time, but when it happened, she would have to be there with him. The dilemma Anne had, was what should she do in the meantime when Mark asked her questions about the blank piece of his memory? All she could do was to stall for time, and she answered him in a casual, matter of fact way.

'Not now Mark....'

Anne was conscious that she should answer in a way that made it sound like it was unimportant, but she hoped she didn't overdo it and appear to be holding something back. Anne casually remarked;

'In time all their memories would return, but they might not all be pleasant, and you will need to be ready to face them, she warned.

By speaking generally, she hoped she had disguised her concern for Mark by seemingly being concerned for all of them. Anne knew full well that, although each of them had regained a lot of their long-forgotten memories, there were still parts of their consciousness that lay dormant. How would they react when those hidden images resurfaced? What effect would it have upon them? For now, all she could do was wait and let fate follow its intended path. Annes' thoughts were suddenly interrupted by Jock. He had been sitting on the packing crate, absorbed deeply in his own thoughts. He abruptly looked up and said;

'Teach!' He had obviously spoken aloud, a reference to something he was thinking about.

'Teach what?' Mark asked puzzled by Jocks' sudden question.

Jock rose to his feet, evidently focusing on

something in his mind.

'Teach! Edward Teach! You remember Edward Teach, don't you Anne?'

'Aye!' she replied.

Anne was instantly transported back to those days long ago, before she became a pirate. She had worked as an office clerk back in Nassau during the day, and although not a job usually undertaken by women, her father had secured her the position through one of his contacts. He felt it would do her good to have a job, partly to educate her, and partly to keep her out of mischief. Her father, couldn't have been more wrong about the latter reason though, because by being employed in a shipping office, she regularly got to meet sailors, and worse, pirates! She saw how they would frequent Inns and Taverns and she envied their energetic social activities, wishing desperately that she could join in. Unfortunately, being a girl of only fifteen, this was a lifestyle that would have been far too dangerous. It was a lifestyle that attracted her though, nonetheless. The shipping merchant she worked for, bought, and sold cargo from the constant flow of ships that entered the docks of Nassau, and although most of the ship's captains were honest tradesmen, her employer was not adverse to the odd shady deal with pirates. In fact, many shipping magnets were involved with pirates as it was a way of life, and even the Governor himself would often turn a blind eye to the illegal activities of the brigands, if there was something in it for himself. Annes' job was to keep the records of all the goods traded through her employer's Office. Every item bought or sold, had to be listed in the big leather-bound ledger, along with the price, well, all the legitimate articles of business were. Dealings with not so legitimate transactions, i.e. dealings with outlaws and pirates, were recorded on bits of paper and kept in an old tin that was stored under a loose floorboard in the corner of the Office. If ever there were disputes about contracts with vagabonds, her employer could produce written records, albeit not documents that would have any status in law, but bonds that could act as an insurance, and be provided as evidence to condemn any unscrupulous pirate captain that tried to cross him. As her father had been through a difficult time with business not being so good, Anne thought to herself, that some of this ill-gotten wealth could go a long way to helping him in his current situation. Afterall, it was illegal money, and no one was going to ask any questions if certain pirates had some of their money stolen! It was customary for Anne to take bags of coins from her employer, down to the docks and pay the various pirate captains their share of the profits from the sales of cargo. It would be easy enough if a bag or two of money went missing! The problem was though that the pirates would turn the town upside down in search of anyone who crossed them. At noon, on a balmy hot day in June, Anne made her way down to the dockside with her usual bags of money, thinking how she could possibly cheat the pirates out of some of their booty. Fate was with her that day, because when she reached the quayside, she saw a large schooner docked in Port with some furore happening on board. She could see the bright red jackets of the British soldiers swarming all over the deck of the large vessel. As she watched, she saw several chests surreptitiously being dumped in the water at the bow end of the ship, evidently to conceal them from the Soldiers, and no doubt to be retrieved later. A young seaman called James Bonny, was coiling some ropes on the ground, and she called over to him;

'What's afoot, James?'

The young man glanced up and said

'Oh, just British inspection.'

The British were fond of their so-called inspections. They would board a ship suspected of being crewed by pirates, and blackmail the captain into handing over gold or other valuable goods they had amassed, in return for not reporting them to the harbour master or the governor. When the soldiers were satisfied with their recompense, they would disembark and let the pirates carry on unmolested. On this occasion, the schooner in the dock, belonged to none other than Edward Teach, otherwise known as Blackbeard. Blackbeard was a fiendish individual, who took delight in torturing his victims before finally killing them. He would frequently put lighted tapers in his long black beard, so as to scare the living daylights out of those unfortunate merchant seamen he came across, in his perpetual plundering of the seas around the Caribbean. Although Anne didn't want to dwell more than necessary on the memory of James Bonny, she did however, think about how they had swum out into the harbour that night, and somehow managed to retrieve one of the trunks that had been discarded from the schooner, when the British army had boarded. Once they had wrestled it onto the beach, they forced it open and found it full of Spanish gold! Anne smiled, as she remembered seeing all that money, and how it had helped her father as well as setting herself up with a considerable fortune. For a second, she remembered how it was also the beginning of her relationship with James Bonny, but she quickly came back to reality, and put the thought of him out of her mind. She turned to Jock and exclaimed:

'Blackbeard! Oh yes, I remember him well. I remember the great service you did for all the privateers in relation to Mr Teach, Jock!'

'What did you do, Jock?' Mark Asked.

'I killed him!' came the casual reply, and everyone fell about laughing.

Before becoming a full-time pirate, Jock had spent his time working with whoever would employ him. He was often employed because of his commanding stature and his warrior like qualities. "Jock the mercenary," people called him, although he wasn't particularly fond of that name, as he felt it made him sound like an unprincipled thug. Invariably the enemies of his employers would back down at the mere sight of Jock, advancing towards them with sword and pistol in his giant hands. On one occasion, the British army enlisted as many men they could, in an attempt to take down Edward Teach, as he had become too much of a liability, for not only the Governor, but for other pirates as well. Teach was upsetting the natural balance of moderate piracy and many stood to lose the comfortable and profitable lives they all enjoyed. Teach had to be rid of. On the day of the attack, Teach, a big man himself, was not intimidated by the giant Scotsman and had engaged him in combat. Jock remembered it was one of those days where he'd literally fought for his life. Jock felt, it was more luck than skill that he was finally victorious, as Teach seemingly stumbled in their battle. This gave Jock enough time to recover his wits, and he thrust his sword right through the chest of the odious Blackbeard.

Jack wandered back on deck having lowered the anchor and fastening the ship, so they were no longer adrift. Seeing Jack, Anne remarked with a sort of pride in her tone,

'It seems much of the memories of your former selves have returned.'

Everyone nodded with broad grins on their faces. Jack was still in a good mood and was evidently ready to resume his pirate life once more, as he proclaimed, that now they knew who they were and what they were, they should set sail and prepare for attack. Anne had to reign in his wild enthusiasm once again, and chided him for his lack of consideration.

'NO! Stand-to, there Jack. Remembering our time as pirates is not enough!' she bellowed. Jack had never been one to climb down quickly, even if he knew Anne had a point, he would still push his argument as far as he could.

'What do you mean, not enough?' He pulled rank and spoke with authority, 'now is the time says I, now fall in Bonny!'

Jack knew it and Anne knew it; the argument would not end there. Both Jack and Anne, always battled to have the last word in any argument, and so Anne retorted back:

'For God's sake, Rackham, for once in your life, think man, THINK!'

Taken aback by her ferocity, the only words he could muster were,

'You what?'

He did manage to make himself quite fierce in their delivery, or so he thought. Anne paused before responding, allowing Jack to interject with some other foolish remark, for which she could admonish him for, but none came. Jack stood there glowering. After several seconds and with a calmer, gentler voice, Anne continued;

'There is still much in our minds that is hidden from us. It is imperative that we fight to unlock those deep, forgotten times of so long ago! That is why we are alive again! We must not fall into our old ways of delinquency; we must aim beyond that.'

In her mind, she could hear the voice in the wind, telling her about the importance of their long-forgotten memories, and she knew the secrets locked inside their minds held the key to the puzzle of their resurrection. Anne felt she had impressed upon them a well-reasoned argument as to why they should not revert to their old pirate ways. But she had been overconfident in the delivery of her words. She was startled by Mark, who suddenly spoke up with much more confidence than would have been expected, and in a somewhat scathing tone, he attacked Anne verbally.

'Don't be so sanctimonious, Anne! Jacks' right. We are pirates and that is how we survive.' Before Anne could respond, Jock joined in with his verbal disapproval.

'I respect yer, lassie, but yer sound like the preacher, with yer fine words. Fine words spoken by those with comfortable lives are easy, but we have tae fight to live. We cannae live by fine words!'

This was too much for Anne. She could be a wonderful diplomat when situations demanded it, and she was skilled at manipulating a situation, but Annes' biggest weakness was she was quick to temper when she thought she was being criticized personally. She turned on Jock and spat back;

'Fine words are they? Tell me Jock, what exactly is out there in this new world, huh? What dangers lurk in the corners, we have no knowledge of? Tell me! I want to know!'

Metaphorically putting her foot down, she told them in no uncertain terms that exploring their past was the path they would now have to take, and that future adventures would have to wait. Nobody said anything. Mark and Jock went back and sat on the packing cases in a way that could only be described as deflated, while Jack, just stood there staring into space. Anne stormed up onto the raised platform by the wheel in silence. Taking the wheel roughly in her hands, she gazed out across the horizon. As the ship was at anchor, there was no necessity for navigation, but it helped her to focus her anger. Jack broke the ominous silence and spoke softly and slowly, almost as if he were testing Annes' mood, and partly anticipating a tirade of abuse at his point of view.

'Whether our destiny lies in the past, or out

there in the future, at this moment, it is irrelevant.'

There was no response from Anne. She kept her gaze on the distant horizon and gripped the wheel tightly. She was rigid and tense, but she showed no emotion. Thinking he was safe to continue relaying his thoughts, Jack went on.

'What is important is the here and now. You all remember I was your captain before, and now I am your captain again.'

Still Anne did not move or make any indication of her feelings. It was Jock who answered, and he was not in the mood to take Jacks domineering attitude.

'Hold fast, there laddie,' he spat.

He told Jack in no uncertain terms, that although he had been captain in the past, it didn't give him the right to be captain now. Mark entered the debate and offered his opinion that many captains had been overthrown in the past, for less than what Jack had done.

'And prey tell me, what exactly have I done that is so terrible?' Jack spluttered in reply. Without adverting her eyes or making any movement whatsoever, Anne responded.

'Because of you, we were taken.'

The repost was perfect, and it stunned Jack spectacularly. He just gazed at her with a pained expression, his mouth open and unable to make any comment. Mark, marched up to him and yelled in his face.

'I died 'cause of you, John Rackham!'
Jumping to Marks' defence, Jock confirmed that allowing one's crew to be taken, was a good enough reason to depose a captain. Jack was incensed and retaliated in a more aggressive way than any of them had ever experienced from him before, or at least, in a way that they could remember. Jack seemed to almost double in size as he reared himself up and thrust out his chest. He threw his head back and laughed in a cruel and condescending manner, and then posed the question.

'Who's going to depose me?'
He turned on Jock, and insultingly indicated that the Scotsman was incapable of being captain, because of his tendency to take so long thinking everything through, before making any kind of decision. He accused Jock of being so fastidious that in battle, everyone would be dead before he could bark out an order. For a moment, Mark thought Jock was going to burst into tears, like a little boy being bullied by his elders, but Jock held his position and glared hard into Jacks eyes. Jack avoided Jocks' gaze by turning his focus on Mark.

'I suppose you think you'd make a good captain, do you boy? 'Cause that is all you are, a boy!'
Mark just shook his head and said,

'Not I, but you're forgetting Anne?'
There was a darkness in Marks words, and just as with Jack, Marks' manner was totally out of character, but he stood up to Jack and confronted

him. Jock felt there was a bit of Anne in the young lad, and perhaps her influence was starting to rub off on the boy. Jack responded arrogantly and sarcastically.

'What? Anne? A woman?' and he guffawed so much, tears welled up in his eyes with joy.

If it were possible for anyone to suddenly turn into a hideous monster, at that moment, Jack did just that. The contrast of his manic laughter and his thunderous words was quite frightening, but Anne recognised this trait in her lover. She had seen it before, although mainly when he was engaged in battle with other ships. She had hardly ever seen this side of his personality privately or when talking to the crew. She wondered if the sudden remembrance of his past execution was now having the effect she had feared. Jack spat at Mark, reminding him that there were stiff penalties for mutinous talk on his ship, and any that harboured such thoughts, would feel his wrath, and would wish they had stayed within the bosom of Davy Jones' Locker. He yelled at Mark that he was the captain, and he would do well to remember that. Jock immediately sprang to Marks' defence again, and reminded Jack that it was customary for the crew to hold a captain's vote when there was dissatisfaction with a captain. Jock could see in Jacks' expression that there was no possibility of him allowing a vote, so he resorted to the only action open to him, a challenge!

'We shall have to settle this in the traditional way!' Jock yelled at Jack, as he drew a sword from his baldrick that was hanging from a marlin spike on the wall of the ship.

As he pointed his sword at Jack, Mark launched into action as well, and he too brandished a sword in Jacks' face.

'Have at you, Jack Calico!' he screamed, as he brought his sword down as if to cleave Jack in two!

Jack was an experienced swordsman and easily parried the blow, but as he did so, he caught the sight of Jocks' sword slashing towards him out of the corner of his eyes. Spinning in an instant, he managed to parry Jocks' attack, but Mark was on him again. The more Jack parried them, the more aggressive they became. The fight was over as suddenly as it had begun by a fourth sword joining the affray.

'Desist I say! Desist this minute!' Anne bellowed at them.

This was exactly what she didn't want to happen! Anne had been very much aware, that as their memories returned, there was a strong possibility that they could fall back into their old ways, before taking the path that was intended for them. Using all her cunning and strength, she had to nip these skirmishes in the bud. Anne was a great reasoner, but she knew there were times no amount of reasoning would work, and that resorting to violence was the only way to exhort her authority. Fortunately, the three of them immediately put their swords away on her intervention. Glaring at them, Anne spoke to them in a voice they all recognised. Anne had the knack of exerting her authority by speaking slowly and quietly, but devoid of any sense of emotion. Her words were cold, and chilling. She had induced a deep fear in many a pirate over the years and it was this tone that she now adopted.

'There is only one true captain here, and anyone who disagrees, will have me to deal with, right?' Her eyes pierced into each of them as she spoke, daring anyone to contest her, but of course, they didn't. Jock was about to protest about Jacks' attitude, but Anne shut him down, telling him to shut it. After a long pause, while each of them allowed the tension to dissipate before speaking, Jack whispered under his breath that he was still the captain. He miscalculated the mood however, as Anne heard him, and she rounded on him, telling him to shut it as well! Before he could argue back, Anne cut him off and warned him to quit while he was ahead. When Anne was in these moods, Jack knew it was pointless to argue with her. He had learned long ago that it was best to let her calm down on her own, while he busied himself with captains' duties. He could always revisit the argument later, when Anne was not in such a defiant frame of mind. For whatever reason, Jack went against his usual reaction and fought back with a thrust as deadly as a red-hot dagger, where Anne was concerned.

'Just be very careful, Andy Cormack!' Jack viciously spat.

Anne had very precise boundaries where "Andy Cormack" was concerned. Everyone, or at least, everyone who knew her, knew about Andy Cormack. She considered Andy Cormack as a completely different person to herself, a kind of alternative personality, she liked to think of him. When she dressed as a man, it was for a reason. A reason usually, where Anne wanted to gain an advantage that would not be possible as a woman. However, degrading this was to her, she knew she could not fight against the male prejudices of the time, but she could play against them by being Andy Cormack. The certainty was, that Anne knew her own mind and was savagely proud of herself as a woman, standing up for herself in a man's world. She was independent and lived her life by her own rules. She did not need the guise of a man to be who she was, only to take advantage of men, and their corrupt ideology of women. Calling her Andy Cormack, Jack had insulted her to the core, as he was accusing her of being a weak woman, who could only achieve success in the world by being a man. For a second, this insult shook Anne, and the tone in her reply indicated he had got to her.

'What did you say?' she responded, with a slight tremor in her voice.

It was only slight, but it was enough for Mark to notice. Jack knew he had the advantage of her and pressed on with his verbal attack.

'You see! I do remember. I remember, the ever so strong woman, that had to hide by pretending to be a man!'

What made the atrocious slur much worse for Anne, was that if it had been any ordinary roughneck in a Tavern, she would have fought back violently, even though she wouldn't have taken it too personally, as she was used to this kind of abuse. But when it came from her lover, the one person who should respect and know her better, it hurt and hurt like hell. It hurt like the cold steel of a rapier piercing her heart. Anne was incensed and went to attack him. She raised her sword above her head, but suddenly without warning, the young lad, who up to now, had been quite docile, albeit a little arrogant, launched into a violent attack against Jack. His manner was even more violent and aggressive than when he'd questioned Jacks' claim to be captain. It was as if he'd been possessed by some terrible demon, and he seemed to be reacting as if Jack had directed his comments at him, rather than at Anne. Everyone was shocked by this outburst and even Jack pulled back in alarm. Anne leapt on the boy and restrained him physically. It was an act of gallantry on Marks' part, but it was rather stupid to attack Jack as he could have easily been killed in the fight. In his confusion at the outburst from Mark, Jack was evidently shaken, and he had completely lost his advantage. The only course of action open to him, was to withdraw below and wait for the atmosphere to calm down. Retreat and rebuild your strength, he reasoned. With a parting word, he spluttered;

'Just watch yer back, Anne Bonny, I don't take kindly to being crossed!'

With that, he stormed off through the right-hand door and disappeared into the bowels of the ship. Anne felt Mark struggling against her grip, ready to attack Jack again.

'Be careful,' she warned Mark. 'Don't push him too far.'

Jock had been standing watching the foray with a confused look on his face. He was stunned at the boy's outburst, and never dreamed the young laddie had it in him.

'Yer a feisty one, laddie, I'll give yer that!' Jock said, but Mark rounded on him, and told him he was more than feisty, and warned him to watch out for himself in future.

The best policy, Anne thought, was to get them all apart until things calmed down. She ordered Jock to go below and talk to Jack. Anne was concerned. Not just because of Marks' sudden attack on Jack, but because it could have led to a more volatile situation. Anne was fully aware of her part in this strange situation they had all found themselves in, and had focused on what she presumed was expected of her. The voice in the wind had told her she had to lead them to their ultimate destiny, and although the voice had been very ambiguous, Anne had reasoned her role was that of guardian of her shipmates. She knew they had lost their memories, yet she hadn't, and she knew that when their memories returned, it would cause each of them a considerable trauma. There were many questions, but for now, Annes' role was to guide them through the ordeal of remembering their tragic pasts, and then to guide them to recollect other times in their lives. What this would lead to, she was unsure, but she believed answers would become clearer in due course. There was an exception to all this however, and it confused Anne. Why do they not remember Mark? She asked herself. They should know! There is nothing traumatic about remembering Mark, so why do they not remember? Had the truth come out during the spat with Jack, who knows what would have happened? As Jock went below deck, she took Mark by the shoulders and led him to the large treasure chest and sat him on it.

'You calmed down now?' she asked.

Mark was evidently a lot calmer as he sat on the chest, like a little child with his legs dangling, as they didn't quite reach the floor. He simply replied:

'Yes,' and just sat there looking forlorn and regretting his tirade.

Anne smiled at him and said;

'You look silly!' Looking up at Anne, Mark replied puzzled
'Silly? How Silly?'
'With that stupid caterpillar stuck to your face.'
Every time Anne had looked at Mark since they had awoken, she'd often had to stifle a chuckle. Seeing her friend of so long ago with that ridiculous looking moustache was absurd. It didn't even look real. It could have been quiet concerning had the whole thing not been so comical. Mark didn't think it was funny though, and defended his moustache. He explained how he didn't want Jack or Jock to know the truth. Anne was puzzled, because they had all known in the past, so why all the secrecy now? But Mark kept to his belief that it was better they didn't know. Mark was wary of Jock, because he noticed things, and so he had to be extremely careful around the Scotsman. Yes, he was a good man, but Mark couldn't afford to let him find out as he was afraid of the reaction from his old friend. Mark went on and said, he didn't fear Jack so much, as he wouldn't notice the truth, even if it struck him in the face. They both chuckled at the thought of Jacks' inability to grasp the simplest of things that happened around him. But Mark looked at Anne sadly, and told her that Jack was a good man deep down, but that he was nothing without her. Was it jealousy or resentment? or was Mark just sorry that he hadn't been as lucky as Anne in having someone close. They were

both so alike in so many ways, Anne thought. She couldn't help wondering that in his previous life, had Mark found someone who had stuck by him instead of using him, he might not have died in the way he had. Could that all change this time? Who knew, but if it did, that would answer many questions as to the purpose for their resurrection.

'Jack has you Anne, and that is why I have Mark,' the boy continued. 'He protects me, he keeps me safe. I feel I can be myself with Mark.'

'I know,' Anne said softly. 'I really do know. That is why I always kept the boundaries between myself and Andy Cormack. You see,' Anne continued, 'It is all very well being Mark, and I understand why, but sometimes, just occasionally, you have to simply be, yourself.'

Anne reached out to Mark, and taking his hair between her fingers, she gently tugged at his curly locks. The wig came away easily and was replaced by a shock of blond short, cropped hair. She then gently pulled the ridiculous false moustache from his top lip and flicked it away across the deck. As she did so, she gazed at the young woman who now sat on the treasure chest where Mark Read had sat a moment ago. Anne smiled at her and said gently,

'Hello, Mary Read.'

# CHAPTER 7

## **The Isle of Skye**

Jack was lying on the bunk in the cabin where he'd found his clothes. He would often take up residency of a single berth rather than using his own captain's cabin, because he had to share that with Anne. Sometimes, it was nice to have some space of his own, away from her. He lay there, gazing up at the ceiling and kicking the wall like a petulant child. He hated it when Anne belittled him in front of everyone, and when she did, he would storm off in a fit of pique to console his battered ego. Jack was his own worst enemy and never for a moment did it ever occur to him that he brought many of his problems on himself. Jack was too dogmatic, although he couldn't see it. It was that one negative trait of his, that Anne was constantly battling against. If only he could just stop for a minute and consider the point of view of others, he might actually be drawn to the right conclusions and in turn, take the right decisions. He always had to have the last word, even if it was obvious he was totally wrong. To Jack, it was about being right, regardless of whether the facts backed up his argument or not, and to back down was a sign of weakness. Anne believed it blindingly obvious that if he would only wait before spouting his argument and listened to all the other proposals first, it would make him appear more of a diplomat, rather than a hot-headed idiot. This reasoning, however, was not in Jacks' personality and he lay there just kicking the wall. What advantages were there to kicking the wall was anyone's guess, but it made Jack feel better and that was all that mattered to him. With the constant thump, thump, thump of his foot against the wooden panelling, Jack didn't hear the footsteps outside, and suddenly the door to his cabin burst open and the massive frame of Jock stood in the doorway.

'Make yer feel better, does it laddie?'

'What?' replied Jack stroppily.

'Kickin' the wall,' said Jock, in his thick Scottish brogue.

Jack leapt to his feet and faced the Scotsman. In a snarling, self-pitying manner, he asked Jock what it was to do with him what he did in his own cabin. Jack was aggressive, and many would have responded with an equal amount of aggression in the past, even Jock himself would have risen to the threat, but Jock just smiled, as he knew Jack of old. He knew when Jacks' ego was bruised that he would always be on the defensive. Like Anne, Jock knew how to deal with Jack in these situations. He placed his hand on Jacks' shoulder and gently pushed him down on to the bunk.

'Does yer head hurt, laddie?' Jock asked, as he stroked Jacks' brow.

Jack looked puzzled.

'No.' he blankly replied.

'Does yer heart hurt, laddie?' he continued, jabbing his finger in Jacks' chest.

Jack looked at him curiously, wondering why the hell he was asking him such odd questions.

'No.' Jack responded dismissively.

'Does yer foot hurt?' Jock then asked.

Without thinking, Jack responded, saying that he did have an ache in his foot and that he must have sprained it slightly coming down the stairs. Jock stared up at the ceiling and almost as if he was talking to himself, he declared that it was funny how some people who had received no physical injury from a tongue lashing, were quite prepared to injure themselves physically by continuously kicking their foot against a wall, making it sore in the process.

'Aye!' Jock continued, 'the only reason in my mind that someone would punish themselves like that, is to atone for their own feelings of guilt.'

Jack just sat there looking up at the highlander without any spark of expression, except that his jaw dropped open and remained like that for several seconds, not knowing how to respond. Jock sat himself down on the bunk next to Jack. He didn't look at him, but just stared at the wall opposite. He told Jack about the times in the past when he had been engaged in battle and how he had been revered as an expert swordsman. It was true, Jock had been a master of the sword and had fought and won many skirmishes, but he went on, that he didn't really have any special abilities, just a good strategy. He explained how he would provoke his enemy with taunts and doing very little in the way of physical aggression.

'By doin' this,' he went on, 'I would inflame my opponent's anger and aggression to the point that they would explode their pent-up energy into a violent and forceful attack upon me. Because I was calm and relaxed, I had more strength, and it was easy for me to simply parry a forceful onslaught and simply thrust me sword into their belly.'

Jack frowned, and looked at Jock and glibly asked why he was telling him this?, as he wasn't remotely bit interested.

'But don't yer see. laddie? By conservin' yer strength and takin' yer time, yer come out on top. Let the other person get all flustered, not you.'

Mary was uncomfortable. She was uncomfortable being herself and she felt exposed without her disguise. Hiding her true identity behind the facade of "Mark," gave her confidence; and as she sat there on the treasure chest, her exposure became more and more distressing for her as the seconds ticked by. When she could bear it no longer, she reached out for her wig that Anne was holding in her hand.

'Please, Anne?' she begged, but Anne moved the wig further from her reach.

Anne knew she had to be cruel to be kind and force Mary to give up the ridiculous disguise.

'Look, Mary, I know exactly how exhilarating adopting a false personality can be. The danger is though, it can take you over. Andy Cormack was always a separate person to me in my mind, so it was easy to transit between my two personalities. Ultimately, you are you, and any other persona you adopt is not real, but the danger is, that your soul can become buried beneath a lie.'

Mary sat there rigid with her fingers digging into the wooden lid of the chest as Anne spoke. Ever since she had been very young she had pretended to be a man more than she'd ever been herself. To begin with, it enabled her mother to receive an income and later for her to gain good commissions at sea. In a way, she had fallen into the habit of being Mark Read and the more she had indulged in the ruse, the deeper Mary Read had been submerged in her consciousness. Mary stressed to Anne, that being Mark, made her strong and she needed Mark to do the things she wanted, but Anne dismissed her, telling her that she could still do anything she wanted as herself and the disguise was no more than a prop that was now working against her.

'Identify as a man if you wish to, but do so as yourself. Don't hide behind a false character to please others, just be you.'

As she spoke, Anne thought she saw a tear in Marys' eye, and it concerned her. If Mary were to be this emotional about giving up the habit of living as Mark, how in God's name will she cope when she remembers the truth about the child? Anne put out her arms and gathered Mary into her bosom. Mary welcomed the motherly embrace from Anne as it made her feel secure again. At that moment she wanted to remain in Annes' arms forever.

Jock had finally managed to talk some sense into Jack, and they began reminiscing about the times they had sailed together as pirates and the adventures they had had. Jock could be quite a raconteur and had Jack laughing with his tales of seafaring ventures. As they chatted and laughed over events from so long ago, Jock led Jack back out onto the upper deck. Jock felt it best to get Jack back with the others as soon as possible before resentment set in. Jock was well aware that in a defeated argument, Jack could quite well sulk for days on end, which could have long term repercussions with members of the crew, as he would often give the appearance that he held on to grudges. As they walked back onto the deck through the door to the left, with Jock in front, he delivered the climax to a tale about a pirate they had once known. Jack let out a hearty laugh as he remembered the foolishness of that particular mariner. His laughter suddenly stopped short though, when his eyes fell upon Anne standing by the treasure chest with someone in her arms. It was that Read lad, Jack concluded. He couldn't see his face, but he recognised the clothes of the cuckold, and he felt his temper surging up inside him. He stormed across to Anne and tore her away from the boy and almost succeeded in throwing her across the deck.

'What's goin' on here then!' He screamed. 'Who is this dog that you are so enamoured with?' As he spoke, he turned to face the wretch that was taking advantage, not only of his woman, but of himself. For a brief second, Jack was taken aback. The face of the upstart was not who he expected. Staring back at him was the face of a woman. In fact, the face was vaguely familiar, but he couldn't quite place it. Jack was stunned by what he saw and struggled to remember where he'd seen her before.

'Oh, don't be so stupid!' Annes' yell rang in his ears, and he realised he'd made another mistake, but rather than explode again, he just stood meekly looking at Mary. 'We've been here before, remember?'

Anne went on, but no matter how hard he thought, he just could not remember who this person was and said so.

'Remember her? I've absolutely no idea who this woman is.'

Anne was exasperated at his lack of memory. She grabbed him by the scruff of the neck, Jack let out a little yelp of surprise, and she physically forced him to look into the strange woman's face.

'Mary!' Anne hissed. 'Mary Read!'

Jacks' mind seemed to shift gear into slow motion, and he was conscious of waves of memories slowly swimming into the forefront of his brain. The image of Mary emerged out of the mist in his head, and he suddenly remembered her.

'Mary Read!' he beamed. 'You're Mary Read!'

Anne thought he was about to launch into some silly little dance and clap his hands, but he didn't. If Jock McTavish were prone to instances of blushing through embarrassment, this would have been one of them. The moment he realised Mark was really a woman, his mind raced back to earlier when they had first introduced themselves to each other and he had whipped off his birthing robe and stood there completely naked. At the time, he had been puzzled by Marks' reaction, but now it all made sense. In an attempt to conceal his awkwardness, he suddenly blurted out;

'Och, well I always knew!'

Everyone turned to look at the giant Scotsman with a look of incredible disbelief, as if to say he was talking balderdash. Jock, seeing the look on everyone's faces, knew they didn't believe him, so he changed tactic. 'I mean, I always thought there was somethin' odd about him.'

'Her!' Jack immediately interjected, but Mary cut in with,

'Him!'

'What?' Jack asked.

'Him,' repeated Mary, I prefer to be him, but yes, I am Mary Read.'

Mary smiled and Anne noticed her entire posture suddenly changed. Her shoulders weren't as hunched, and she thought she detected a slight reddish hue to her cheeks, which up and till now, had been pale and wan.

'Well, your secret's out now and you can relax,' Anne said warmly.

Mary felt her unmasking had been a bit of an anticlimax. She had expected, at the very least, an air of disapproval from her shipmates but none came. Jack took it all in his stride and just told her to be herself, like they all did, and with that, he took Jocks' arm, and led him to the raised platform. The two men sat down, and Jack took out a couple of dice from his pocket and started playing with the Scotsman. Although Mary was glad her secret was out and everyone still accepted her, she still felt naked being Mary and a wave of self-doubt swam over her and she yearned to be Mark again. She felt vulnerable without the protection of her alter ego, and she reached out to take back her wig from Anne, which she still held in her hand. Anne saw Marys' hand out of the corner of her eye as it crept slowly towards the hair piece and immediately turned to face Mary.

'What you doin'?' Anne questioned.

'My disguise,' Mary answered sheepishly.

Anne responded in her best mothering tone and told her that she didn't need it anymore, but Mary was insistent and implored Anne to give her the wig, insisting that she wanted to be seen as a man. Anne of course knew that the problem was not with how Mary identified herself, but that she had come to rely on the disguise as a form of safety and comfort to hide behind. Immersing oneself with another identity was harmless when it was done to achieve certain results, like she had done in the past, where the persona of a man enabled her to enjoy drinking and dancing in the Taverns or winning the advantage over unscrupulous sea captains, but the very real danger was when you allowed that false personality to take you over. This was nothing to do with how Mary wished to identify herself, it was purely a bad habit she had to break for her own sanity. Besides, thought Anne, she needs to be rid of the unhealthy emotional attachment to Mark before the truth finally dawns. Anne grasped Mary by the shoulders and looked deep into her eyes.

'Look, identify as a man if that is what is in your soul, but do so by just being you. You dress like a man and as far as we are concerned you are a man and that should be enough. What you know in your heart should be what you show to the world. Don't hide behind a disguise for the sake of others. They accept you or they don't.'

Mary knew Anne was right, but she still had reservations.

'What if people don't accept me?' she asked.

'Then I'll cut their bleedin' heads off!' Jock didn't even look up from his game of dice with Jack as he spoke, which only further demonstrated the strong bond they all had with each other.

Mary was a member of the crew, albeit a very small one, and however or whatever or whoever she was, she was one of them and anyone who disrespected any of them would feel the full force of their wrath. Anne smiled to herself. Seeing this strong bond of empathy growing between them was heartwarming. It wasn't because they had never been sympathetic or cared for others, it was because when they were pirates they had to suppress their emotions and appear cold and detached from emotions just to survive. Anne couldn't help drawing the analogy between their pirate personas and Marys' strong dependency on the fictitious Mark. They had all buried their true selves one way or another, due to the harshness of piracy, but now their real selves were starting to emerge from the darkness, and Anne thought it was wonderful. A cheer suddenly went up from the dice players. Jack had won a round and was like a big kid as he taunted Jock mercilessly, revelling in his win, as if it were some great skill on his part, rather than pure luck. It was all in fun though, and as Jack punched the air, he noticed Mary standing next to Anne watching them. Mary looked like a kid herself, but a kid new in town and was reluctant to join in.

'Come and join us, Mark!' Jack called across to her, as he took up the dice in his hands and began to shake them in his palms, ready for his next big win.

The sincerity in which he invited Mary to join them did not go unnoticed by Anne. Jack didn't invite her to join them out of pity or with any thought, he was casual and simply invited his friend to join in, as he would any other friend. The relationship between them went on as if the unmasking of Mark Read had never happened, and it proved the point, that Mary did not need the disguise to be herself and to be accepted.

Mary eagerly dragged the treasure chest nearer to the platform and sat down just as Jack threw the dice, but as the dice rolled and slid across the floor, the expression on Jacks' face changed from pure excitement to one of defeat. The dice came to a stop and the pips clearly showed that he had lost this round, much to the delight of his opponent. Jock, however, was more composed and gracious in his win than Jack had been. He simply looked up and smiled at Jack with a knowing twinkle in his eye, then turned to Mary and winked. There was something quite comical about it that made Mary laugh out loud, but in reality, she laughed because she was comfortable being herself with her two friends. Anne left the three of them to enjoy their game and wandered over to one of the packing crates and sat on it. She watched them as they played and took a moment to gather her thoughts. She was puzzled as to why neither Jack nor Jock had remembered Mark was really Mary. They had known in their previous life, so why had they not remembered now? Her mind retraced their steps over the past few hours from the moment they had awoken on the ship. It was remarkable she thought, as she watched them together, how they were so sociable with each other. It wasn't just camaraderie or friendly banter; they seemed more like a family that had been close to each other for years. More astonishingly, Anne thought, it was only half an hour since they were ready to tear each other to pieces. She was proud of them, and it was clear they were changing and changing fast. They truly were becoming the people they really had always been deep inside, but now, the personalities that had been lost for a very long time, were returning. Even though they were changing into more decent human beings than they could have been described when they were pirates, it would have been a mistake to believe they were in some way becoming spineless. Their individual traits remained intact, and in many ways, they were still hard and ready for action, and they could still be devious, forthright, and cunning. The realisation hit Anne with a jolt, she sat rigidly upright on the crate and her mouth fell open.

'Of course!' she muttered to herself.

She was sure the reason for their memory loss was in some way, to protect their fragile minds as they were thrust into the world of the living once more, after leaving it in such harrowing circumstances. It was logical that they should regain their memories slowly, so as not to damage their mental faculties permanently with the sudden realisation of who and what they had been. But it was more complex than that, Anne realised. They had not remembered Mark was really Mary because it was some kind of test. It was some kind of assessment of them as to how they would react to the situation as they evolved. Pirates, Anne knew, would always accept you if you were ready to risk your life for every member of the crew and it didn't matter who or what you were, as long as you could fight, and plunder. But what if one's situation were different?, and it was not just a question of survival that made you accept another person. How would you accept someone different to yourself if your life didn't depend on it? What prejudices might affect your reaction? And that was it. Both Jack and Jock accepted Mary in an instant without batting an eyelid. Not because they relied on her to fight the cause, but because they were her friends. It was proof of the emphatic humanity they had deep in their souls. The more Anne pondered this hypothesis, the more a warm glow spread through her. She looked up at the inky black sky and smiled, wondering if the entity that spoke to her in the wind was watching her now, and if they were, she wanted them to know she understood. Jack, Mary, and Jock were engrossed in the dice game, and it did seem that Mary was winning hands down. Anne smiled wryly as she remembered the times when Mary, who although could fight with the best of them, had a penchant for trickery at the games table. It didn't matter if it were dice or cards, Mary had the knack of lightening many a sailor's pockets of their hard-earned cash. It was just as well Jack and Jock didn't remember clearly, that fact about Mary. As she watched them, Anne suddenly felt something she had not felt for nigh on three-hundred years! The pangs erupted in her abdomen, and she started to laugh. The feeling was glorious and proved she was indeed alive again. Anne Bonny was hungry! She could have let the hunger pangs go on all night as she loved the feeling because it reminded her that she was human, but sensibly, she knew they needed to eat. But where could she find food? It was highly unlikely that there were fresh provisions on the ship, and if anything was still on board from the past, it would probably be rotten as Hell by now. In the old times, she would stash a small sack of ship's biscuits in Jacks' cabin as a precaution against any unfortunate situation that may have occurred, which forced them to remain inside. Whether that be an attack, Navy inspection or worse, a mutiny, then they could sustain themselves during any potential siege and not fall due to hunger. Would any of those biscuits still be there? She wondered, and if so, what condition would they be in. Anne wandered off to her and Jacks' cabin and left the others to their game. As she entered the room she was amazed at the scene before her. When she had come in earlier for the pistol, she had been in too much of a hurry to take much notice of the room, but this time, she let it all wash over her. Their cabin had not changed in three-hundred years, and it had the strange feel about it as if they had only popped out for a few minutes and would return at any moment. The feeling was odd, yet comforting and impossible to believe that its inhabitants had not been there for more than a quarter of a millennia. Anne hurried across to the little cubby hole in the corner where she used to stash the biscuits, or "hard tack" as they were known. Incredulously sitting in the crevice of the cubby hole, was a very familiar tin which like the rest of the room, was exactly as she had left it so long ago. Taking the tin down from the little shelf she could hardly contain herself. She felt a shiver run down her spine as she wondered if the biscuits themselves would still be edible after all this time, and if they were, what implications would that have? She hardly dared open the tin, but when she did, her gut feelings had been right, the biscuits looked as fresh as the day they were baked. Anne marvelled at everything in that moment. It made sense that if their awakening was part of some plan by an unknown force for some given purpose, sustenance would also have been provided to aid their survival. Who or what that unknown force was that was behind everything, was not a question she dared to answer for now. All that mattered, for the time being, was she had a part to play, and she would fulfil her obligations, but she couldn't help being in awe of it all. She supposed it was reasonable to assume that if they had been asleep for three-hundred years and had awoken without too much physical change, then so could the ship. She whispered to herself;

'It's as though everything has been frozen in time…. including us!'

It was uncommon for sailors to eat ships biscuits by themselves as they were so hard that one risked the danger of breaking several teeth. The usual method was to dunk them in their stew or water to soften them a little. Anne was sure there were no cauldrons of stew knocking about the place. Even though it seemed the impossible was possible on the ship, it was unlikely the powers had stretched to providing piping hot stew, although it would have been lovely if they had. Water though was a vital necessity, she thought, and bound to be some, but where? She then remembered the small barrel out on the deck and smiled to herself. Snatching up the tin of biscuits, four tankards and a ladle, Anne headed back on deck.

'You lot still playin' dice?' she asked with a mock disbelief.

'Aye!' Jock responded, 'got to win at least one game here against young Mark.'

Anne knew the frustration Jock and Jack were going through. She had seen it so many times when Mary would fleece the sailors. To begin with, they treated a loss as nothing more than beginner's luck, but the more she kept winning the more frustrated the other players became, and it seemed the longer the game went on, the more difficult it became to win. Anne put the tin, the tankards and ladle on a crate and went over to the small barrel, took the lid off and there inside was the welcoming sight of clean, clear, fresh drinking water!

'Right, you lot,' Anne thundered. 'Enough of the game now. Time for food!'

She sounded like a bossy mother calling her offspring together for a meal. Jack wondered if Anne were going to insist they go and wash their hands. It made him smile, and it was then they all realised they had not eaten anything yet and they were very hungry.

'What's on the menu, wench?' Jocks' dulcet tones rang out.

'Just be careful I don't brain yer with this 'ere ladle, McTavish!' Anne roared back.

It was all in jest though, and they were thankful to Anne for somehow managing to find food and water. Anne handed each of them a tankard of water, that she had filled from the keg, and invited them to take biscuits from the old tin. It was funny to watch them as they all sat down again and together banged their biscuits on the floor in unison. It was a habit of sailors to bang their biscuits on something hard before eating them so as to knock out any insects that had burrowed into them. It was one of those necessary actions that became a habit over time. For the first time since their awakening, a wave of peace and quiet hung around the deck, as they all sat there eating their biscuits and drinking the water. Anne knew these provisions would only temporarily fulfil their immediate needs. The biscuits would satisfy them for now, but they had to start to think about going ashore in search of real food and drink. The thought of that venture filled Anne with dread. Not for the first time she wondered what they would find out there. What were the people going to be like? What kind of civilisation would they discover? But moreover, was this new world brimming with hostility that they could not defend themselves against? Wiping her mouth on her sleeve, Anne stood up and went to the wheel, while Jock sauntered over to the tin on the crate and helped himself to another fistful of biscuits. Jack had been right when he warned them all about the ship being adrift, and it was right to lower the anchor, but Anne was now curious to know exactly where they were. She gazed up at the sky, wondering if the starry formations had changed that much during the long time they'd been asleep, and could she still pinpoint their position by the constellations? Anne concentrated hard as she pieced together the pattern of the stars in the sky. It was difficult, not because she didn't recognise or know the patterns, but because she had never seen them laid out in this formation before, or had she? A whisper in the back of her mind suggested there had been a time when she'd seen the stars laid out in this configuration, or at least a very similar arrangement. It had been some years after their pirating life had come to an end and she had been sailing as a passenger from Dublin back to California. The ship she was on had weighed anchor unexpectedly, and she remembered gazing up at the stars to try and work out their position, which in turn, might have offered a clue as to why they had stopped. Was this the same formation? She wondered, and was the ship now where the stars suggested they were? For clarity, she grabbed the spyglass that was fixed to the side of the wheel and looked out across the bow at the ocean ahead. In the moonlight her observation confirmed her assumption but there was something more to what she had seen. What Anne had observed had some deep hidden meaning for her, and as she lowered the spyglass slowly, she whispered knowingly to herself

'After all this time! Skye! The Isle of Skye!'

# CHAPTER 8

## The Battle of Culloden

The simple meal of biscuits and water was over and Jack, Jock and Mary, or Mark as she still preferred to be called, sat there staring into space. It was as though everything had come to an abrupt halt. They had been through so much in the short time since they had awoken, but now they were getting bored. The silence was broken by Anne, who was still standing at the wheel.

'You still feel the sword in yer belly, Jock?' she suddenly asked.

'Well, it's not as bad now I've had somethin' tae eat!' the Scotsman replied.

It had been a difficult hour, what with the skirmishes between everyone, and the unmasking of Mary, but finally everything had settled down and they were getting along much better. Maybe it was discovering Marks' secret that had helped to calm things down, things had certainly been much more conducive since. In an hour or so, they had all regained their memories of the time they were pirates together, but there was still a long way to go, thought Anne. The next stage of their evolution was to restore everyone's memories of other times when they hadn't been pirates. She was not too sure why that was necessary, but nonetheless she had a duty to lead them back into their own past. The voice in the wind had distinctly told her they must all face their long forgotten haunting memories and that was what she must do. Although Anne was committed to the task she had been given, it sometimes felt that she wasn't really making that much of a difference in the grand scheme of things. Yes, she had intervened when fighting broke out and she had taken charge, but she felt the results they had achieved so far, would have happened whether she were involved or not. Anne did not know what to do next. Although not easy, it hadn't been that difficult to stimulate general memories of their past, but she had no idea or plan as to how to reignite their personal memories, or how to restore them completely. The one clue Anne had as to the way forward, was when she discovered their exact location. At first, it seemed odd when she had worked out the pattern of the constellations, which suggested they were anchored off the northwest coast of Scotland, but why were they there? Most of their pirating lives had been spent around the Caribbean, so why set them so far away from the area they used to inhabit? But when she'd used the spyglass to confirm her theory as to their location and saw the Isle of Skye, a period long past, shot into her mind and she remembered the tragedy that had unfolded all those years ago. What was at the forefront of Annes' mind, was the time between just after they had been captured, and up to the death of Jock? Being in close proximity to the Isle of Skye and what that represented, Anne knew it was time to reveal that particular piece of the puzzle. Could it be that what she had to do, was to encourage the others to face their previous deaths? It made sense, as that was what had happened with Jack. None of them remembered anything until Jack was faced with the lead up to his own execution. Not only did Jacks' memory of their time as pirates return, but Mark and Jocks' memories improved somewhat too. The sighting of the Isle of Skye was evidently a sign that the next step in their strange and unworldly journey, was the death of Angus "Jock" McTavish. Although Anne knew everything about that period, the others didn't, and Anne was concerned that to just blurt out what she knew could be shocking for the others, not just the truth about Jock, but also the truth of her own untold story, so she had to tread carefully. The first thing to do, she thought, was to introduce them all gently to what they had to do next; build up their confidence and make them feel good about themselves, that was the right approach. This might just protect them somewhat from the distressing and shocking facts they were about to discover. Anne turned and looked down at her shipmates who were just sitting there staring into space with bored looks on their faces.

'It's good that we are getting along better, instead of squabbling and fighting each other like we did before,' Anne casually said. After a slight pause, she continued softly, 'and, although many of our memories have returned, things are still not yet clear.'

'She's off on one of her fantasies and speaking nonsense again,' thought Jack, but he welcomed it as it relieved the boredom and he played along.

'Such as?' he asked.

'I don't know,' Anne replied.

But she went on to say how she thought they should all try and remember more of their past lives and that they could help each other do that. Anne was not being very clear in her meaning, and even Mark asked her what she meant, but she carried on speaking in riddles, or that's how it appeared to everyone. She told them to rid their minds of who they were now and think back to a time they weren't pirates. She implied that the questions they had to find the answers to, lay somewhere in their distant memories.

'We have proved to ourselves that we are not just thugs and murderers and that we have feelings and compassion for others, but we must discover more about that side of our personalities, and I believe we will discover more when we realise who we once were and why we became pirates in the first place. It will teach us that we are basically good people.' Anne was not just lecturing everyone, but also speaking her thoughts aloud. Her concentration was broken however, when Jock yawned and stretched and informed them all that he had no goodness in himself and that he became a pirate because of the lure of riches and adventure.

'You sure of that?' Anne quizzically asked him. 'You say you can feel an ache you believe to be the feeling of a sword in yer belly, right?'

'Aye,' Jock replied. 'I dinnae ken what it means though.'

Thinking about all the biscuits Jock had devoured, Jack said,

'Probably indigestion!'

'Shut it Jack,' Anne cut him off, and then continued, telling them how Jock had escaped when they had all been captured and had returned to Scotland to join his clan.

Jock didn't know why, but his mouth became very dry as she spoke. He reached for his tankard and took a long swig of water. What Anne was saying was news to him, as this episode in his life was still a blank in his mind, but he accepted what Anne said all the same. What shocked everyone was what she said next.

'Of course, that's when yer became a hero!' Jock choked on a mouthful of water and spluttered violently, while Jack and Mark fell into fits of laughter. Anne just stood there watching them with a look of distain on her face.

'Me! A hero?' Jock coughed and spluttered incredulously, as he regained his composure.

'Angus McTavish the Jacobite!' Anne exclaimed. It didn't make much sense to Jack or Mark, but a look of confused recognition crossed Jocks' face.

'Jacobite,' he whispered slowly, and as the mist in his mind cleared somewhat, he continued slowly

'I was a Jacobite! and fought against the monarchy.'

'Yer mean yer was a traitor!' Jack declared, but Anne quickly cut him off.

'It doesn't matter if you disagree Jack, the important fact was that Jock fought for somethin' he believed in. Somethin' he felt was just.'

Anne knew that both Jack and Mary were dead by this point in time and didn't know about events twenty-five years after their death, so she explained to them that Jock and the Jacobites believed "Charles Edward Stuart," known as Bonny Prince Charles, should have been the rightful King and they fought to instate him as the rightful monarch. Anne paused before continuing and stared hard at Jock. How would he take it? How will he react? After what seemed an age to everyone, Anne finally spoke again.

'It were when yer fought with the Jacobites, Jock, that…..' She felt really uncomfortable saying it, and could hardly finish her sentence. But she didn't have to, because Jock finished it for her.

'I was slain…'

He remembered the moment a few hours before, when he and Anne had first spoken, after the awakening and the niggling belief in his unresponsive mind that he had somehow been slain. He had even asked her if he were dead. At the time, he didn't know what it meant, but now it was very clear. He had been killed and the memory was lurking deep within his unconsciousness, although he could not reach it then. While all the information about his death sunk in, Jocks' mind raced to connect all the information. He looked up at Anne and very seriously he asked her if that was why he had the feeling of a sword in his belly.

'Yes.' She replied sadly.

Jock was not the only one trying to piece together the facts as Anne recounted them, Jack was too, and he couldn't make any sense out of it.

'If Jock had escaped after we were all taken and was killed in battle sometime after, how come

you know all about it?' he asked.
But she was in no mood to go into details of her own memories at this stage and she just replied dismissively and said

'Because I was there!'

Before Jack could continue with his interrogation, Jock suddenly spoke

'Culloden! That were the name of the battle!'

It was a name that had come into his mind twice within the last few hours. The first time it meant nothing, but now it meant everything. It had been successful, thought Anne. Jock had regained some more of his memory, and thus far, without too much distress, but it wasn't enough though, she felt. It was one thing to remember the basic facts of the event, yet it was quite different from actually reliving those moments again. If she could get Jock to relive the battle of Culloden in his mind, it might unearth memories and feelings about himself and his character. But how could she do that? It was then, her eyes fell upon the pile of discarded clothes that had now been kicked into a pile in a corner by the taffrail. Bounding over to the pile, she rummaged through the bundle and when she found what she was looking for, she stood up and held out a British Marine's uniform coat. They had always gathered clothing like this on raids as they could be useful, especially if they wanted to disguise themselves as part of a ruse when raiding other vessels. Why the off casts were here on the ship now though, she didn't know, but she assumed it was all part of the grand plan.

'Mary…' She stopped herself, 'Mark, put this on for me.'

She handed the coat to Mark, who slipped it on. Next she found a black battered tricorn hat and plonked it on her head. Next she tossed a piece of tartan cloth to Jack and told him to drape it around his shoulders.

'What the hell are we doin?' Jack asked indignantly.

'You'll see,' Anne replied. 'Now, Jock, go and stand over there.'

She pointed to a spot on the deck to the left, near the taffrail, and further towards the bow. Jock meekly obeyed, even though he too had no idea what she was up to. Anne went back up and stood by the wheel so she could look down on her three crewmates. She directed Mark to stand opposite Jock and Jack, to stand just to Jocks' right. Anne looked like she was about to start a peculiar game of chess but with real people as the pieces. Jack certainly felt like a "pawn" in her game!

'Now Jock, I want you to look at Mark and really concentrate.'

This was all getting ridiculous thought Jack, but he played along, if nothing more than to keep the piece. Anne wasn't exactly having a go at him for a change, and it was certainly better than just sitting there wondering what to do next.

'I know you all think I have lost my mind,' Anne pronounced, 'but I've had an idea.'

'You're not going to get us to join hands and dance round in a circle, are you?' Jack asked sarcastically.

Mark and Jock began to laugh, only to be shot down by Anne.

'Be serious, Jack!'

Addressing Jock, she told him to focus on Mark and try and remember the battle of Culloden. Anne knew it was all rather bizarre, but she had this idea that if Jock were to really look hard at Mark dressed as a British redcoat, his enemy at the battle of Culloden, then it might trigger some deep forgotten memory. Create a pictorial representation, she reasoned. It was a long shot, but she could think of no other way to stimulate Jocks' memory of the battle. As she had already explained, she didn't believe that just talking about the past was enough, she somehow believed they had to actually experience the past in their mind's eye. Getting Mark and Jack to represent the British and Scots at the battle might just achieve that. Jock did as he was instructed, and stared hard at Mark, who found it very difficult to keep her composure. She bit her lip, trying to stifle the laugh that so desperately wanted to come out as she looked at the expression on Jocks' face. One eye bulged out and the other was concealed behind a squint. With the veins of his neck sticking out and just visible behind his beard, he looked like some demented halfwit! The blinding light came from nowhere. The crash of the thunder quickly followed. It came upon them so suddenly that none of them had time to physically react. They all froze to the spot as the howling gale ripped up and swirled around them. The peculiar thing was the sails seemed unaffected, they just hung limply as they had done so ever since Jack had lowered the anchor. The sea remained calm, and the ship stayed reasonably steady. It was as if the storm was ACTUALLY on the deck with them! The second blast of intense white light seemed to engulf Jock whilst the others could just stand and stare rigidly. Jock saw Mark vanish in the bright light in front of him and he could hear the deafening thunder in his ears. He could just make out Anne vaguely standing at the ship's wheel, and he was aware of Jack standing just behind him. In the roar of the thunder and the howling wind, he thought he heard a familiar sound.

'Was that the sound of the pipes?'

Jocks' head was spinning, and he concentrated on Marks' face more and more, but the more he focused on her, the harder it became for him to see her. He glanced up towards Anne, but she was so distant in his vision he could not make her out. Yes! It was the distant sound of bagpipes that he could hear and turning to concentrate on

Mark again, he was baffled as to why she was changing right in front of him. Was she wearing that ridiculous wig again?, he thought, because her hair was now dark underneath the black tricorn. Her clothes changed too. The redcoat remained but her clothes under that became the full uniform of an 18th century British Soldier! He glanced toward Anne at the wheel, but she was gone, and up on the hill was another "lobster". The gun's smoke from the cannons was thick, and the roar of the explosives was deafening. He felt a hand grab his shoulder;

'This way, Jock!' the voice cried!

It was not the voice of Jack, in fact his shipmates were no longer there, neither was the ship. McTavish was standing in the middle of the battlefield of Culloden.

'Get under cover, Man!' The Jacobite screamed at Jock, and forcibly pulled him down behind an old, demolished cart, with hessian rags and peat spilling everywhere.

Just as they hit the ground behind the cart, the place they had been standing in a second or two ago, erupted in mud and fire as a mortar shell landed and exploded with a mighty force. Jock immediately went to stand up, but his saviour pulled him sharply back down again.

'You got a death wish laddie?' the young Scotsman shouted at him.

As Jock ducked down again he recognised the young man as the son of a friend of his, Jamie

Maclean.

'We cannae just lay here and do nothin'!' Jock shouted back. 'Yer nae got pistols laddie?'

'Got pistols, no powder!' came the reply.

Jock then had an idea.

'Pass me that lamp,' he yelled.

Young Jamie Maclean, reached out and grasped an oil lamp that was flickering just behind them on the ground. It had probably fallen off the cart they were now hiding behind when it had been attacked.

'Lucky it dinnae break! exclaimed Jock as he held it up so he could see how much fuel was left in the glass reservoir.

Satisfied it had enough oil for his purpose, Jock stood up and holding the lamp high in the air, brought it crashing down onto the remains of the wooden cart. The glass of the lamp smashed, the oil ran over the hessian rags and the flame ignited it; then with a tremendous amount of strength, Jock heaved the entire blazing cart and tipped it down the incline of the small hill they were stood upon. The fiery wreckage rolled down the incline and into a group of soldiers who were on the verge of overpowering a small group of Scots.

'Take that, yer Sassenach bastards!' he screamed, as the fireball smashed into them.

As the soldiers scattered, with one or two of them desperately trying to extinguish the flames burning their clothes, Jock jumped up and down and waved his arms in the air out of pure excitement. He then grabbed the young Jamie Maclean and embraced him in a bearhug.

'Get off me, yer great bampot!' Jamie yelled, as a musket ball whistled past his ear.

As Jock set the lad down again, Jamie grabbed Jock by the arm and started running, leading him towards a nearby cottage. At first, he thought the lad was trying to run away and take Jock with him. Before he could protest they arrived at the cottage which was filled with an array of Scotsmen from various clans. Jock recognised most of the Tartans there. Some were friends and others not so friendly, but at that moment they were all on the same side.

'Jamie! well done, yer got McTavish!' One of the elders of the MacDougal clan came over to Jock, and put his arm around his shoulders.

He was about as big as Jock, but somewhat older, probably in his mid-sixties. At this point in time, McTavish was around fifty years old, twenty-six years after the crew had been captured and he'd made his escape. He'd lived a comparatively quiet life after his fellow pirates had been taken, partly to keep a low profile and partly to live a quieter life. He had worked his way back to Europe spending time working on farms and plantations as he travelled. It was whilst on the crossing back to England from the Americas, that he learned of the Jacobite uprising and vowed to join the rebellion in a cause he believed was just and honourable. That cause had led him to Culloden and the climax of the movement.

'Listen, McTavish,' the old man hissed, 'it's done.'

The Jacobites had put up a tremendous fight, but they were too outnumbered by the British and defeat was imminent.

'Nae, yer cannae give up till the last man is standin'!' McTavish insisted, but the chieftain shook his head and told Jock that they had lost so many, and it was not right that more Scots should perish when there was no chance of victory.

Jock couldn't accept that they had lost and tried desperately to come up with new strategies, he had no knowledge of the past few hours on the ship with Anne, Jack, and Mary, because to him, none of that had happened yet. This was Angus "Jock" McTavish as he was back in 1746 and the future had not yet been written on the ancient scroll of time. Although there was nothing that could avert the Jacobite loss, the old Scot had a mission for Jock.

'Withdraw, regroup and plan again.' the old man said.

This campaign was over, but the Jacobites held on to the thin possibility that they could fight another day, but deep in their hearts they knew that the prospect of Charles becoming King was fading by the hour. There was only one goal now, with defeat so close, and that was to get Charles out of the country. The Jacobites weren't an aggressive rabble, they were an organised army, and they may well have won the day had it not been for the sheer numbers of the British. Long before the actual battle took place, there had been meetings and discussions about tactics and planning and although they were out to win, they had to consider the possibility of defeat and what steps should be taken if the unthinkable occurred. And so it was, that their worst fears had been realised. Here they were now, staring into the face of defeat and the plans that had been drawn up in the months preceding the battle, were now badly needed. The old man told Jock of the plan to get Charles away and out of danger. It was too obvious to organise the escape via the coast, as the British had foreseen the possibility of that route of escape and had already based men around the coastal ports. Instead, the plan was to move Charles west, across country towards the Isle of Skye, and get him aboard a ship bound for France. Several men were required to accompany the heavily disguised Prince on the hazardous journey westward, and Jock was chosen to be one of those men. There was no time to lose, they had to get Charles away that night and so, within the hour of arriving at the cottage where the elders were meeting, Angus "Jock" McTavish, along with several others, together with "Bonny Prince Charles", set off on their perilous journey.

Surprisingly, they met no resistance, and the roads were quiet; obviously the Jacobites had planned well and had accurately predicted the strategies of the British in that they would have focused more on the coastal areas nearer to Culloden, rather than the roads westward. The small party proceeded for several days without much trouble. But their luck was about to change. They emerged from the cover of the trees onto an open moor with virtually little cover. Over the crest of the land, about a mile in front, they could see the sunlight glinting on the sea in the far distance. Perhaps it was because their journey had been so uneventful that the sight of the sea gave them the false knowledge that they had succeeded. But as they neared the brow of the hill, a sudden surge of British Marines swarmed over the bank to meet them. They were exposed on open ground with no means of cover. It was too far back to the safety of the forest, and they were totally outnumbered. Jock called to a young Scot of the Stuart clan, yelling at him to get the Prince away while the rest of them would engage the British to give them more time. The young lad and the Prince moved off quickly in the direction of the forest behind them, while the others faced up to the oncoming Marines. A tall fair-haired lad dressed in a redcoat that seemed a little too large for him, rushed at Jock, brandishing his sword above his head, and yelling with as much force as his lungs would allow. Stupid idiot, thought Jock, as the lad hurled himself towards the giant Scotsman. Using all his energy running and screaming like that would tire him before he even engaged in the fight. Jock stood his ground cooly and waited for the lad to strike. With all the force he could muster, the boy brought his sword down towards Jocks' head, but Jock simply parried the blow and with a quick flourish, slashed out at the Marine's stomach, neatly spilling his guts over the ground moments before his lifeless body collapsed into the bloody gore of his Innards. Jock didn't have time to revel in his victory as another Marine was on him in an instant, but it was a simple action to dispatch this one too. As he fell, Jock noticed this lad was no older than fourteen.

'They're just bairns!' he exclaimed, as another leapt upon him and into the arms of death. Jock was disgusted at the waste of life. He knew he had to fight back for the sake of his own life, but he hated the nonsensicality of the situation and the unnecessary killings on both sides. Just as suddenly as they had appeared, the Marines turned and fled back the way they had come, leaving the corpses of the dead scattered about the field. Not just British bodies but several Scots also, lay fatally wounded in the mud of the churned-up ground. Jock gazed at the aftermath of the brutal battle and felt the bile rise in his throat as he wearily sat down on a boulder jutting from the sodden earth. The Jacobite campaign was right and just, he believed, and they had a right to demonstrate their case for the enthronement of Charles Edward Stuart, but all this senseless killing in pursuit of the goal was unacceptable. Jock stared at the body of a young Marine now laying lifeless at his feet. He imagined the boy bidding farewell to his mother as he left for battle with courage and patriotism in his heart. He thought of the mother proudly watching and waving to her offspring as he set off with pride in her soul. Where did all that pride and courage get them? A few terrifying seconds, the clash of swords and the mother's son, of whom she was so proud, fell in an instant, like a lifeless doll. To Jock, there had to be a better way to pursue one's beliefs. As the Marines fled, Jock McTavish had time to gaze at the aftermath of the skirmish with a sense of anguish that now rose within him at the carnage that lay all around. He looked to see if the Prince had escaped, but there was no sign of him, either dead on the field or fleeing towards the forest. As he looked towards the line of trees he thought he saw movement, it wasn't the Prince, but who was it? He stood up to get a better view and saw the figure was moving in his direction, but it wasn't a Marine as there was no sign of the unmistakable red jacket. Neither was one of his own as he couldn't see any tartan plaid flapping in the wind. As he stared at the ever-approaching person, desperately trying to make out their identity, was when the blow struck. Jock had made the unforgiveable mistake; he had let his focus turn from the face of danger. Unbeknown to Jock, a rifleman had crept up behind him and swinging the butt of his musket, brought it swiftly down onto the back of Jocks' head. In a whirl of confusion and dizziness, the Scotsman sank to his knees, scrabbling desperately to determine where the attack had come from. Someone was shouting. Was it a woman? The sound of a woman's voice shouting just added to his turmoil. Who was she? What the hell was a woman doing here? The cold, soggy mud slapped him hard in the face as he collapsed onto the sodden ground. It was only momentary, for no sooner had he hit the soil, he felt himself rising up again, but not under his own effort. He was conscious of someone lifting him as he felt the strong arms of his unknown saviour under his axilla, slowly lifting him upward. But just as his eyes met those of his liberator, she screamed:

'NO!'

As her shrill cry echoed in his ears, a searing pain surged through his chest and looking down, he saw the tip of a sword blade projecting from his stomach, dripping with his own blood. The pain subsided just as quickly as it came, and he felt a strange deep, Inner peace. He slumped backwards onto the ground, exhausted, and she cradled him in her arms. Gazing up, he looked into the eyes of the woman and with every ounce of his remaining strength, he focused hard on her face, and as the thin veil in his eyes cleared and the vision of the woman swam clearly into focus, he knew her. Was this his life flashing before him as he died? Or was she actually here? It didn't matter to Jock McTavish, all that mattered now was as the final sleep of death enveloped him, it was comforting to leave this world in the arms of his old friend, Anne Bonny.

# CHAPTER 9

## Fare Thee Well

The sound of someone calling out his name echoed around the darkness in his brain, as he tumbled headlong into an inky black vacuum.

'Jock... Jock!'

The voice sounded familiar, but he couldn't place it. Then a pinpoint of light became visible in the far distance. This light was where he had to get to, he reasoned, this light meant salvation. As he concentrated hard on the tiny spot of bright light, it grew larger and nearer, and the more he focused, so it speedily got closer. As the blinding light rushed and engulfed him, he became aware of a face staring out of the brightness. The features were blurred and indistinguishable, but the more he strained his mind to make sense of the vision, the more the face became clearer. He heard his name again, but this time it was louder and more urgent. It became clear that the voice was coming from the face in the light, for he could see the lips of the face mouthing his name in time with the sound. Then came the rushing noise, like a thousand winds all blowing at the same time from different directions as if to distract him from his goal. With determination, he forced his mental attention upon the face and as he did so, it swam into a clear focus, and he knew who it was. He summoned up all his energy and with every ounce of breath in his lungs, he shouted to her,

'Anne!'

'Is he dead?' Mark whispered, as Anne knelt by the body of Jock McTavish, laying on the deck.

Jack stood dumbfounded. He was concerned for his crew mate, but he was also alarmed because of what had just happened. This very strange incident proved that the life they were now experiencing was very far from normal. One minute they had been playing along with Annes' ridiculous game of dressing up and pretending to be at some Scottish battle, and the next minute, Jock had been struck by lightning. The concerning thing was, that any sailor worth his salt, knew when a storm was approaching long before it actually hit. This storm though, came from nowhere. Everything had been calm and still in the early hours of the morning. There had been no wind and no signs of an approaching storm. The lightning had just suddenly appeared and had engulfed Jock in a violent explosion, knocking him hard to the ground. The moment the Scotsman hit the deck; the storm was gone but this strange incident unsettled Jack.

'He's coming round!' Anne exclaimed, as she knelt over the prostrate form of Jock, calling his name and gently slapping the side of his face in an attempt to rouse him.

Jock began moaning about being hit and not being on his guard, as his whole body began to slowly writhe on the ground. His eyes suddenly shot open, he half sat up, and looking at Anne, he shouted her name.

'It's alright, Jock,' she soothed. 'You've had a nasty shock from a bolt of lightning.'

'Aye,' he replied, breathlessly.

Anne smiled as her old friend regained consciousness and she felt a deep sense of happiness, unlike the last time she had held her friend like this, three-hundred years ago on that remote Scottish moor. As Jock struggled to compose himself and to rise to his feet, Jack and Mark rushed to help him.

'Sit him on the crate,' Anne instructed, as she rose to her feet again. 'I think you need to rest awhile,' she said to Jock, as he sat on the wooden box visibly shaking.

'Och, I'll be a right,' he sighed. 'A wee bit of lightning's not gonna beat me! Besides, its nothin' compared to the traumas me fellow Jacobites had to endure, or the harshness of life me Ma and Pa had to bear.'

Anne stood bolt upright, and knew from Jocks' words, that his memory had returned in full. On one hand this was encouraging, but she had to be diligent and watch for any signs of degeneration in his personality that such as sudden realisation of his past might have on him. Outwardly, Jock appeared not to have been unduly affected by his ordeal, physically anyway, but it was his mental state she was concerned about. For now though, she reasoned, the best course of action was to let him rest and not to engage him in any stressful activity, especially any arguments that might spring up between herself, Jack, and Mark. Not that there seemed to be any reason for an argument, but she had to make sure nothing would disturb him in his current delicate state. Anne wandered over to the smouldering brazier and casually warmed her hands, reflecting on the several times she had done this in the last few hours, in an attempt to convey a sense of normality. She really had to think of other ways of appearing disaffected by events around her than warming herself on the fire! It was becoming a habit and one the others would see through if she did it often enough. The thoughts of her own mortality entered her head again, and she knew Jock would have remembered her being with him as he died, and he could ask about that at any moment. She had put off telling them how she had escaped execution and how she went on to live out her natural life. She wasn't looking forward to explaining that, as she felt there was a sense of injustice about it. They had died and she had lived. How would they take it? For now, that was a confession yet to be revealed and there were other things to be getting on with. Mark was fussing around Jock, and Jack was cracking jokes about how lightning works, and how it "suddenly struck" him, but Jock seemed uncomfortable with all the attention. Anne called Mark and Jack over to the brazier, telling them there was work to do.

'What work?' Jack blurted out as he crossed over to her.

'For one thing, we have to get this ship moving. We can't idle here indefinitely.'

Anne then whispered to Mark,

'You stay here and keep an eye on Jock, but don't let it appear too obvious. Make out you are busy with something?'

'Like what?' Mark answered puzzled.

'I don't know.., sort out that bundle of rags on the floor, but just keep an eye on him!'

In a loud voice so that Jock could hear, Anne ordered Mark to clear up the deck and then turned to Jack and ordered him to go below with her to study the charts. She knew Jack was about to respond with, what charts? but she anticipated his reply and shot him a sharp look, which he understood before he could open his mouth. She glanced across at Jock and told him to rest awhile.

'Aye, I'll do that lassie,' he replied. 'And yer know something, lassie, that ache in me belly has gone, gone I tell ye!'

He smiled broadly and then fell back into the world of his Inner thoughts.

As the three of them set about their tasks, Jock sat in a world of his own. Everything was much clearer now, and he understood what had just happened. He had been forced by that strange lightning to relive his last days on earth in his previous life. It hadn't been real of course; the vision had only been in his head. A bit like a dream, he reasoned, but more vivid. Nonetheless, the shock of reliving the battle of Culloden had somehow unlocked all the other memories that had been locked up in the deep recesses of his mind ever since he and the others had awoken earlier. Although it was very strange and in some ways disturbing what was happening to them, he felt a sense of Inner peace and tranquillity. He remembered back to when he was a boy and how he had found his mother dead, and he felt a great sense of sympathy and understanding of the harrowing life his parents had undertaken, in the belief they were doing it to give him a better chance of life. A tear trickled down his cheek as he remembered waving to his father from the ship that took him away, never to see him again. His mind then moved ahead to the memories he had just revisited in the aftermath of the battle of Culloden. He was moved by the death of those young marines, several of them at his own hands. There was no feeling of remorse on his part because in battle it was a simple choice, your life, or your opponent's. What he was disgusted by, was those that allowed such situations to arise in the first place. The King and all the politicians did not care one fig for the life of a young boy on the battlefield. What they cared about, was gaining political power at whatever price as long as it did not affect them personally. Jock was sickened by the thought of Innocent lives wasted unnecessarily in pursuit of some overlord's ambition of power and wealth. When they were pirates, they had attacked and stolen, and although it was criminal and wrong, they had done so in order to survive. Yes they were guilty of murder, but where was the difference in killing to survive as a pirate and killing to survive in battle? In both situations the authorities created these hostile environments in their never-ending thirst for power. The political wranglings that resulted in war, was not that far removed from the King abandoning privateers after the war with Spain and the resulting corruption that festered amongst the gentry. Lawlessness was rife, but the gentry were excused, and the poor man persecuted. In every case the ordinary people were the victims, but took all the blame.

Mark was busy sorting through the rags that lay strewn across the deck. As she sifted through the clothing, she came across the wig she had worn when dressed as a man. She picked it up and fingered the loose curls and thought how Mark Read had been her protector. It was funny that she felt more confident as a person now, without the disguise, having initially not believed she could be her true self, unless she was hidden by the alter ego of Mark. She smiled to herself as she thought how everyone still referred to her as Mark rather than Mary. She knew they didn't do it out of any kind of respectful duty or because she had asked them to, but rather because they had always taken her for Mark, and after Anne dismantled her appearance, they continued to do so without any judgement. It seemed like her unmasking was no more than someone just simply removing a hat or cloak they were known to usually wear. The person did not change, just the garments, and that's how they thought of her, and it was nice. She knew the next step in her advancement was to feel comfortable being Mary Read, the woman again. That was really the problem, as being Mark had become an ingrained habit and her womanhood had succumbed beneath the façade. Now she had to regain her femininity, but so much of her personality had been developed by her experiences as a man and she desperately wanted to hold onto those traits in her persona. This was where her confliction lay. It was as if she wanted Mark and Mary Read to be combined in one soul, but she didn't quite know how to achieve that balance. All she had was the conviction Anne and the others had instilled in her, that she simply had to just be herself. But in reality, just being herself didn't seem that easy.

'Och, that were a battle and a half, that was! Funny how I remember everythin' now!' Jocks' dulcet Scottish tones rang out around the deck as he voiced his thoughts aloud, without actually speaking to anyone.

The sound of his voice brought Mark back into reality, and she turned to him.

'You alright, Jock?' she enquired, in her soft northern dialect.

Her voice was gentle, with an air of genuine passion that came from within the still locked door of her Inner soul. Jock stirred from his musings and looked up at her and smiled weakly.

'Aye,' he confirmed, 'I was just rememberin' all those that were slain....'

He paused as he thought deeply about all those killed in battle and then continued in a low gentle whisper

'Wasted lives... on both sides...'

His voice petered out as he sank once more into his own thoughts of his past experiences. Mark smiled and turned to continue sorting out the bundle of clothing when Jock suddenly spoke to her.

'What yer doin?' he asked, as if her interjection into his thoughts had stirred him into reacting to her activities, and taking his mind way from his own deep thoughts.

'Just sorting out this lot.' She casually replied. Jock noticed she was holding the foolish wig she had worn earlier, and he knew his friend was thinking about the times she would dress as a man. He knew it was not healthy for her to dwell on certain episodes of her past as such thoughts could draw her backwards instead of allowing her to move forwards. Yes, they had all accepted Mary as Mark, but perhaps she needed a little more prodding, to wheedle out of her, the reasons she began hiding behind the face of a man in the first place.

'Tell me lass...'

It was the first time he'd actually addressed her in the feminine, and it wasn't a slip of the tongue. He meant it. He continued

'Why did ye start dressin' as a "Jack" in the first place?'

'Oh, you know,' she casually remarked, 'nothin' were ever planned. Just sort of happened. Yer see, me mother and her husband had a son, but her husband soon died thereafter.'

'Aye, nothin' so tragic as losin' yer spouse.' Jock cut in, remembering when his mother died and witnessing the sadness his father experienced.

'Well, yes.' Mark responded, 'although, all that were before I was born. But, as I were sayin' me mother's husband died soon after the baby were born, and her mother-in-law, who were comfortable financially, agreed to pay me mother, a sum of money each month for the upkeep of the boy.' Mark then went on to describe how her mother fell pregnant again by another man when the boy was about one year old, and for the sake of appearances, she went to the country to have the baby.

'That baby was me,' Mark said, and continued the account of how soon after her mother had given birth to her, the first-born son by her deceased husband, suddenly died. 'Me mother knew, her mother-in-law would disown her, if she'd found out she'd been with child by another man, yer see,' she explained.

'I dinnae ken what this has to do with you dressing as a man?' Jock asked puzzled.

'Well,' Mark went on, 'me mother pretended I were the son that had just died, so her mother-in-law would continue with the payments. Me mother would dress me in boy's clothes and as I grew older, I was forbidden to reveal me true self. I had to be a boy for me mother's sake!'

Jock stared at her with bewilderment.

'I can see that yer ma wanted to keep the money comin' in, but it were a bit unfair on you, though.'

'Maybe,' Mark whispered, as she thought about those days so long ago.

As she pondered her upbringing, she was puzzled that she could remember all about her early years, yet she couldn't break through the wall of her memory where the image of another child was lurking. The pain in her temples hit once more and she slumped onto the decking near to the plinth of the ships wheel. Jock sprang to his feet and moved towards her with concern, but as he put his arms out to embrace her, a bolt of blue spark, shot from his fingertips and into Marks' slumped body. For a moment, the two of them remained motionless as the electrical charge crossed between them and for an instance, they resembled the fresco of Michelangelo on the ceiling of the Sistine chapel. Marks' body arched and became rigid, forcing her into a standing position, where she stood frozen to the spot as the powerful current surged through her body. Literally shocked at the spectacle of sparks coming from his own fingers, and more so at the sight of them hitting his friend, Jock forced himself backwards in an attempt to deflect the arcs emanating from his body away from Mark. The flashes stopped as abruptly as they had begun, but Jock was concerned for Mark as he stood there motionless and rigid with wild staring eyes.

Mary stood by the London dockside with the outline of the new St. Paul's Cathedral dominating the skyline in the distance. The old

Cathedral had been destroyed by the great fire, thirty years ago in 1666, but the new one was very impressive with its copper dome. Mary was watching a woman with a young boy of about four or five years old. At first she didn't think much of it, but the more she was drawn to the figures, she realised she was watching herself and her mother. In a sombre way it was fascinating to watch her younger self dressed in boyish attire, but there was something rather unnatural about her mother's attention to her. The woman in front of her, did not just act as if she were pretending her daughter were a boy, it was clear she actually believed it. This was clear by her actions and the way she spoke to the young Mary. She pointed to the ships docked in the harbour and said

'One day me lad, you're gonna be someone on a ship like that. Yer might be a mid-shipman or a left tenant. Wouldn't that be nice?'

It was as though her mother had totally buried the truth about her daughter's birth and her son's death, mentally replacing the dead boy with her. She was totally possessed by the false narrative she had invented in her mind. What had started out as a mere ruse, had now morphed into an unsettling, fabricated reality in her consciousness. Perhaps she herself had inherited her mother's odd affliction of burying reality in favour of a false idealism because it felt more comfortable, Mary thought. The vision then blurred and the woman and child were gone. She was now stood at the side of the roadside, watching a coach trundle past. She remembered that journey vividly. She remembered hearing that there was work aplenty on the shipping lanes out of Liverpool in the North of England, and with the few coins her mother had given her, she had bought her passage on the coach to the Northwest coast. Her mother had been delighted that her "son" was eager to join the merchant navy and willingly gave her the cost of the fare. Mary had been born in the countryside just outside London, but had spent her young years in the great Metropolis with her mother, living the life of a young man growing up in a male world. It was all a lie of course, but the young Mary knew no different. Her mother never spoke of the child she had lost. To her, she only had one child, a son. Mary didn't blame her mother, as she understood that all the trauma she had been through, the loss of both her husband and her son, had ultimately affected her rational. She was to be pitied, Mary thought. And so it was, that Mary grew up as Mark, and to her this was normal. It was perfectly natural to the young Mary Read to be known as Mark and to seek out a respectful career in the merchant navy.

The vision blurred again, and this time the image was replaced by a young lad standing at the dockside, staring at a tall ship in the harbour.

The lad was about 14 years of age and Mary remembered how she had spent several weeks in Liverpool looking for a commission on a merchant ship. Every morning she had gone early to the docks, enquiring about any vacancies, and every morning the answer was negative. She could have soon become despondent, but her spirits were kept up by the various northern sailors of whom, she'd struck up friendship with. She would often chat with them and occasionally join in the revelries with them at the local Inn. Mary was convinced seeing all this in the vision, that this was where she had picked up the northern twang in her dialect. She watched herself as a young man, standing before the tall ship on the quayside. The young man was full of excitement and glee at his first commission, but Mary knew only too well, that what her younger self was about to embark on, was not going to be a pleasant experience. The vision faded once again, but this time it was not replaced by another scene from her early life. Instead, she heard echoes in her mind of her early career at sea. She remembered her first commission was tough and much harder than she had expected. She recalled how she then fought for the British on one of their powerful ships of war. The memories of the victories, the battles, and the commendations she received, especially those she won whilst fighting alongside the Dutch in the war against the

Spanish, all flooded into her mind. But then, the visual images returned, and she saw herself standing behind the counter of a hostelry. Mary gasped, as she knew where she was and what it meant. Throughout all the visions she had watched so far, her younger self had always been dressed as a man. But now seeing herself in the Tavern, clothed in a lovely silk dress, she knew what was coming. A young man entered the Tavern, carrying a bucket of water, he smiled at her as he lifted the hatch of the counter and came behind to join her. Putting the bucket down, the fair-haired man grabbed her and kissed her passionately on the mouth. Mary was happy in those days when she married Louis, a Flemish soldier, and she remembered the time they had first met. They had both returned to the billet after a day's battle, and as was customary with soldiers returning covered in mud, sweat and blood, they sought water and possibly soap for a good wash down. Many of the soldiers took to bathing fully clothed in horse-troughs or streams, claiming it was easier to wash both themselves and their uniforms at the same time. For Mary, however, she craved a more thorough bathe to cleanse her body. She had been great friends with Louis, and they had fought well together, supporting each other in the melee of battle. She had developed a deeper liking for the young man, deeper than the usual camaraderie between allied soldiers, and she knew that the liking she felt for him as a woman would be frowned upon, especially given that everyone assumed she was male. She had naturally hidden her feelings or so she thought. Louis, in recent weeks had started to become a little distant from her and she worried that her feelings were showing, in the manner she behaved towards him. In actual reality, the young soldier had begun to develop deeper feelings for the young lad himself, and it worried him. He thought it best to put distance between the boy and his own feelings. So it was that on that fateful day, Mary wandered off to find a quiet stream away from prying eyes, where she could bathe herself properly. Finding herself in a thick forest with no sounds of life except for the birds twittering in the foliage way above her head, she looked for water. As she trudged through the deep undergrowth, she parted a rather dense bush of branches and leaves and came across a small pond at the end of a trickling stream. The spot was ideal! The pond was well hidden, and the water flowed enough to remain free and clean of algae. Tearing off her clothes, Mary plunged herself into the cool, blue water and sighed with the pleasure of feeling all the dirt washing itself from her body, and the feeling of peacefulness as the water caressed her naked flesh. She suddenly jolted out of her pleasurable moments of relaxation by the snapping of a twig somewhere nearby in the trees behind her.

'Who's there?' she called out in a half shout half whisper.

She was fearful someone may see her and wanted to know if anyone was there, but at the same time she didn't want to draw attention to herself unnecessarily. There was a rustle in the bushes to her left and she instinctively turned to face the direction the sound came from. As she did so, another body slid into the water beside her. Hearing the sound of the water gently splashing, she turned to her right and she let out a stifled scream. There, in the cool water beside her was Louis. He didn't speak or make a sound, instead, he gently placed his finger over her lips, indicating her to be quiet, whilst he just beamed at her with a twinkle in his eyes. Apparently, he was curious when she wandered off and he decided to follow her. He was having difficulty battling against his feeling for the young lad, Mark Read, and although he tried so hard to keep his feelings at bay, they soon got the better of him and he instinctively knew that if he followed Mark as he disappeared into the wood, something delightful would happen. Why he had developed such strong feelings for the boy soon became clear when he saw the lad strip off before plunging into the water. His heart pounded faster and faster and he broke out in a cold clammy sweat as he gazed at the nakedness of the boy, only it was not the body of a boy, but the body of a beautiful young woman.

As Mary stood and watched the drama of her memories play out in front of her, a tear trickled down her cheek. She was happy then, happier than she had ever been, both before and after this time. She had loved Louis because he was the only person in her entire life who was able to break down the façade of Mark Read and bring out the true woman of Mary Read. But just as she became overwhelmed with the joyous memories of that time with Louis, everything came crashing down around her, like it usually did. The image faded, only to be replaced by herself still wearing the silk dress, but this time she was sat on the ground cradling Louis's body in her arms, and she was sobbing her heart out. Mary wanted to smash the vision that was happening all around her, just like she would smash a mirror into a thousand shards if it reflected an image she'd rather not see. But she couldn't. Mary had no alternative than to witness the devastation of her early life that was replaying itself in front of her, as the dreadful pain seared through her temples once more. In an instant the pain stopped, and she found herself once again on the quayside of the docks in Liverpool where her younger self was boarding a merchant ship. This time though, her younger self was somewhat older and was dressed in a mid-shipman's uniform. As she stared at her younger self walking up the gang plank, she had the strange sensation of floating very quickly towards her younger self and then everything around her blurred and she became enveloped in a peculiar mist. When the mist cleared, Mary Read was back in the body of her younger self boarding the ship and just like with Jock McTavish earlier, when he was transported back to Culloden, all knowledge of the present was gone. Mary Read was boarding the ship captained by Burgess, which would become known as "the floating hell!"

    Captain Burgess was a bully, and no sooner had she reported to him, he began the first of many onslaughts against her.

'Name?' he barked gruffly.

'Read, sir, Mark Read, sir,' she responded meekly. After the death of her beloved Louis and with all their money gone, Mary decided the only course of action open to her was to don male clothing, become Mark Read and obtain a commission at sea, once again. Her blissful married life was over, and now she had to resume the path the fate had obviously set out for her from the beginning. She had set off from Flanders three weeks before and made her way back to Liverpool. When she had married Louis, all their former colleagues naturally got to know Mark was really a woman and the news had travelled amongst many of the sailing community on the continent and even into the southern areas of England, she feared. The news probably had not reached Liverpool yet, and so she believed she could once again become Mark, and no one would be the wiser. Mary had made many friends in her previous visit to the northwestern port, and she was sure those old friends would help her secure a commission.

'Oh, Mark Read, is it?' Burgess mocked, with a lilting tone to his voice, implying Mark had ideas above his station. 'Oh, me little lah-de-dah!' he spat in her face. 'Think yer a cut above everyone do yer?' he bellowed. 'Only, I don't like little jumped up little lah-de-dahs on my ship, yer get my meanin' lad?'

Mark felt the stench of his stale rum-breath consume her as he yelled, and she screwed her eyes up tight in an attempt to reduce the odious smell in her nose. Burgess then screamed at her to fetch a bucket and start swabbing the deck. Mark did as she was told and fetched a pail half full of dirty water and containing a scrubbing brush, which she took out, got on her knees, and vigorously started scrubbing the wooden planks of the deck. Burgess began to laugh in a harsh crowing sort of way as he stood over her as she worked.

'I'll make a man out o' yer, yer little worm!' the brute shrieked 'Yeh, a little worm is wot yer is, yer little shit! What are yer?

'A little worm,' Mark Mumbled.

'A little worm, WHAT?' he yelled at her.

'A little shit worm.' Mark replied, with a quiver

in her voice, trying desperately to placate the ogre standing over her.

'SIR!' he screamed, with his face turning bright purple. 'Yer calls me sir!'

'Aye, s.. s.. sir,' Mark stammered.

But it was not enough to satisfy the odious tyrant, and he continued his brutish verbal attack.

'So, me little lah-de-dah, I'll ask yer again, what are yer?'

'A little shit worm, sir,' Mark breathlessly replied.

He then asked her if she had a sweetheart. The question brought flood-loads of memories of Louis, crashing into her mind and how they had planned out their lives, and all the happiness that was waiting for them in their future. But of course that life had died with Louis. He was still with her, but only in her heart and so she answered Burgess with

'Yes!'

'Did'ave... yer mean!'

Mark looked at him puzzled. He couldn't surely know about Louis, could he? But Burgess was in total ignorance of her life and misfortune, as he continued.

'Yer won't be seeing yer lovely little whore for a very long time, and by the time you is back in Liverpool, she'd'ave forgotten all about the little shit worm, that left her for a life at sea. She'll be shacked up with some other blighter, by the time yer get back!'

Although she was shaking with fear at the tirade from this inhuman monster, she couldn't help smiling inwardly at the little victory she felt in her heart. The brute thought she was a man, and likewise, assumed her "sweetheart" was a woman, and this proved what an ignorant beast he actually was. She furthered her little personal victory by playing him at his own game, and Innocently replied.

'She said she'd wait for me, sir.'

It was delicious to see the hulking brute continue with his insult of women, unaware that the young man who he now took such delight in bullying, was in fact a woman. This thought gave Mary courage, and it delighted her inside. She had often taken pleasure when others were unable to align the correct pronoun when referring to, or about her. She found great amusement when people would refer to her as "he" when all the time she was a "she!" For a few seconds she was distracted by her thoughts, and momentarily she had forgotten about Burgess, but that soon changed when he started up again.

'Wait for yer…? Ha, Ha, Ha…! Listen lad, these women folk, they're all the same. 'Soon as we left port, she'd'ave been on her back, wavin' her legs in the air and takin' another man's pleasure with her sweet little….'

Before he could finish, Mary was on her feet, swinging the bucket above her head. It had been amusing to see the oaf completely unaware of what he was saying and the actual truth that lay before him, but as he continued with his debasement of the character of women, it became too much for Mary and she brought the bucket crashing down onto his head. To strike a captain was a capital offence and Mary regretted her actions the moment the wood of the bucket cracked against his skull, splashing water all over the place and virtually soaking the monster. She froze, realising what she had done and braced herself for the inevitable violence that would soon be inflicted upon her. She squeezed her eyes tight shut and tensed all the muscles in her body ready for the battering she knew she was going to get. But nothing happened. After a few seconds she cautiously opened her eyes. Burgess, soaking wet, was glaring at her, but as she stared at his ugly features they began to soften and the wrinkles around his mouth grew and spread. His blackened teeth stood out like craggy rocks as his lips receded and his eyes began to sparkle like little droplets of dew in the early morning. Burgess began to laugh! He laughed and laughed until tears began streaming down his cheek.

'Oh, yer a right one sure enough, lad,' he laughed, 'I likes a lad that stands up to a bully!' Mark began to smile too, but it was a mistake, for Burgess suddenly changed mood again.

'Listen lad,' he spat, 'I admire yer pluck, but yer

does not go around bashin' yer captain over the 'ead!'

Burgess was not a forgiving man, and he certainly had no intention of forgiving the young lad for what he had done, but as he admired the way he'd stood up for himself, he decided punishment would not be too harsh. In Burgess' eyes, not too harsh meant anything but hanging. He ordered two crew members to tie Mark to the main mast, sentencing him to remain tied there throughout the night until sunrise. He told Mark, the time would help him reflect on his actions and to work on his temper so that no similar disobedience would happen in future. So, it was that Mark tied to the mast, gazed out across the ocean, and watched the port of Liverpool that stood way off in the distance grow smaller, as the ship sailed further out to sea. She thought about her beloved, and how Flanders was a long way from Liverpool, but just as the ship sailed further away, she felt herself being pulled further away from Louis. Up until this moment there had been so many distractions to focus on, that the pain of losing Louis had been kept at bay. But now confined to the embrace of the mast and the night creeping over her, she could do nothing but think of him. Almost silently she whispered.

'Fare thee well my own true love, I know now, I will never see you again.....'

# CHAPTER 10

## Prepare for Battle

The voyage on captain Burgess' ship was a long one. Several months in fact, they were heading for California with a cargo of goods, including leather, bolts of cloth, wool and manufactured tools and farming equipment. On many occasions, Mark was the focus of Burgess' bullying. On one occasion she took to writing a letter to a friend back in Liverpool, the same friend who had warned her about Burgess. This friend had told Mark to let him know how the voyage went and what Burgess got up to. There was an unofficial blacklist developing amongst naval hands around the northern ports where many sailors refused to sail with the tyrannical captain. Others though, were sceptical and would only listen to the tales of bullying, if proof were to hand. Marks' letter would go some way to providing that proof, once his letter arrived home after they reached land. Unfortunately, Burgess discovered Mark writing the letter and literally beat him to a pulp. There were many severe forms of naval punishment, but nothing in the articles ever described the sort of punishments Burgess handed out. Unfortunately, the actions of the captain of a ship were regarded as law and there was no legal way to depose a captain. That was why the mariners at home were trying to build a blacklist. Without a crew, Burgess could never be a captain again. It was after Burgess had assaulted Mark for writing the letter, and he had later read the contents, that Mark found himself once more tied to the mast. Burgess seemed to have a liking for this method of punishment, for Mark anyway, as he never resorted to punishing anyone else like this. Fortunately for Mark, Burgess' punishments for many of the other sailors were far worse.

It was early in the morning and the sun was yet to rise. The body of Mark Read was tied to the mast as it had been all night. They were nearing their destination and soon, life on this hell-hole of a ship would be over. Mark dozed off somewhat, albeit briefly, as it was not the most comfortable of places to sleep. He deeply breathed in the cool morning breeze, and lifted his head, his bruises were sore, but at least the many cuts about his face had scabbed over in the salt air. As he looked upward, a tiny speck on the horizon caught his eye. It was still very early, and no one was about. Many of them were sleeping off the effects of the rum and ale consumed the night before. That was one good point in Burgess' favour. He allowed the crew to drink as much as they could take in the evenings. That was probably because he was such a drunkard himself and would drink most of the crew under the table. The only ones about, were a couple of the crew on watch and another soul being punished, who was busy scrubbing the deck. Mark strained to make out the object on the horizon. It had to be a ship. What else could it be? As he stared at the object, it suddenly began growing in size. That meant only one thing, whatever it was on the horizon, had turned and was coming their way. Mark continued to look out towards the approaching ship, as he had nothing else he could be getting on with, until someone untied him from the mast. He had confirmed to himself that it was a ship, as now he could make out the masts and sails as it sailed ever closer. It was still too far away to identify, but Mark wondered whom did it belong to? Spanish? French? Or maybe another British ship? After several minutes of watching the little dot grow bigger and bigger, Mark jumped at the cry from one of the crew on watch.

'Pirates!' he bellowed.

Suddenly all hell let loose on the ship. Sailors were running everywhere. It all seemed very busy until one realised they were not actually doing anything except running about in a panic. Then the captain's cabin door burst open and the unsightly figure of Burgess in his underclothes, came shambling out onto the deck. In one hand he had managed to grab his breeches, and was hastily trying to drag them on whilst performing a strange little dance, as he fought with the garment.

'Get to the canons yer dogs!' he screamed. 'Every man arm themselves!' he cried.

He then went back into his cabin briefly, and returned with his leather tunic around his shoulders, and holding a cutlass in his hand. In the melee, everyone forgot Mark tied to the mast. All she could do was watch the undisciplined rabble as they attempted to form a fighting force to combat the pirates, and were failing miserably. The pirate ship was very close now, and Burgess rushed to the bow, waving his sword in the air and shouting obscenities, but the moment the pirates canon rang out, he darted back down the deck and threw himself into his cabin and locked the door. Typical of a bully thought Mark, can dish it out like a good un' but when it comes to a real fight with others just as forceful as themselves, they run and hide. Mary, or rather Mark, as that was who she currently was masquerading as, struggled at her bonds that held her fast against the mast. It was actually really frightening seeing the pirates board the ship, slashing with their swords at every sailor who tried to stop them. The noise was deafening, with men shouting, gun-shots and canon-fire and the air was filled with the acrid smoke from the artillery. Many of the crew were screaming and praying for their lives, but the pirates were merciless as they advanced, but no one took much notice of Mark tied to the mast. A rather vicious looking cove, suddenly ran past her and broke down the door of the captain's cabin. There was the sound of a kerfuffle, then a scream, then the cove reemerged holding the head of Burgess in his hand. He held his trophy aloft, laughed, and then threw it in the air where it became entangled in the rigging. The dead eyes of the captain looked down at the devastation that was unfolding on his ship below. Someone was grappling at her bonds behind her, Mark gasped and felt the fear rising, but then a face appeared round the mast and winked at her! Did she imagine it? But, no, the brigand had actually winked at her. Then he laughed and said;

'Come with us lad, yer'd be better off wiv us than ever yer would 'ave been wiv that bastard.' The pirate finally released Mark from the mast, and she felt herself swept along with the other invaders as they returned to their vessel. Standing on the deck of the pirate ship, Mark felt the fresh air blowing through her hair. It was strange! here she was on a pirate ship with a crew of murderous cutthroats, but she felt freer than she had ever done in her life. And it felt wonderful. The pirates were kind to Mark and accepted her without question, but even as they felt like the family she had never had, she was not confident enough to reveal her secret. It worried her though, when they brought fresh clothes and began undressing her, but luckily they only removed her old uniform and redressed her in fresh breeches and a leather tunic, complete with a thick heavy belt. Everyone was laughing and slapping Mark on the back, spirits were high, and it was not long before the grog came out. Mark took a moment to look out across the ocean as the sun glinted on a distant harbour, she remembered her past life as a merchant seaman, a British marine, and a wife, but at that moment, she knew she would never see that life again.

'Mary?' The voice called her, did they know? 'Mary!' the voice called again.

She blinked, and in an instant, she was back. It was as if she had just been distracted for a moment.

'You alright, Mary?' Anne asked.

'Yes, fine thanks,' Mary responded, and felt stupid the moment she said it.

Of course, she was not fine, her whole past life had just passed before her, and viewed as a whole, she realised just how traumatic her previous life had been. Anne was taken aback as Mary just lifted her arms and reached out and cuddled her.

'I'm safe now,' Mary whispered.

Embracing Anne was like the time they had first met, thought Mary. She had taken the Kings' pardon and relinquished her pirate life and spent her days around Nassau as Mark, looking for suitable employment, but without much joy. It hadn't helped that after giving up piracy she had landed a fairly short but decent commission on a trading ship. The captain had been a pig and not wanting a repetition of Burgess, she willingly joined the mutiny against him. Although the captain was known as a useless bounder and deserved to be mutinied against, those who actually carried it out were viewed with suspicion and regarded as untrustworthy. This made it hard for Mary to find any further work.

One late afternoon she had been sitting on the quayside feeling dejected with the lack of opportunities, when a young man approached her.

'You alright, lad?' the youth had enquired.

They both got into conversation about the lack of seafaring work and they both bemoaned their luck. The young man said he did have a lead, but it was all very secretive and asked Mark if he might be interested. Anything was better than nothing, she thought, and they agreed to talk further at the small Inn, on the edge of the dock. Whether it was the alcohol they consumed as they sat at the little table in the Tavern or because the young man seemed so kind, but she found herself snuggling up to the lad. He didn't seem to mind, and so she pushed herself further. It was only when she went to kiss him on the mouth did he pull away.

'What yer doin?' the boy said in alarm.
Mary wished the ground would open up and swallow her. Why did she keep making these stupid mistakes and ruin everything, she tersely muttered to herself. She desperately tried to think of an excuse to make her exit when the lad started laughing.

'I know I was out of line,' Mark moaned grumpily, 'but there is no need to laugh at me!'
The boy didn't answer, but he stopped laughing and moved his stool closer to her.

'Sorry,' he said, 'no offence, but I'm spoken for, and....,' he hesitated, and Mary wondered what was coming next. She didn't really want to hear all about his sordid marital affairs, but the lad who had recently introduced himself as Andy Cormack, removed his hat letting his jet-black hair to cascade down around his shoulders, as he held out his hand and said

'Anne Bonny! How do you do!'

Anne burst out laughing at the expression on the young lad's face as he sat there gobsmacked, and soon stopped laughing though, when Mark Read removed his hat, held out his hand and said

'Mary Read, nice to meet you!'

After revealing their true identity to each other in the Tavern, Anne had taken Mark to meet her lover, John Rackham. All of them were finding life tough in Nassau, and Rackham had a plan! And so, it was for the second time in her life, Mary Read became a pirate.

Anne held onto Mary and squeezed her affectionately. The pair of them had been through a lot together and they had a kind of unspoken bond, made stronger by the fact they were the only two women in Rackhams' crew, and had a harder time to prove themselves.

'Just came oot me fingers, it did!' Jock was protesting his innocence in case anyone thought he'd been responsible for Marys' or "Marks'," affliction.

'Yeh, well you shouldn't keep touchin' things that don't concern yer, should yer!' Jack hollered back.

It was only a rebuke in jest, and referred to Jocks' habit of meddling with things he shouldn't. Everyone laughed and it broke the tension that was evidently amongst all of them after both Jock, and now Marys' strange disorder.

'I were just tellin' Jock about how me mother,

RESURRECTION

who made out I was a boy when I was young.' Mary spluttered, as if in some way she was to blame for what had happened.

Jack reminded her that it was down to Jock that she had suffered the blackout, but Anne interjected, proffering her wisdom, as Jack would describe it.

'We must just accept these odd manifestations. They are obviously part of the process which we are all going through.'

Although Anne was right in her supposition, she had an even greater perplexity. It was evident that Mary had undergone an experience similar to Jock and her general memories had returned, but there was no sign that Mary had remembered about the baby and the prison cell. Why was that? Anne wondered. As Anne was pondering the conundrum, Mary spoke suddenly, evidently with her new remembered thoughts of the past, still fresh in her mind.

'I'd have done anything for me mother. Loved me mother I did. Even suffered under captain Burgess, the captain from hell, for her. Just so she had money....'

No one said anything, they just stood there almost ashamed of themselves for not being as kind and compassionate as Mary so obviously was. Perhaps that was the reason why her previous life had been such a tragedy, thought Anne. Always putting others first, when they were not necessarily worthy of such consideration, always putting herself in second place, Anne affirmed in her mind. Although Anne probably knew Mary much better than anyone else, given the amount of time they had spent together, they all knew, and now remembered Mary from before, and it was satisfying to see the old Mary back with them once again. Of course, they didn't experience what Mary had just relived and didn't know all the facts about her early life, but what they did know, was that their true friend Mary Read was just as they remembered her.

'Och, I'm glad yer alright, Mark laddie!' Jock said breaking the silence. For some reason Mary giggled and said

'It's alright, Jock. Yer can call me Mary yer know, 'cause that's who I am. Mark is just me back up!'
Everyone laughed again. Not because it was funny, but because Mary was speaking how she used to speak back in the old days, with a sort of mocking mischievousness in her voice, and it was lovely to have her back.

The traumas of Jock and Mary being hit by the strange lightning, had lasted till long after sun-up. Not that the incidents themselves had lasted that long, they had only lasted a minute or two. It was all the talk and questioning that went on afterwards, that had engaged the crew for some considerable time. With all that happened to them since they awoke, they were now feeling somewhat tired from the events of the early hours of the morning, and so they all agreed to go below and get some rest for a few hours. They agreed to meet back on deck at dusk, for they felt it was better to tackle anything that might be inflicted upon them during the night, so they could remain hidden by the cloak of darkness. The ship swayed and rocked gently in the daylight hours, as her crew slept below. The location of the ship where it had appeared some hours earlier was perfect, as it didn't lie in any major shipping lanes and was too far from the shore to be seen. Just as the sun, sank below the edge of the horizon, a faint noise could be detected coming from the bowels of the ship and gradually was getting louder. It wasn't anything of importance, just the crew waking up and clambering up the steps to the deck. The main source of the noise naturally came from Jock as he banged and knocked himself in the narrow passageways. Sheepishly and sluggishly, all four of them emerged out of the two doors and stepped onto the deck, yawning, and stretching themselves.

'I've got an ache in me belly!' Jock suddenly ejected.

'Yer feelin' the sword again?' Anne asked slightly shocked, as this didn't make any sense. Jock just laughed and shook his head.

'Nay, lassie! I mean I'm hungry!'

Jack immediately took the opportunity to mock

the giant Scotsman and reminded him of all the ship's biscuits he'd consumed less than an hour ago.

'That were nae proper food, laddie!' he responded, but Anne cut in with her usual sanctimonious, "I know best!" attitude.

She wasn't purposely trying to be domineering, she just wanted to add a mood of sensibility to the proceedings.

'Ship's biscuits are not a substitute for a proper meal, they are just a temporary solution to hunger pangs.' Anne declared.

Jack stared at her incredulously.

'Not a staple meal? We always used to eat ship's biscuits; a real meal was a luxury in them old days!'

'Aye, and it wasn't right, was it? Think about all those sailors that suffered ill health, like scurvy, because of the lack of proper nourishment.' Anne continued.

'You're now ship's surgeon?' Jack asked in a rather sarcastic tone.

Of course, to Jack, his eating habits on board ship during his time as a pirate, were just as he said they were, and no one ever complained about not having a healthy lifestyle and he couldn't understand why Anne was speaking like this. Anne though, had outlived Jack by many considerable years and had the luxury of being able to look back on her life at sea, and to account for all the things that were wrong with that lifestyle, no matter how romantic it might have seemed at the time.

'Look!' said Anne, 'What are we doin' standin' around arguing over ship's biscuits? Jocks' right, we need provisions. Not just decent food, but drink, warm clothing, and fresh water! We're not going to get far without them.'

'But that means goin' ashore,' Jack spluttered.

'Well obviously.' Anne responded.

But Jack didn't like the idea. He was cautious and felt that any trip ashore required planning and preparation. He was right. Three-hundred years had passed since they last walked the earth, and there was no telling what might be waiting for them ashore. For one thing, the British army might control much more of the country now, the place could be overrun with them. They could be massacred in an instant, Jack feared. He was no coward and although he outwardly came across as reckless, he wasn't stupid. Jack had always been a clever and cunning captain, made even better by having Anne at his side with her astute intellect, and it made no sense to go into battle without any knowledge whatsoever of the enemy you were about to engage with. Unlike some of the larger and more ruthless pirate crews who had tackled Spanish men of war ships, and large cargo vessels, Rackham had concentrated on smaller fishing and trade ships that sailed nearer to the shore. With only a small crew, compared to the likes of Blackbeard, it would have been foolish to tackle prey much larger and more equipped than he was. Know your limits, Jack had always preached. This was why just walking into a society that had advanced three-hundred years more than they had, and without knowing anything about these people, was foolish in Jacks' eyes. Jock agreed with Jack that there was a certain amount of danger, going ashore without any knowledge of what the people of this modern world would be like. But, although Anne knew they spoke sense, she also questioned how they were supposed to find out what to expect without actually going and seeing for themselves. In normal circumstances, planning a raid was the right thing to do, but in the past they more or less knew what they were up against. Now though, they didn't have the slightest clue, and so planning was impossible due to the total lack of facts at their disposal.

'All we can do, is ready ourselves.' Mary said, in an attempt to back up Anne, as it seemed the men were building a case against her idea of going ashore.

'I don't really think we've got a choice. We have no food and water on board, so we either starve to death or we face what is out there.' Anne reinforced her argument by adding,

'Choice 1, we definitely don't survive! Choice 2, we have a chance!'

Jack and Jock reluctantly agreed that they should

go ashore, but Jack still insisted they prepare as much as possible. Anne thought for a moment, and reflected back on the incident earlier where Mary and Jock had their set-to with Jack and she'd intervened. It was a vicious foray, but she had noticed at the time that their fighting skills were somewhat lacking. Picking up her own rapier, which she had replaced in her baldrick that was hanging on the broken stair post, she regarded it attentively.

'The only real danger we face, is the aggression of these new people and how adept they are in battle, which we cannot possibly gauge. That means that the danger we face is for our own lives, and to protect these, our battle skills must be perfect and our reflexes razor sharp!'

Anne suggested they take their rapiers and engage in sparring sessions with each other, to sharpen up their sword technique. Although none of them had taken up a sword for battle in over three-hundred years, their skill had not deteriorated that much. A little rusty perhaps, but otherwise they were in good condition. Anne was pleased. At least they could hold their own in battle. Whether they could win with these modern people was another matter, but at least if they did perish, it would not be through lack of skill and discipline in the field of battle.

'Now remember,' Anne lectured. 'It is not just about protecting ourselves against the possible aggression of these new people, we are going to get provisions. We must avoid all confrontation if we can. We only fight to protect ourselves if the situation arises. We must not instigate that situation ourselves.'

The others nodded in agreement, as this was the language they all understood. It was funny how young and new recruits would often imagine the life of a pirate was to charge in, gung-ho with pistols blazing and swords slashing and simply collect the booty. A seasoned pirate on the other hand, knew that the exact opposite was how one actually succeeded. Be unseen, be quiet and be cunning. Only fight when confronted.

'We should be like a burglar!' Anne expressed. 'Unseen, quiet and cunning!'

'Can hardly see Jock being quiet interjected Jack, 'especially if he finds something to fiddle with!'

The laugh that came from everyone broke the tension that was now building inside of them. The anticipation and the unknown began to fuel the adrenaline. The ship was still at anchor off the northwest coast of Scotland, and although they believed it was prudent not to sail too close to the shoreline in case they should be seen, they were still too far out to make the trip ashore by dinghy. Everyone set-to and prepared the ship for sail. The anchor was raised, and the jib adjusted to set the angle of the sail. They didn't need to ready the ship for a major ocean-going voyage, but just enough to move them several nautical miles closer to land. Once they reached a suitable point, they weighed anchor and lowered the rowing boat. As they stepped into the dinghy, now fully dressed in coats, hats, weaponry and belts, Anne reminded them to be "cat like" in their endeavours.

'Remember, we must move stealthily and quietly,' as she said quietly, she gave Jock a withering glance. 'We must move with the stealth of a cat!' she whispered, as Jock and Mary took up the oars and began to steer the boat away from the protection of their ship.

Anne was pleased with the way they had prepared themselves for this venture into the unknown, but what none of them realised, was that they were being prepared for something much more adventurous, but that was still in the future. Jock and Mary were now primed following their mental trips into the past, and soon it would be time for Jack and Anne to undergo a similar process. That was yet to come, but for now, they all sat in silence in the darkness as Jock and Mary paddled slowly and quietly towards the shore.

# CHAPTER 11

## Shore Leave

The people of Smugglers Cove, a small village on the western side of Scotland on one of the outlying islands, were an isolated community, and they liked it that way. Apart from the odd tourist on a walking holiday in summer, they rarely had strangers in town. Like with so many small, isolated villages scattered across the British Isles, everyone knew everyone else. Not only did they know each other, but they knew each other's business. To many people, this situation would not be attractive, but to the people of Smugglers Cove it was a happy private place. Many of the locals worked the land, and some made an occupation from fishing. The village had come into existence several hundred years ago as the rocky coastline made it ideal for smugglers, who would move their illicit goods from ship to shore. The village name came from those days of smuggling; long past. There weren't many amenities, except for a small village shop and a pub; The Dog and Duck. This was where many of the locals would meet in the evenings after a long day's toil, and many of them were there drinking ale and whiskey on that late September evening as the small wooden dinghy floated ever nearer to their shore.

Mrs MacIntyre owned and ran the village shop, which she had inherited from her father, ten years before, when he retired. He'd been dead these past three years, but he had left her a decent little business which kept her comfortable. Her husband was a delivery driver, and twice a week, he would take his van on the ferry, across to the mainland to pick up stock for the shop. He would also collect any post, parcels and other goods intended for the inhabitants of Smugglers Cove, from the main Post Office in the large town. He would often set off in the late afternoon, spend the night at his usual guest house on the mainland, and then spend the following day picking up all the necessaries for the island. After a wee dram or three at a local bar, he would retire to the hotel for the second night, and on the third day, make his way back home. On this particular night, Robert MacIntyre was pleasantly sipping his whiskey in the bar on mainland.

The evening was still and unusually warm for the time of year, but no one was about. The locals were either in the Dog and Duck or returning home after a long day's labour in the fields. Even the little fishing boats were safely moored and their owners snuggly in bed, resting before early rising the following day to resume their daily activities at sea. Had anyone been on the shore that evening, they would have borne witness to a very strange spectacle. Nothing was visible at first, just the plop, plop, plop, sound of the oars of a rowing boat. Then out of the gloom, the boat appeared, with the oddest-looking occupants, sitting silently as they drifted ever closer to the natural rocky quay. The four individuals sat in silence while two of them rowed. They were dressed in clothing so out of date for the 21st century with large frock coats and tricorn hats. The spectacle would have been so comical had anyone seen it, but if anyone had known who these eccentric individuals were, it would have been far from amusing. As the boat knocked gently against the rocks, Jack, jumped out of the vessel with a length of rope in his hands. He tied the boat to a large boulder, fastening the little craft close to the flat rocky outcrop. The others then climbed out of the boat to join him.

'Right! We're here!' ventured Jock. 'Now what?'

Everyone looked at him as if he might have the answers. It was then that they all realised that although they had prepared themselves against the threat of attack, and were clothed well; to keep out the possible chill from the sea breeze, they had not actually made any plans as to what they should do once they landed. But in all fairness, they had no idea what to expect and so it was difficult for them to anticipate what they may encounter ashore, and therefore, it was difficult for them to plan. In the old days when they were pirates, they would simply have disembarked onto the quayside and made for the nearest stores to ransack as they pleased, but here on this strange shore there were no quayside buildings in sight.

'There's got to be some warehouses or stores for goods somewhere around here.' Anne declared.

'Yes, but where?' Mary replied.

'Why don't we just go and look!' Jack responded.

'What? And move further inland, away from the safety of the boat?' Jock said with alarm. But Anne agreed that Jack was right; and that there didn't appear to be any imminent threats of danger as there was obviously no one about. If they kept a low profile and kept quiet, they could easily survey the surrounding area without being seen.

Mrs MacIntyre was ready to close the shop. She normally stayed open until around ten o'clock at night, in case any of the locals needed some provisions in a hurry. She didn't mind. She had her little portable telly behind the counter and a kettle to make some tea. She just might as well sit here rather than at home. It didn't look like anyone was going to turn up and so she busied herself cashing up the till; and putting all the change into small bags. Being occupied in sorting out the day's takings, she didn't notice four shadowy figures pass the window. The first she knew of them was when the little bell above the shop door tinkled, ringing out the news that a potential customer was entering. Mrs MacIntyre looked up over the rim of her spectacles to see who, her late-night visitor might be. Naturally she expected to see a familiar face, but she was taken aback at the sight that greeted her. Instead of seeing the familiar face of either Sam Connal, the old fisherman who was constantly running out of tobacco, or Janet Taylor rushing to get a pint of milk for her old man's bedtime drink, her eyes fell upon the extraordinary vision of four people who looked rather like 18th century sailors.

'Good evening.' She said, in her gentle Scottish accent.

She didn't let out any element of surprise, but just regarded them as any other normal customer; and that was the point, they were customers and customers meant profit. It never crossed her mind that they might be thieves, as crime was a seldom occurrence in Smugglers Cove.

'What can I do for you?' she then asked them.

The four pirates just looked at each other dumbfounded. 'What was this place?' Anne thought. She was not alone. The others were confused as well. They had seen the small village shop with the lights blazing, and had headed straight for it as it was the first building they had seen since landing on the shore. They presumed they'd get some food there, but as they gazed around the little shop with its rows of shelves displaying nothing but brightly coloured packets and cylindrical pots with peculiar writing on them, they were confused as to what type of shop this was. They had been used to seeing raw meat displayed, or open barrels of fruit, vegetables, sweetmeats, fish, and pulses in the shops of their time, but none of what was on display here, looked edible or gave any indication of what their purpose was. It was Jock that broke the silence, when he asked the lady behind the counter if she had any food. She looked at him with an air of astonishment and was perplexed by his strange request.

'Look around you, deary!' she replied. 'Plenty of food here. What you're lookin' for?'

None of them answered because they were in a deep state of confusion. Seeing the look on their faces and their strange attire, Mrs MacIntyre wondered for a moment if they had escaped from some secure unit, but as there was no such facility on the island, and she reasoned they could not have made it to her shop, if they had absconded from a mental institution. There had to be another reason these four oddballs were in her shop at ten o'clock at night on a late September evening. The best course of action she thought, was to try and engage them in conversation. That way she might find out more who these strangers were, where they had come from; and why they were here.

'Not seen you round here before, me lovelies,' she said. 'Have you come far?'

Jack opened his mouth to speak but Anne immediately cut in, not trusting what he might come out with and make the situation more awkward.

'Oh yes, we've been travelin' for many days now.' Anne explained.

But then, Jack got his way and interjected.

'We're moored up by that natural harbour you got here.'

This made sense to the shopkeeper, as it was not unheard of for stray sailors, usually those on pleasure trips, to moor their boats there.

'Och, you been on a pleasure cruise have ye?'

'That's right', Anne confirmed. 'We got a little lost, so we thought we'd moor up here for the night and get some provisions.'

It then occurred to Mrs MacIntyre that they were probably on one of those themed sea excursions.

She'd heard of them in other places, especially in the county of Devon in the South of England. She'd read about festivals and cruises where people would dress up as pirates for some jolly. She hadn't heard of any such boat owners in the area that had started such a business, but then it was possible some entrepreneurial people on the mainland were cashing in on the phenomenon. Believing that was the answer, Mrs MacIntyre was worried for they were a long way out and had probably got carried along by the current. There were some forceful and dangerous currents around the island, and it was better to employ a guide if attempting to sail off the coast of Smugglers Cove.

While the difficult conversation was in progress, Mary decided to take a closer look at the different coloured packets on the shelves. The one thing that she found fascinating was the cylindrical metal pots. They had labels on them, such as "potatoes" or "carrots." All these little pots contained vegetables, Mary thought to herself with glee. Looking at other tins, she saw some contained meat too. Picking up a squarish shaped tin, she read the label and put it back down quickly.

'Spam! That don't sound very nice,' she said to herself.

Walking further into the shop, she came across a chest like affair, that was icy cold when you put your hand in it. Here were other types of food that she thought she recognised. "Pork Chops" she read as she picked up a tray of butchered meat.

'Can't eat these,' she said to herself, 'Their frozen solid!'

Mary heard Anne, ask the shop keeper if she kept local delicacies; Anne thought this might be a good way of finding out what food actually existed in this strange building. Before the shop keeper replied, Mary called to the others,

'It's alright, plenty of food down here.'

Anne breathed a sigh of relief and could not thank Mary enough for relieving them of a very difficult conversation.

'Don't mind if we look around?' Anne asked the proprietor.

'You please yer'selves,' Mrs MacIntyre said.

She was a trusting woman, partly as crime was virtually unheard of in these parts, and partly because she felt these young people were on an adventure; and their little village was somewhere they were totally unused to. It will be a good experience for them she thought, discovering a place like our little village. She smiled to herself and closed the till as there was no point cashing up with customers in the shop. She sat down and picked up her knitting.

Anne, Jack, and Jock joined Mary at the back of the shop where she showed them the freezer with all the frozen food. Mary said it was ridiculous to think anyone could eat food that was frozen solid, but Anne saw the advantages and corrected her. She explained that the frozen food would thaw out in time, and they could eat it then. Moreover, the food would last longer whilst it was frozen. Everything was falling into place. There had been no need for violence as there was no threat, and they had come through the very difficult explanation of who they were. Not only that, but they had also found a place with food that would see them right for several weeks if they rationed properly. It was Jack that put the mockers on everything. He whispered fiercely for them to stop collecting the packets of food. Anne was frustrated with him, as here everything was perfect.

'What's the matter?' she hissed at him.

Jack rightly pointed out that they would probably need to pay for the food, and they didn't have any money. Moreover, he was against any form of violence against the older woman, nor was he prepared to steal from her. She had been kind and decent to them and that was worth considering. Anne knew he was right. How would it be, if when they were trying to become better people, they just went out and committed robbery. The conundrum was that they needed to eat, yet had no money to pay for it. What could they do?

'We really should find a way to pay for this lot,'

Jack said.

'The laddie's right,' Jock then declared. 'We really should pay for this! Tell yer what,' he exclaimed, as his hand rummaged in his sporran, 'This lot is on me!' and with that, he pulled out a small cloth purse. When he opened it, it was full of gold sovereigns.

'Where did you get that lot from Jock?' Mary asked incredulously.

'I've been savin' it for a rainy day,' was Jocks' wry answer.

'But it's not rainin'!' Mary responded, in her cheeky humorous way.

Jock gave her a withering look and passed the bag to Anne, who refused to take it, since it belonged to Jock, no matter how he came by it.

'Seriously, where did you get that from, Jock?' Anne asked.

'I found it in one of the wee drawers below deck, when I found me pipe, and was lookin' for tobacco.'

It was settled then; they had money, and so they would take as many provisions as they could.

'How much de yer want for this lot?' Jock asked. They had accepted him as spokesman because they felt his Scottish accent might create a sense of familiarity with the grocer, and she might agree to a bargain. They didn't understand that all the food items were priced, and they believed one could just agree a price, like they used to do in the markets three-hundred years ago.

'Let me see,' said Mrs MacIntyre, as she took the goods from them and piled them up on the counter. She began typing the price for each item into the cash register.

Finally, when the last item had been added to the ever-growing list, she announced loudly,

'Seventy-six Pounds and eighty Pence; please.'

What did that mean, they all wondered. To prevent further embarrassment Jock tossed the small leather purse onto the counter proudly. In fact, it was one of the few occasions he had actually paid for anything in well over three-hundred years. The shop keeper picked up the bag and tipped the contents onto the counter. She was used to children coming into the shop to buy sweeties with their saved pocket money. She would often have to sift through the assortment of coins to find the right amount for the sugary treats. The gold sovereigns clattered out onto the hard wooden surface of the counter and Mrs MacIntyre gasped audibly at the sight. Everyone was so elated to think they had offered a generous price for the goods. But then the grocer looked up at them over the rim of her glasses again, and said;

'I don't think I can accept these!'

'Oh now, please, madam!' Anne articulated. You must take some coinage for all this. 'We insist!'

'But it's nae legal tender!' The shopkeeper replied.

Not for the first time, the four of them were

confused. What was legal tender? they wondered. Gold was gold wasn't it? Seeing their confused and crest fallen faces, Mrs MacIntyre felt pity for them.

'Och, alright, me dearies, I'll just take three of yer coins. That should settle it!'

She had a rough idea of the price of gold and reckoned that three gold sovereigns would cover the cost. She knew her husband could exchange them at a bank on the mainland on his next trip. She then asked them if they would like any carrier bags at ten pence each, but when she looked at their faces, she felt she could have been speaking Mandarin Chinese for all they knew.

'Och, here, away with yer!' she blustered and smiled as she tossed a handful of bags onto the counter.

Jack and Mary stuffed the groceries into the plastic bags and marvelled at the feeling of the texture of the strange material.

'Right! Let's go!' Anne declared, and headed for the door with Jack and Mary struggling with the bags. Jock just stood in the middle of the shop absorbed in his own thoughts, but came too, when Anne called him.

'Be with yer in a moment!' He cheerily waved. 'Just goin' tae get some baccy!'

Anne, Jack, and Mary went out through the door, making the little bell perform its jingly dance once again. Jock reached up and took a litre bottle of whiskey from the shelf and placed it on the counter.

'I'll take that as well, if ye don't mind,' he whispered.

He tossed another sovereign onto the counter, to which the woman smiled, picked it up and spat on it.

'Ye enjoy yer dram, laddie!' She said, and with that; Jock made his exit.

Outside on the pavement, Jack was fiddling with his carrier bags absentmindedly, as he obviously had something on his mind. When Jock came out of the shop, Jack passed all of his bags, except one to Jock, and then began playing with the gold sovereign ring on his finger. Jock didn't mind taking the bags, as it gave him somewhere to conceal his bottle of whiskey. Without saying anything, Jack slipped back into the shop, where they could see him talking quietly with the shop keeper inside. When he came back out, Anne asked him what he'd been up to as she didn't trust his motives. But Jack casually replied he'd been asking the way to the nearest Tavern as he felt they all deserved a tot or two to celebrate their success.

The lane was dark and there was no street lighting to illuminate the surrounding area. Had there been, what they would have made of the street of houses, all with cars parked on the driveway, was anyone's guess. As it was, there were many things they didn't notice on their way down the road in the inky blackness towards the Inn. It wasn't clear who heard the strange rumbling noise coming from behind, first. But they all turned instinctively, as the noise grew louder. It wasn't so much the noise that startled them, but the two bright lights that shone in the darkness like two mini suns. The lights got brighter and brighter and the noise got louder and louder.

'Hell's teeth!' Jack shouted, 'what is it?'

Anne shook her head and said she didn't know. Mary hid behind Jock as they stood there in the middle of the road, transfixed by the hellish beast that was obviously tracking them down. The high-pitched noise rang through their ears forcing them to cover them, and as the monster bore down on their little group, they split and threw themselves to the kerbside. Jock and Mary lurched one way, whilst Anne and Jack stumbled to the other side. They had all witnessed some very strange events in the few hours since they had awoken, and so it was not really a surprise to find this creature, or whatever it was, coming at them at great speed. The natural reaction was to defend themselves, and they each drew their swords from the frogs on their baldricks. Jacks' hand was on his flintlock pistol, which was tucked into his belt, ready to draw and fire, but Anne stopped him as the car past them, because something even stranger occurred. As the vehicle passed, the four of them saw Mrs

MacIntyre INSIDE the beast! She waved at them cheerily as she drove past, and they all stood open-mouthed as they watched the two red lights at the back of the contraption disappear into the night.

'What were that strange beastie?' Jock breathed. But it wasn't Anne for a change, that hit upon the notion of what the unworldly object was that had just passed them.

'It must be some sort of carriage,' Mary reasoned. 'We had carriages in our day, only they were pulled by horses. Perhaps these modern people have made some sort of mechanical horse that fits inside the conveyance.'

'Well, yer a right clever little missy, aren't yer lass!' Jock genuinely meant his comment as praise, but Mary was insulted by his tone, and it seemed he was belittling women, so she slapped him one, right across his right cheek.

Anne intervened before things got out of hand. They were in the middle of the night in an unfamiliar land. They had to be on their guard against any further surprises, this modern world have to throw at them. The last thing they should do, was, squabble amongst themselves.

'There's a light ahead!' Anne pointed out.

'That contraption's not coming back again, is it?' Jack said, as he strained his eyes to focus on the light someway ahead.

'No, the light is not moving, that's definitely a light from a building and we know about lights in buildings, so nothing to fear. Come on!'

Anne strode out, and the others looked at each other with looks of trepidation in their eyes, but they meekly followed her, even though they knew she had no idea what lay ahead.

Scotland had been playing Uruguay in a World Cup Match that had been televised, and most of the inhabitants of Smugglers Cove had watched the match on TV in the Dog and Duck. The game finished in a draw and many of the locals sipped up the last of their beer and headed outside for the short walk home to bed, ready for an early start the next day. People chatted, mainly about the game, and several of them offered their wisdom about how the team should have played in a particular way and thus avoiding a re-match. The chattering voices faded into the blackness of the night, as the village folk dispersed along the road. Soon everyone was gone and normally the streets would have been devoid of human life for about eight hours, until the populace would once more spring into action at dawn. But this night, after everyone had gone home, the street was not deserted. Out of the gloom and into the pale pool of light that spilled from the dim light that hung on the outside wall of the public house, four figures emerged. The one-time 18th Century pirates, had arrived at a modern-day pub, three-hundred years after they'd died!

The little shop they had visited not twenty minutes since, was a bright little place, with its large windows; and what lay inside was obvious to any outside observer. They had clearly seen the premise was empty of people, except for a lady of around sixty years. The shop had no indication of any threat to the out of time explorers, but the Inn was a different matter. The small windows of the crumbling building were dark and dirty, making it hard to distinguish the activities taking place inside. Anne felt uncomfortable, as there was no way of telling what sort of people currently occupied the hostelry. Would they be aggressive? Were there enough people inside, to overpower their small number? Without any obvious signs of life on the inside of the pub from the outside, it was extremely difficult to gauge the reception they might encounter. All they could rely on, was their own experiences of Taverns and Inns from their time; being places to frequent with the sole purpose of drinking alcohol to unwind from the stresses of daily living, they invariably became dens of debauchery; with drunkenness, violence, and lewdness. Anne knew the best course of action to take, although the prospect of walking into the unknown Tavern and the reception they would meet, was unnerving, they also realised that it was something they had to do.

'Are you sure it's wise to go in?' Mary asked.
But Anne, back in the driving seat of reasoning,

explained that they had to live in this unfamiliar age, and they would encounter all manner of unusual situations that were beyond their experience.

'We're going to have to learn to live with the people of this new world.' Anne explained; 'and we'd better make a start here!'

With that, she drew a deep breath, puffed out her chest, and marched through the grimy door with its frosted glass window; into the abyss of the lounge-bar of The Dog and Duck!

Fred Tooley, landlord of The Dog and Duck was behind the bar washing and wiping a mountain of glasses that stood piled on the bar after the busy night. The match had been disappointing, but at least it had been busy and bolstered the profits quite nicely. The television on the wall was still on, with several pundits expressing their thoughts and views of the evenings game. No one was listening in the bar, as there was no one there. Everyone had gone and left the place deserted. With the sound of the main door slamming, Fred looked up to see who had entered. Expecting to see one of the regulars who had no doubt forgotten a packet of cigarettes or their coat or something, he was startled to see a fierce 18th Century female pirate, complete with armaments, standing as bold as brass in the middle of his pub.

Anne was taken aback the moment she

marched in, as the interior was not as she'd expected. She didn't know what to expect, but the sight that greeted her knocked her momentarily. She supposed she expected to see a dark and dingy room; lit by candles and the odd oil lamp, with rough wooden chairs and tables standing on a straw strewn cobbled floor. But the scene before her was like nothing she could ever have imagined. The tables were polished, and the seats upholstered in a way, akin to many of the gentry houses of her time. Even the floor was covered in a rich carpet, or at least it seemed to Anne! In reality, the carpet was threadbare and had beer stains dotted about, but it was certainly a few steps up from straw. She would never have expected to see such grand furniture and décor in a Tavern three-hundred years ago. The strangest thing to catch her eye, though, was the peculiar "window" on the wall next to the counter. 'Was it a window?' She thought. Didn't much look like a window. It had glass, she was sure, but what was unnerving was, that there were people talking to each other behind the glass, and she could hear them loudly! She wondered if this was a window into another room in the Tavern, as there was a door immediately next to it with a simple drawing of a man on it. Just as she was taking it all in, the door swung open, and a man staggered out of there, in the process of adjusting his breeches. He paid no attention to her, but slowly and steadily, he carefully placed one foot in front of the other until he reached a chair, and collapsed into it, sighing with relief. Anne smiled; this was something she was familiar with! A man who had obviously had more than his fair share of ale for the evening. There was no danger though, as the man was clearly well intoxicated. She remembered meeting many men like this in the old days when she used to frequent Taverns as Andy Cormack. Not that she ever got into that state, because if she had, there was no telling what she might have let slip and given the game away. The odd thing though, Anne thought; was if the strange window did look-in on an adjacent room, as the door was so close to the window, surely she would have seen the drunkard pass before it and in front of the others who sat there chatting, just before coming through the door.

'Fancy dress, is it?' The voice of the landlord shook her from her musings, and she turned to face him.

'What yer saying, dog!' she spat.

It was customary for Anne in the guise of Andy Cormack to show dominance from the start. That way, people were wary of you and less likely to start a fight. More often than not, any unwanted attention was halted there and then as strangers would not attempt a confrontation with someone they didn't know, especially if they seemed hostile. The only exception to the rule was when someone full of Dutch courage, due to the copious amounts of rum consumed, believed they could take on anyone. These fools were easily dealt with. The moment they would lurch forward to attack, one would either simply step out of the way and watch them crash into the nearest table or to casually place one's hand on their chest and push them. This latter action invariably had the same result as the first option with the unfortunate sot crashing into a table behind them.

'What?' the landlord replied. 'You'd better speak up, hen, he said as he tapped his ears in an attempt to indicate he was hard of hearing. Anne though, took this to be some impolite gesture and responded; accordingly,

'Get me ale!' Anne ordered, at the same time pulling at her own earlobe, emulating the actions of the Innkeeper.

Stand firm she thought, and return the gesture. 'This way you keep face,' she mentally thought to herself. Seeing the woman indicate her ears, the landlord understood she must suffer the same affliction as himself.

'You 'ard of hearin' yerself, hen?' he enquired.

But before she could answer, the drunk in the corner snored loudly and broke the impasse.

'Just a minute,' the landlord said, and he fiddled with something behind his ear. 'That's better! Always keep it turned down when there's a rowdy match going on.'

Fred had adjusted the volume on his hearing aid,

but the action was totally lost on Anne.

'Now, what was it yer ……wanted?' His voice tailed off as three more people entered tentatively and gathered round the woman.

Nothing like this ever happened in The Dog and Duck, well, perhaps at Halloween when they normally had a fancy-dress party. Fred Tooley was fascinated by the appearance of the four strangers dressed as 18th Century pirates and holding plastic shopping bags full of groceries. Even though the sight that met his eyes was ridiculous, there was something almost sinister about it. The unnerving thing was, their clothes didn't look like fancy dress, they looked much too authentic, especially the weapons they carried. Like Mrs MacIntyre, he had heard of this new craze of, cosplay was it? Well dressing up anyway. Fred liked a friendly pub, but he was conscious that the atmosphere was growing a little tense, so to break the ice, he asked his question again.

'Goin to a fancy-dress party?' he asked.

Of course, they didn't have a clue what he was on about, but Jock stepped in.

'Aye, we're oot for a good time of frivolity!'

Jock thought he could charm the local, after all they were both Scots and he was conscious of the not always healthy relationship between them and the English. Fred instantly took to the highlander, and they began chatting away. Curiously, as they talked, both Jocks' and the landlord's accents became harder to understand! Anne did pick up on the fact they were discussing Scottish history though, and once or twice she heard mention of, the battle of Culloden.

'Don't say you were there, Jock!' Anne begged him in her mind, 'He'll have us thrown out as imbeciles.'

Fred though, had been a barman most of his life and the one thing he knew, was to never judge a customer. Always agree and be pleasant no matter what they say. Many people had deep seated problems and could often only find comfort in a jar or two and a good chat with the barman. Jock ordered everyone a drink and paid for it with another gold sovereign. Fred tossed it in the till without a second thought. If he could exchange it, he would, but it didn't matter. It had been a good night and now these four strangers looked like they could be a lot of fun. Anne, Mary, and Jack took their beer from the bar and went to sit in the plush chairs by the fireside. For the first time that evening, since leaving the ship, they felt somewhat relaxed. Yes, the interior of the Tavern was unusual, but here they were sitting by the fire sipping beer and that was a situation, they were used to. Jack took a long swig from his glass and smacked his lips.

'I tell yer somethin,' he remarked, 'the ale of this time is better than ours. This brew hasn't got any bits floating in it and it tastes lovely!'

Mary agreed and she too took a long draft of the frothy refreshment. Anne just smiled and she felt all the muscles in her body relax and settle. This new world didn't seem so bad after all. The people seemed friendly enough and it was comfortable. Perhaps things had changed for the better in three-hundred years. Her thoughts were interrupted by Mary who suddenly drew attention to the television set on the wall.

'That thing is marvellous isn't it?'
It was obvious to Anne now, that the contraption was not a window as the scene had changed.

'It's a communications device!' Jack cut in. 'Don't understand how it works, but it's clever.'
They sat there for a few minutes discussing the TV and coming up with their own theories as to what it was for and how it worked. Anne called across to Fred and asked him the name of the device on the wall.

'You mean the television?' he answered.

'Television!" Mary mouthed. 'Clever! Tele for far off and vision for seeing!' she continued.

'What?' Jack queried.

'Greek,' Mary responded. 'It's Greek!'
Anne and Jack just stared at each other, then took another swig of their beer. Anne had seen some machines in her time, although they were very basic; such as the powered looms in factories and the electric telegraph. These had been slightly later than both Marys' and Jacks' time, but nonetheless she remembered them. This

television was obviously a more advanced sort of telegraph, one that had pictures and sound with it. A strange thought came into her mind as she considered people of the 15th Century, and how as a girl, she always thought of those people being inferior or less intelligent to the people of her time. Now, here she was, three-hundred years after her era, and she imagined what the people of today would have thought of the people of her time. She smiled as it was clear that they too, would probably regard 18th Century people as being less intelligent and it made her laugh to think how wrong they would be.

Anne was brought back to reality by Jack who nudged her and told her to look at the screen. The news had just come on and the three of them quickly became absorbed by what they were witnessing. The programme told of the wars taking place and about poverty in many parts of the world. There were speeches by politicians and bureaucrats, promising better conditions, only to contradict themselves with posturing and boasts of their own cleverness. Anne felt the bile rise in her throat as she witnessed pictures of the poor and the masses with their heads down taking everything that life threw at them without fighting back. She saw the obvious signs of corruption from governments, and the injustices suffered by so many. It made her angry to think mankind had obviously made many technical advancements in three-hundred years, but the psyche of humanity had not only stagnated, it had also regressed.

Jock and the landlord had finished their conversation. Fred was flicking through the pages of a newspaper and Jock, just like the others, had become engrossed by the images on the television. The mood in the bar was sombre, and Fred had picked up on this. The news programme was depressing everyone, he thought. That was no real surprise because the news these days made everyone miserable. His belief was strengthened, especially when Anne got to her feet and was marching to the door.

'We're going!' she barked.

But before she reached the door, Fred flicked the remote control of the TV and changed channels. He'd been scanning the "What's On" TV guide in the paper, looking for something more appropriate for his current clientele. He noticed a docudrama was showing on one of the lesser-known channels and thought this would be a welcome diversion from the news. The series was about the "Golden Age of Piracy" and the moment the programme came up on the screen, one of the characters shouted out, "Anne Bonny!" Anne froze to the spot as she heard her name ring out round the room. She spun round to face the screen on the wall and was shocked to see a young actress, dressed in rather shabby and dirty clothes, scowling at the person who had called her name. Anne was incensed! It was not just the apparel of her doppelganger that enraged her, but the girl's physical appearance. Her eyes bulged and the veins stood out on her neck, and she fiercely yelled at the screen.

'Red hair? I don't have red hair!'

Annes' mother had lovely jet-black hair and Anne had often wondered if her mother had gypsy blood in her. Perhaps that's why she always chided her daughter for mixing with them when they came to town. To Anne, it was a nice idea, but was it true? There was no way of finding out after all this time, but she liked to believe there might be some truth in it. It would explain though, the colour of her own hair and why she had a natural affinity with the gypsies.

'John Rackham yer dog!' the character on the screen yelled, and Jack was about to respond to the portrayal of himself by the actor, but Jock cut in.

'Well, it's been a lovely fine evenin' Landlord, so we'll bid yer a good night!'

And with that, he and Mary ushered the unsettled Anne and Jack from the Inn.

Out on the pavement, Anne was moaning to Jack that she would never dress like that. She protested that she had always kept herself tidy and clean. But Jack said he thought it was a fair portrayal, which angered Anne even further.

'The actor playing you was spot on though!' she hissed, 'insipid and weak!' This inflamed the anger within him, but before one of Annes' and Jacks' infamous rows erupted, Jock reminded them that it was late, and they should head back to the ship. Mary had picked up all the shopping bags from the corner by the bar and passed them around, so she didn't have to carry the entire load back to the rowing boat on her own.

They all walked back to the harbour where they had moored the boat, in silence. They had learned a lot about the modern world that evening, and they were each processing the information they had gleaned. In less than half an hour, they were back sitting in the boat with Jocks' strong arms pulling at the oars, as they headed back across the still waters of the sea to the comfort of their ship. This new world was strange and mystifying, but they were here now, whether they liked it or not!

# CHAPTER 12

## The Devil's Child

The voyage back to the ship had been sombre and non-eventful. For most of the trip they had all sat in silence contemplating this new world, they now found themselves in. The gentle lapping of the water as Jock pulled at the oars that cut through the sea, was relaxing and on several occasions Jack would suddenly jolt upright as he found himself falling asleep. When they finally came alongside their ship, he tied the small boat at the foot of the rope ladder and they all clambered up onto the deck, not an easy task when laden with plastic bags of groceries. Once back on board, Mary and Jock placed their bags; including an orange bag Jack had given them to hold, behind the old chest, and then hung up their sword belts. Jack hung his, on one of the newels at the foot of the steps, and disappeared briefly with the bag he was holding, into the captain's cabin where he dumped it, and returned on deck almost immediately. Anne slung her baldrick on the other newel and stormed across the deck, flinging her bags in the corner at the foot of the ship's wheel. She then plonked herself on one of the packing crates.

'Three-hundred years! And nothing's sodding changed!' she grumbled.

Jack was in a more jovial mood and declared that he thought a lot had changed. He felt a sense of excitement at the things they had seen, and he knew there was a lot more to discover in this new world, and part of him couldn't wait to get back on shore and begin exploring. Jock and Mary were also excited about their adventure, with the Scotsman babbling about the "horseless carriages" and Mary couldn't stop talking about the Greek invention called "television!" She had naturally assumed that the appliance was Greek from the name. She didn't realise that the inventor of the "magical window" had actually been born not far from where they were now, in Scotland! Anne, however, was still lost in her own thoughts about what she had seen, and began mumbling to herself about how some things had changed, but not necessarily for the better. Jack felt she was putting the downers on the present happy mood of everyone, and chided her.

'What you on about now?' he wearily questioned, hoping she would snap out of this negative attitude she seemed to have adopted.
Anne looked up, her eyes had a faraway look in them and half responding to Jack and half speaking to herself, she whispered in a melancholy tone,

'Did yer not see them?'

Sometimes Anne could be unfathomable, and this was one of them, thought Jack. Before going ashore, they had all been apprehensive about what they might find on land and nervous about how the people of today, would react to them. As it had turned out, it had all been very pleasant and much better than in their day. He was determined not to let Anne ruin the general good spirits with her depressive ramblings, and with a terse tone in his voice, asked who she was talking about. None of the people they had met, albeit it had only been three people, were unfriendly or aggressive, in fact they had all been extremely welcoming and seemed happy in their lives. Unfortunately, Annes' mood was starting to affect everyone and both Mary and Jock sluggishly sat down, Mary on a barrel and Jock on the other packing crate. The sombreness of the return journey was starting to manifest itself again. But just as Jack thought the mood couldn't get any darker, Anne launched into one of her self-righteous sermons. Jack slapped his forehead and mentally begged her not to, but

Anne was already on her feet pacing up and down.

'Those people with dull eyes, struggling under the strain of just getting by. At least in our day we had more freedom and fire in our belly to fight back.'

For a moment, Jack thought she was about to burst into tears, but then he realised the moisture in her eyes was not tears, but just the effect of the cold night air. Besides, the thought of Anne Bonny bursting into tears was ridiculous! Instead, her anger became fiercer.

'These people seemed to be more oppressed than we were. Perhaps they've more to lose than we did. Whoever is in charge of this new world seems worse, than what we had to put up with. At least we knew those in authority were dishonest!'

For a several moments, the silence that hung around the deck was oppressive, and no one spoke. When Anne was in one of these moods, it was always prudent not to interrupt or make any comment, especially if you didn't want the full force of Annes' tirade directed at you personally. It was Jock who took the brave step to speak first, and he asked her how she had fathomed all this from the brief time ashore. She could not possibly make a declaration like that without further proof. Jock regretted speaking out, as Anne lifted her head and her fierce bright blue eyes pierced into his brain just as effectively as red-hot pokers.

'You want proof?' she yelled, as she grabbed one of her bags and pulled out the newspaper the barman of The Dog and Duck had been reading, and slung it at him. 'Read that!' she spat. It wasn't Annes' tone or the words she spoke that upset Jock, it was the fact she had thrown a journal at him, and as he toyed with it in his hands, he was somewhat dismayed that she had embarrassed him like this. For all his adventures and for all his good deeds, the one thing Jock had never got to grips with, was learning to read. Anne knew he was self-conscious of the fact he couldn't read, and it upset him to think she could toss the paper at him like she had done. Mary latched on to Jocks' discomfort and went to him and putting her arm around his shoulder, she gently took the offending item from him and whispered in his ear that he shouldn't take it personally.

Anne was standing by the brazier warming her hands again! Although she had vowed to stop doing that, this time it was out of sheer habit and with no thought whatsoever. She continued with her rant and talked about the people she had seen on the television with their dead eyes. There was no life in these people. They seemed to be completely consumed by everything that happened around them. She was struck by how lonely they all looked and how totally self-absorbed they appeared to be. It was as if only their own single existence had any importance. She thought about how the people of her time would have stood up and rebelled, not just for themselves but for the sake of each other. But these modern people seemed to have had the passion knocked out of them. All Anne could think, was that these modern people were afraid of something, but afraid of what? It was as if they had lost faith in everything and no longer believed in anything. To Anne, this was not only a tragedy, but three-hundred years of opportunity, to improve the lives of everyone which has been terribly wasted. Anne gazed down at the embers of the fire, which was virtually out now, but she didn't notice as she was totally absorbed in her thoughts. She looked up and casually scanned the deck as if taking stock of everything around her, including her small crew. It was then, her eyes fell on the assortment of carrier bags containing the groceries, but something was out of place. All the bags Mrs MacIntyre had given them, had a blue and white design, but one of them stood out from the rest because it was bright orange. She stormed over to it and picked it up.

'What the hell is this?" she yelled.

Jacks' face paled with guilt as he knew it was his turn to feel Annes' wrath.

'Just a bag,' Jack mumbled.

'And where did you get it?' she barked.

She knew perfectly well where it had come from,

because she had seen it behind the chair of the old drunk in the Tavern. She knew that's where Jack had got it from. But it was not where he got it from that angered her, it was the fact that Jack had obviously stolen it from the old man.

'You stole it you dog!' she vehemently screeched, and Jack just held his head in his hands. Not because he was embarrassed, but because Anne now had a reason to have a proper go at him. He was tired and not in the mood for a verbal onslaught, and so he just waited for her to run out of steam.

'What the hell have you done?'

It wasn't a question, but a rebuke, as she went raving on about how Jack, had fallen back into his old ways of thievery by just marching in there and casually taking something that didn't belong to him.

'Oh come on, we've got to eat! And we don't know how long the stuff we bought is going to last. I just thought a little bit extra wouldn't go amiss.'

Although Jack was quite prepared to let Anne go rambling on just to get the situation over with, he wasn't too keen on her chiding him like this in front of the others. He was right to be concerned about Jock and Mary, but then, Jock joined in the admonishment of him. He accused Jack of not having any honour, especially given what they had all learnt about themselves.

'Bout time yer grew up, laddie! We're nae in the

Caribbean now, yer know!'

So now Jack, had both Anne and Jock on his back, but it got worse because Mary then put in her two-penneth-worth.

'Jocks' right, Jack. If yer abandon yer honour and selfishly act alone, yer no better than captain Burgess!'

Anne then agreed with Mary, and Jock agreed with them both, and Jack felt himself drowning in a sea of verbal condemnation. There was only one thing he could do to save himself, and that was to stop listening and to absorb himself in some distraction or another. He crawled over to the heap of bags, and especially to the orange one that Anne had so ceremonially chucked back on top of the heap. Picking up the bag, he casually rummaged through the contents inside. He was now familiar with the packets and metal cylinders of food they had discovered in the small store on land, but the contents of this bag were different. There was a fish wrapped in the same type of paper Anne had thrown at McTavish and there were bags of small objects of different colours. Curiously he took one and popped it in his mouth to see what it was. It tasted sweet and rather pleasant. As he sucked on the sweet, the words of the others, who continued to berate him, seemed to fade into the distance and Jack started daydreaming about what other wonders there were to discover in this new land. As he dwelt on the prospect of adventures new, he inadvertently took a thin flat box out of the bag and read the inscription. There was a lull in the chatter from the others as they took time to think of more accusations and criticisms they could fire at him. In the pause, Jack broke the brief silence with a question as he contemplated the label on the thin packet.

'What's a pizza?' he asked.

'What?' yelled Anne.

'A pizza, look! it says, take away pizza! Well, that's what I did! I took it away! and he roared with laughter at his joke.

The others just stared at him stony faced, and he did not realise the irony of what he had said. Anne was furious, as he had obviously had not taken heed of anything they had said. He wasn't remorseful or seemed to understand that their days of thievery were over. They had been given this second chance of life, to prove that they were not necessarily the people history had painted. For some reason, the image of the girl portraying her on the television in the Tavern, came into Annes' mind, and she was both flattered and annoyed. It was wonderful for her ego to think history had remembered her, but it was annoying that history seemed to have bastardised her memory. What she had seen was only brief, but it was enough for her to know that many of the facts about herself had obviously been skewed by the passage of time. She made a conscious note that she would somehow have to change that, and set the records straight, but at a later date. Now though, there were other more pressing items on her agenda, such as getting Jack to understand what was expected of him. It was curious she thought, that although Jack had regained some of his memories, especially of their pirating days, the strange forces that had taken over Jock and Mary had not focused on him.

'I wonder why? she whispered to herself.

As she gazed at her lover, now sitting on the floor rummaging through the bags of groceries, examining everything else they had bought, he reminded her of a little boy lucky enough to have received many presents for some special occasion. Much of Jacks' personality had returned. He was still rash and had the occasional mood swings with aggressive outbursts, but at other times, he was much calmer than he used to be. One could almost say there was a sense of innocence about him.

'Innocent! Jack!' she thought and began to laugh out loud.

Everyone was startled by the sudden change in Annes' mood. One minute she had been raging and now abruptly she had burst out laughing.

'You alright, Anne?' Mary asked.

'Hmmm?" Anne responded with a casual grunt.

'You alright?' Mary persisted.

'Of course, I'm alright!' she snapped back, but everyone was cautious.

It wasn't like Anne to suffer such mood swings, one minute berating Jack and the next laughing hysterically. Although her outward appearance was troubling, inside she was relatively calm. It was just the thought of the people of the modern world and how it seemed so much injustice remained, and that after three-hundred years, mankind had failed to address the problems that had existed in her time. Her thoughts actually kindled a fire within her, and she grew eager to right many of the wrongs she believed existed today. She felt sure this was what was required of them and why they had been reborn. The voice of the wind echoed in her mind and images of all that had happened in the last few hours, flooded into her consciousness. How she could achieve this goal though, was another matter, but Jacks' attitude had annoyed her because they couldn't rise to the challenge when he was so blasé about everything. What angered her the most, was that the fire that used to burn in his belly, seemed to have been reduced to a smouldering ember, not unlike the coals of the brazier. That same fire and zest for life that had attracted her to him in the first place, had now seemingly been extinguished. If they were to achieve their goal, she had to get Jack to change his ways and instil the fight he used to have, back into his soul.

Anne thought for a moment, and considered how Jock had been forced to relive his past. Yes, it had been the lightning that had caused him to remember, but it was her plan that everyone re-enacts a physical representation of the battle of Culloden, that had set the train of circumstances in motion. Could it work with Jack? She wondered. Could she stimulate his memories of the long distant past and reignite the passion he once had? It was worth a try she thought.

'Jock, put on the redcoat uniform!' she commanded.

But Jock was having none of it; especially because of how she had embarrassed him with the journal. In truth though, the thought of dressing as one of the "enemy" from Culloden, filled him with disgust.

'I'm not wearing that Sassenach uniform for anything!' he indignantly replied.

Anne wasn't to be put off by his flat refusal though, as she knew Jock was susceptible to bribery, and offered him a flagon of whiskey as a reward. Naturally, the Scotsman grasped the opportunity and immediately sprung to his feet.

'Right!' he exclaimed, and marched across the deck to where the army jacket had fallen after Mary had discarded it, picked it up and put it on.

'Now what you up to?' Jack sighed.

It was the middle of the night, and everyone was tired after their adventures ashore and a better course of action would have been to go below and get some sleep. Unfortunately, when Anne got an idea fixed in her head, she had to carry out her plans immediately, and not wait until morning, when the idea might not seem as attractive. This manner of hers' really annoyed Jack, and when she then stated that it was now his turn, to relive his past, his patience ran out and he flatly refused to have anything to do with her stupid plans that night, and he emphatically told her so. Anne just stood aghast and was lost for words because she realised she had gone too far. She wasn't beaten though, and after a slight pause, she turned towards the back of the ship and announced that they would all meet on deck at sun-up. With that, she flounced off through one of the doors into the interior of the ship. Before anyone could react, she popped her head back around the door frame and ordered Jack to take first watch, then she was gone.

'That's a relief, I don't mind tellin' yer!' Jock exclaimed, taking off the red coat. 'I'm ready for me bunk!'

And with that, he tossed the army jacket over his shoulders and marched off through the other door to his cabin to get a well-earned rest.

'Anyone would think she's the captain!' Jack quipped crossly.

He always let Anne act on a long rope, as sometimes she had good ideas and strategies, but he was the captain in name and sometimes she overstepped the mark and needed reigning in.

'But I thought she was the captain,' Mary responded, and Jack spun round to face her, ready to admonish her for disrespecting him, but as he faced her, he could see the twinkle in her eyes and the slight upturn of the corners of her mouth and knew she was teasing him. Jack relaxed and smiled. A lot of what Anne did, angered him, not specifically for what she said, but because of this frustrating ability she had of belittling him in front of everyone. Seeing Mary tease him though, reminded him that both her and Jock were very much aware of Annes' character and that they didn't think any less of him when Anne would belittle him. In a way, he and Anne were both the captain with two separate personalities, and when they worked in unison, it worked perfectly. The trouble was, when one of them upset that balance, it became uncomfortable for everyone else. He also admitted to himself, that it wasn't always Anne that spoke out of line, he was guilty of it too, and he believed that the other two were very much aware of this fact, also.

'It was Anne that turned me to piracy, you know.' Jack suddenly announced huffily. 'I was a decent bloke until she turned me from the straight and narrow.'

Mary asked him if that was during their time in Nassau, as she knew that Jack had taken the Kings' pardon and only returned to piracy after he had met Anne. That was just before she, herself had met Anne in the Tavern on the quayside and had been invited to join them. Mary was astounded when Jack confessed that he had known Anne a long time before that.

'It's not something we talk about much, or at least we didn't in the old days. We didn't want people knowing our business, mind you, we were only young, not much more than children, well, at least she was.'

It was funny, he thought that now, he came to mention all this, he could actually remember many of the details of his life then. He paused and thought back to those times. There were a lot of gaps in his memory, and although he remembered certain facts, much of the detail surrounding those times was still sketchy in his head. Jack then launched into the tale of how he had first met Anne in Ireland around 1711 when he was twenty-eight, and she was only fourteen. Jack told Mary he had gone to Ireland in search of adventure and to get away from London, and how he met this young gypsy girl in the streets of Cork. He found out later when introduced to her father, William McCormack, a lawyer, that she wasn't really a gypsy but liked to pretend she was. Jack liked her father, primarily because it was he who had saved him from deportation after Anne had stolen a watch and made out Jack had stolen it. McCormack didn't care much for him though, and forbade Anne to ever see him again. Not long after that, Jack heard that McCormack had moved the family to the Americas.

'I didn't know!' Mary said, and was fascinated by this piece of history she had never known about. 'I think it is rather romantic that you found each other again in Nassau. Did you follow her to the Americas, Jack?' Mary then asked him, but the idyllic romantic tale Mary wanted to believe, didn't materialise as Jack laughed at the idea.

'Good God No!' he scoffed.

He related how he had taken work on merchant ships and because of certain circumstances, ended up as quartermaster on captain Vane's pirate ship. It was only by chance that one day in Nassau, after he had taken the Kings' pardon and relinquished piracy, that he met her by chance. He had been wandering the streets looking for honest work when this ruffian came tearing out of an ale house and crashed straight into him.

''Ere! Watch where you're goin'!' he hollered. But the lad didn't take any notice of the rebuke and instead looked up into his eyes and said;

'Well, bless me! If it ain't John Rackham as I live and breathe!'

The lad of course was Anne, masquerading as Andy Cormack. Mary was fascinated by the story and mumbled something about them being obviously meant for each other, but it was late, and she was tired. She yawned and stretched herself.

'Think I'll get some sleep, meself!' she said, and with that, she wandered off to her bunk down below, leaving Jack alone in the darkness of the upper deck.

He sat there for several minutes thinking about the past and trying to remember the finer details of those times. He couldn't though. His mind would not unlock its full secrets, and so he decided, sleep was more important than trying to remember details of things that happened all those years ago. He rubbed his eyes, stretched himself as he stood up and he began walking towards the door to his cabin, when he heard the distinctive rumble of thunder in the distance. A storm was coming. He'd better check everything was tied down securely, no telling how ferocious the storm might be and what damage it might cause, especially if they were all asleep. Jack wandered to the bow of the ship and looked out towards the horizon to see if he could determine where the storm was and whether it was likely to come in their direction, but there was nothing. Out of the corner of his eye he spied a bright light coming from somewhere and as he turned to find out where it was coming from, he gasped with wonder at the sight that met his eyes. All the upper masts and rigging were glowing with a bright fluorescent blue light. At the end of several of the yardarms the light twinkled and danced like flames of blue fire. 'St Elmo's fire!' he whispered excitedly to himself. St Elmo's fire was a familiar sight to sailors, but although often regarded with caution, it was certainly awe inspiring. Although he didn't know it then, sometime in the future, Jack would be introduced to the wonders of science and he would learn that the phenomena was created by highly charged ion particles in the plasma of the air, often created when storms were close. The effect wasn't dangerous, and it certainly wasn't real fire or lightning as many had conjectured that it might have been. But that knowledge was yet to be learned; and for now, Jack stood and enjoyed the spectacle. Taking a step nearer to the main mast to get a closer look at the display, he inadvertently grasped the lower rung of one of the many rope ladders that stretched aloft. His eyes were transfixed on the intense blue glow as it shimmered around the rigging, but then it seemed to snake its way along the ropes. His eyes followed it as it slowly moved along the many cables holding the sails to the yardarms. As he watched it, it began flowing down the rope ladder that he was holding. Jack was fascinated by the way the cool blue light enveloped his hand as it reached him. He wasn't afraid, as he knew it wouldn't harm him. His attention was suddenly broken by someone shouting, "Dublin! All ashore!" Just like Jock and Mary before him, John Rackham was in a different time and a different place.

Johnny Rackham picked up his kit bag and made for the gangplank that would take him onto the soil of Ireland, and with any luck, to where a new and successful life was waiting for him. The life that was waiting for him, however, was not the one he would have expected; by stepping off the ship on that chilly April morning in 1711, he set in motion a chain of events that would lead him to piracy and hundreds of years in the future, to a new life in the 21st Century. All that lay ahead of him. For now, he had to begin that incredible journey of life here in the bright new city of Dublin.

Rackham was a reserved and quiet young man. He liked to keep himself to himself. He wouldn't describe himself as shy, but he would rather hold back before rushing in, to new situations. He had been born in London in 1682 and soon after, his father had left him and his mother to fend for themselves. He never knew his father, but he resented him. He remembered how his mother had struggled to bring him up in poverty and the condemnation she received for being a single woman with a baby. The only way his poor mother could survive was to offer her services to young sailors around the docks and invariably suffer the exploitation such a position in life ultimately brought. His mother had managed to find a hovel in the Eastend of

London in a place called Wapping. It was very basic, but it had two rooms, one for them to live in and one in which she could conduct business. Many a night was spent listening through the crumbling walls to the horrific abuse his mother was made to endure. The sailors, from many places around the world, were bad enough, but by far the worst of his mother's clients were the soldiers from the marines. Whenever a "Lobster" had called upon his mother in the evening, it was not unusual to find her with cuts and bruises the following morning. It was no exaggeration to say, that the young Johnny Rackham despised them! Finding gainful employment in London was not that difficult as there were plenty of opportunities, but nothing excited him. He wanted adventure, he wanted something stimulating and nothing he could find on offer, fulfilled that criteria. He had never taken up an apprenticeship so that was to his disadvantage, as many trades required skilled workmen and he wasn't skilled. He didn't fancy enlisting for the Merchant Navy, as he hated being 'told what to do!' especially by the likes of those that had mistreated his mother! So, he managed to save a few pounds from odd jobs he'd undertaken over several years, with a view to exploring Ireland. The only reason he chose Ireland in his quest for fulfilment, was because it was the cheaper option. Passage to the Americas would have cost him a lot more and he wasn't prepared to shovel shit for another five years, just to raise the fare! For several long years he took odd jobs so he could provide for his mother, and he put a bit aside each week, saving up for his passage out of London and off onto adventure. When, that day would arrive, he didn't know, but it was the thought of that adventure that kept him going. That was until, the day his mother died and the responsibility he had had for her suddenly ceased. He was now on his own and the day to begin his adventure had abruptly arrived.

So, Johnny Rackham stood on the quayside of Dublin dock's with just his kit bag and wondered, where to go next. The obvious thing to do was to head into the centre of the Metropolis as that was the most likely place to find suitable employment. Although he was ultimately looking for adventure, he was not stupid enough to think the right opportunity would land in his lap the moment he arrived. He was quite prepared to take up temporary work to fund his way around the country in his continued search for satisfaction. It was whilst he was walking along the main street in Ireland's capital city with its market traders, merchants, and street vendors, that he came across a small, dilapidated shop. The place looked forgotten and dejected with its filthy windows and flaking paintwork, but it was not the décor that he was drawn to, it was a tatty piece of paper in the window announcing a vacancy for an apprentice carriage driver. Johnny was curious as it seemed this might be something that would suit him. He wouldn't be working under the watchful eye of some sadistic employer, instead he would be out and about where he could be free to explore the country and get paid for it at the same time. As he entered the cold dark interior of the shop, an elderly man looked up from behind the counter and snapped,

'What you want?'

The old man was hunched, with a hooked nose, and looked like he had just resurfaced from hell itself. His eyes scanned the young man standing in his shop, with scrutiny, as if looking to uncover any dark secrets hiding in his soul.

'I'm here about the apprenticeship!' he told the old man, but the wizened proprietor just waved his hand dismissively and told him he wanted someone much younger.

Although Rackham was somewhat a loner, it didn't mean he was weak. Throughout his young life he'd learnt to be cunning and astute as a means to survive.

'How long you had that notice in the window?' he asked the old man.

''Bout six months,' he mumbled.

'Six months?' Johnny roared with laughter. 'Six months and you've still not found anyone! Seems no one is interested in yer position, old man. I expect the young have got more adventurous occupations to focus on in this fair city!'

With that, he turned to go, but just as his hand was on the doorknob, the old man called him back. It had worked! By showing contempt for the job after the refusal, it had forced the old man to realise that his need for a coach driver was very unlikely to come to fruition, given no one had applied in six months. Here was a young man willing to do the job and he was turning him away, turning away the only applicant he'd had in half a year.

At length, it was decided that Johnny Rackham would take up the post as carriage driver for a trial period of three months. In that time, he was expected to learn the trade, which included getting to know the routes, the clients he was to visit and making sure that deliveries were made on time. It transpired, that the old man ran a transportation company and provided a service, to many of the manufacturers in the city, who required their goods to be distributed around the country. There was also a good trade in transporting goods from the recently arrived merchant ships at the docks. It was a lucrative business for the old man initially, having had ten carriages to begin with. However, times were changing and with the outbreak of the war of the Spanish Succession in 1702, trade was declining sharply, resulting in the old man having to lay off many of his drivers. Now, however, the war was coming to an end, and he foresaw the increase in trade once again; as hostilities ended, and he wanted to be prepared before others snuck in and relieved him of all the possible new assignments. He had retained three drivers, but a fourth would be necessary now if the increase in traffic was to be realised.

It was sometime in early June, when Johhny Rackham drove his carriage into the town of Cork in the south of the island. He had a full load and after distributing the various goods to the clients on his list, he looked for a reasonable Inn to spend the night. When his round took him long distances from Dublin, he would often complete his deliveries and spend the night locally before heading back to the city. Invariably there was often extra money to be made by those wishing to send goods to Dublin, which he would collect and pocket the fees. A suitable resting place was easily found and after tying up the horse with the empty carriage still attached, he ventured into the small Tavern, in the heart of the town and bought himself a tankard of ale and some bread and cheese. It was a pleasantly warm evening and so he took his meal outside, where several rustic chairs and tables were situated. For all his protestations about not accepting this job or that job back in London, the situation he now found himself in, was rather idyllic. He was able to travel, be his own boss more or less, and he had some money in his pocket; and for the first time in his life Johnny Rackham, felt content. As he sipped his ale, he casually gazed around the street watching all the traders packing up their wares for the day, when his eyes fell on a young girl skipping and dancing on the patch of grass opposite. As she danced, she was singing to herself a jolly little tune of love and adventure. Something in the words of her song, resonated with him and he concentrated on her more, fascinated by her performance. She was evidently a gypsy as her skirt was a deep shade of purple, decorated with beads and colourful embroidered flowers. She had long jet-black wavy hair and round her head she wore a headband of velvet just as black as her hair. He was transfixed by her, as she had an air of mystery about her and in a funny sort of way there was a sadness, that hung about her. She was not much more than a child, but something about her gave the impression she was a lot more mature for her age, but that didn't mean she was physically attractive to Rackham, she was far too young for those sorts of attentions.

Whilst he sat there captivated by the girl, she suddenly caught sight of him watching her and she stopped her dance abruptly, and began marching towards him.

'What you about mister?' she asked, in her gently lilting Irish accent.

What amused Rackham, was the question was not hostile as one might think, when a young girl spies a man watching her. Her tone was more inquisitive as if she wanted to know more about him.

'Oh, nothin'' he replied. 'I was just watchin' yer dance.'

'Did yer like it?' she asked, almost seductively, which slightly unnerved him.

He replied that he thought she was entertaining, as that was the only thing he could think of to say that wasn't in any way suggestive or encouraging. Just then, a large wasp landed on his shoulder, and quick as a flash, the girl brushed it onto the table, and picking up his pocketknife he had been using to slice the cheese with, thrust it right through the abdomen of the offending insect. It wasn't a thrust with just the necessary force to kill it that alarmed Rackham, but the sheer ferocity of the way she stabbed the creature. The force was so hard that the knife penetrated the flesh and stuck fast in the wooden tabletop. Her face was demonic, he thought, and she snarled like some rabid dog. But as soon as her action served its purpose, her demeanour returned to normal. Although the girl's actions at the time were shocking and one could of easily have considered her disturbed, John Rackham would in time, get to understand that Anne was immensely loyal, and would stop at nothing to defend anyone she liked and befriended. Anyone or anything, that threatened those she cared for, could expect to feel her violent wrath. She was harsh, but she cared. After killing the insect and all signs of a mentally unbalanced child has passed, she casually asked him his name. Rackham replied and asked her name.

'Annie' she said. 'Annie McCormack.'

The strange alluring child plagued him for several days, as business suddenly required him to stay in town longer than he had planned. A particular client had some merchandise intended for Dublin, but it was not quite ready for transportation, and Rackham had been asked if he would mind waiting a couple of days. The payment offered was too good to refuse and so he agreed to stay until the cargo was ready to be dispatched. He could always make up an excuse for his late return to the depot, blaming the weather or conditions on the road.

Those few days in Cork were to change his life forever. The young girl Annie McCormack, followed him everywhere he went, pestering him at every turn. With not much else to do while he waited for his shipment to be prepared, he spent most of his time walking in the parks, and it was here, that Annie would often, uncomfortably accompany him. On the second day of his stay, he was walking through the park as usual, when Annie came dancing and skipping up to him.

'Yer goin' to marry me, Johnny Rackham?' she asked.

Rackham was shocked by the unsettling forwardness of the girl.

'No,' he responded. 'I'm too old for yer; I expects, that a nice young man will come along when yer a bit older and make a fine husband.'

His response was not the one she obviously wanted to hear, as that same look came into her eyes that had possessed her, when she had stabbed the wasp. He took a step back, feeling very uncomfortable and wondered what she might do next. The image of her stabbing the wasp was very clear in his mind, and he prepared himself for the physical assault he expected her to inflict on him. She didn't lash out at him though, she just stood there with a blank expression, which was just as worrying, because it was impossible to read what she might do next. About forty or fifty feet from them, a gentleman was taking a stroll and he stopped momentarily to consult his pocket watch. After taking note of the time, he replaced the watch in his pocket, and continued on his way, with a slightly faster step. Rackham noticed the girl watching the gentleman intently, with a strange look in her eyes, not so much a look of aggression, but rather like the look a wild beast has in its eyes as it stalks its prey. In an instant, she skipped off in the direction of the man and danced around him. She then appeared to engage him in conversation, although he couldn't hear what she said. She didn't appear to be annoying the stranger as he smiled and chatted with her briefly. Finally, she skipped away from him with a cheery wave and the man disappeared through the park gate and back out, onto the main street. Annie came skipping up to Rackham and with a glint of glee in her eyes, announced she had got a present for him. A flower or some such token he thought, as she took his hand and placed something hard into it. She folded his fingers around the object and then skipped off laughing loudly.

Rackham felt the fear rise in his stomach and hoped he was wrong, but as he opened his fist, the full realisation of not only what the girl had done, but the position it placed him in, hit him hard. There, laying in the palm of his hand, was the gentleman's watch! The girl had blatantly stolen the watch from the gentleman's pocket! Before he could do anything he saw two redcoats running towards him, and just behind them he could make out the gentleman who, no doubt had discovered the robbery of his person and had immediately reported it to the authorities.

'John Rackham, you have been found guilty of theft and this court sentences you to be taken to the colonies where you will suffer hard labour for a total of five years!'

The words of the Judge echoed in his mind as he sat in the tiny cell, waiting for the guards to escort him to the waiting ship, and the long journey to "Van Diemen's Land" and the start of his sentence. He was frightened and angry at the same time. How could he have let the girl get one over on him like that? He should have just walked away. He should have told her firmly to leave him alone, but he hadn't, and here he was, a condemned man.

Outside the gaolhouse, the guards were chatting away amongst themselves and laughing at each other's amusing tales about certain prisoners they'd had to deal with. It was true to say, they weren't exactly focused on the job in hand, but then, who would be stupid enough to attempt to break into a prison? The girl appeared out of nowhere and rudely interrupted their banter.

'What you want, Girl?' one of them gruffly asked her.

'What's it like in there, mister?' she answered with a question of her own. 'Do the cells 'ave spiders and creepy crawlies in 'em?'

'Yeh! And if yer don't 'op it this instant, yer gonna find out!' another of the guards barked. The sternness of the guards didn't shake her, and she continued with her unwelcome interrogation about life in prison. As she talked and gabbled about wanting to be a soldier herself one day, so she could get to killing people in battle, she casually took a stone flagon of ale out of the large cloth bag she was carrying and began sipping the intoxicating brew.

'You shouldn't be drinkin' that stuff!' one of the sentries chided, but the girl kept on sipping and even asked the men if they'd like a drink, after all it was a hot day.

All three of them were taken aback, but still, they accepted the small flasks, as Annie took them out of her bag and handed them around. After about an hour, what with the heat of the day and the alcohol consumed, the guards relaxed on some boxes that lay outside the guard house, that were waiting for collection, and it wasn't long before the temptation of sleep became too much and each of them nodded off; whilst Anne, for her trick had been successful, slipped into the depths of the gaol.

Johnny Rackham had resigned himself to the fact that his life path had now changed and not in the direction he would have liked. He was going to the penal colonies for five years. What he was going to do after that, was not something that warranted planning now.

'Five years!' he sighed to himself.

His thoughts were interrupted by the sound of a key in the lock of his cell.

'Well, this is it!' he thought.

He expected the door to open and the guards to

escort him to the waiting prison ship, ready for the long voyage halfway around the world; when the door opened, and Annie came wandering in. He could have dropped dead with the shock, there and then.

'What the hell you doin' here?' he asked with astonishment.

'No time for talkin, Johnny Rackham. We've got to get yer out of here.'

And with that, she led him back along the dingy corridors, to the main entrance, where the guards still sat sleeping on the packing crates. He was free, but for how long? Surely the guards would notice he'd escaped and come looking for him. Worse still, they might even extend his sentence.

'We can't do this!' he pleaded to Annie. 'They'll come for me, and it will make matters worse!'

She told him not to worry, as her father was a very clever lawyer, and he would sort it all out.

After about half an hour of walking, they came to a large cottage on the outskirts of Cork. It was a fine house, built of stone and evidently the residence of some local dignitary. The finery of the house and the idea that the girl actually lived here, was completely implausible and Rackham did not believe the girl was telling the truth, when she said this was where her father lived. As the doorbell rang and echoed down the hall, Rackham felt himself trembling with fear.

Whatever important person lived here, would soon have them ejected from the grounds, and how was it going to look, when the guards finally caught up with him? The door opened, and a man in his forties stood in the doorway. He was dressed like any dignitary would be, and he had a mop of long grey hair, tied in a queue at the back with a black silk ribbon.

'Hello, Annie,' the man said, and Rackham was shocked, really shocked. This man really was her father!

'Hello, father,' Annie chirped. 'This is Johnny Rackham; and I've just helped him, escape from the gaol, and we are going to get married!'

As she spoke to her father, the child squeezed his hand. Whether it was because what she had said shocked him, or whether it was because he felt uncomfortable being a twenty-eight-year-old man, standing with a girl who was no more than a child, who had just told her father they were to be married; he didn't know, but he snatched his hand away. As his hand passed in front of his face, he was aware of a bright blue light glowing around his fingers. Rackham knew he was standing on their ship in the 21st Century, but at the same time he was aware that he was standing at the front door of William McCormacks' house, over three-hundred years ago. He could clearly see himself, Annie, and McCormack in the blue haze between his fingers. The experience wasn't frightening, but fascinating.

Jack was absorbed by the vision playing out between his fingers, and at the same time he was experiencing the same emotions he'd once had. It was rather like looking at a picture of the past but instead of just remembering the occasion, one actually relived the event at the same time. Long forgotten memories came flooding into his mind, along with all the feelings he'd once had, that had been consigned to the archive of his consciousness long ago. He was reliving the time when William McCormack flew at him in rage, over the suggestion he might marry his daughter, but he also remembered how he'd intervened with the Magistrate on his behalf, and cleared up the unfortunate affair with the watch, on the understanding, that he would never see his daughter again. Staring deeply into the blue aura, he was taken back to when he'd met Annie in private, after her father forbade them to see each other. He had not gone back to Dublin, as the news of his arrest had reached the ears of his employer, and although all charges were quashed, "mud sticks" as they say, and he'd lost his job. He recollected; how he felt the day he heard that the McCormack family, had left Ireland for Americas and how being penniless, he joined a merchant ship out of Dublin, through desperation. All his past life rapidly rebuilt itself; emotions, memories, and feelings of times long past, have all resurfaced.

A face, swam into the forefront of his mind, the face of Charles Vane, under whom he had taken his first pirate commission. The face faded, and another replaced it, the face of Anne Bonny. Seeing Annes' face, and coupled with all the memories of their adventures together in Ireland, he was suddenly aware of how he grew to admire the girl, as she had a wild spirit. Yes, she was unpredictable, and would have bouts of intense rage, but he liked that. There was something about her, that he recognised deep in his own soul. It was as if she unconsciously, taught him how to tap into his own innermost desires and moods, and to free them from the confines of his own inhibitions. He had not realised it at the time, but she had set him free. He smiled to himself as he remembered what he used to call her, 'The Devil's Child!' But now, the newly awoken emotions caused a massive explosion of feelings in his heart, and he felt something; something he'd not experienced for a very long time. He felt an overwhelming sense of love.

# CHAPTER 13

### James Bonny

The blue flames faded, and Jack found himself facing the Anne Bonny of today. Wondering where Jack had got to, Anne came back out on deck, and saw Jack just standing there, staring into space, and she knew; she knew he'd just experienced his past. She smiled at him with compassion, and he flung his arms around her. For several minutes, they just stood there hugging each other. Anne knew that the John Rackham she had fallen in love with all those years ago, had returned and she was happy. Happy for only a few moments though, as the memories she fought to keep at bay began surging into her mind. In an attempt to shrug them off, she sharply pulled away from Jack and stormed across to the barrel and sat on it as if in a fit of pique. Naturally, Jack didn't understand. Here they were, loving each other properly for the first time in over three-hundred years, and she just roughly pulls away and dismisses him. He wasn't going to give up though. He might have humbly retreated recently, but after his experience with St. Elmo's fire, he was himself again and was determined to win Anne over. He sauntered casually across to where she was sitting and knelt by her side. He took her hand in his, half expecting her to snatch it back, but she didn't. She didn't say or do anything for several minutes. She just sat there holding his hand. Eventually she turned to face him and with tears, real tears in her eyes, she whispered;

'What happened, Jack?'

'Life happened.' He responded.

Anne Bonny was a strong woman, but in that moment, even she, struggled to keep the lid on her pent-up memories and emotions and all the hurt from so long ago, came tumbling out.

'A flaming miserable life it was too! You know I was raped? I was abused, and my family's land was taken! What was my crime? Just being a young girl...... and vulnerable,' she sniffed, wiping a tear from the corner of her eye.

Jack tried to cheer her up by jokingly saying, he could think of many words to describe her, but vulnerable; certainly, wasn't one of them! She smiled weakly and continued talking about how her bravado helped keep her sanity and how

Andy Cormack, helped her cope with life. She went on to describe several of the unfortunate events, that had taken place in her life and some of the people who had caused her so much pain.

'Then, there was James Bonny,' Jack said.

He didn't mean anything by it, just that it was he, who had saved Anne from that brute, and naturally this little piece of Annes' troublesome past, involved him. But Anne turned to Jack and sharply told him not to mention that man. Jack wasn't going to stop there. Loving someone was not just about offering sweet compliments, it was also being brave, enough to help one's lover face the traumas of life, so they could move forward. Help them, to let go and dump the emotional baggage of the past.

'Why not? He's part of your past. Alright, a part of your past you'd rather forget; but that's the point, isn't it? We must remember everything no matter how painful.'

Jack's words seared through her brain, and she knew he was right, but the agony she felt when facing those memories was too much for her to bare, and so, she stood up and strode across to the taffrail of the ship, she didn't face him, but she let her chagrin be known as she told him that was enough, and that he must stop it, stop it NOW! Jack knew this was as far as he could push her for now, and decided to let her be alone for a while. He had punctured her outer mental armour, and that was a start. The worst thing one could do to someone like Anne was to show pity, or even kindness at such moments, and as he walked towards the door, he berated her.

'Typical! We all go through the pain of remembering the past but when it gets to you, you can't do it!' he declared.

'Just leave me alone!' Anne snapped back, but Jack had gone.

Anne stood looking out to sea. The dawn would be upon them soon and she wondered what the next day on this new earth would bring. She tried to think of more mundane things in an attempt to stop the ever-increasing memories encroaching on her mind, but it wasn't really working. Her concentration was suddenly broken by Jock. She hadn't heard him come on deck and the first she knew he was there, was when he asked her what the matter was. Not another one trying to wheedle themselves into my business, she thought.

'Nothing's the matter!' she cried, 'Just leave me alone!'

Jock was having none of it. He had known Anne a very long time and he knew when she spoke harshly to her friends, she was trying to build a protective mental wall around herself.

'Och, well, I know yer lassie, and I know what you're thinkin,' He replied.

Anne turned slowly to face Jock as her rage simmered just below the surface. Her nostrils flared, and her eyes sparkled. Not with tears this time, but with pure fury. Jock just stood and looked at her, he knew her wrath was more aimed at herself than it was at him.

'Oh, yer do, do yer?' she hissed, desperately trying to exert her dominance over the Scotsman.

Jock was having none of it though, and stood his ground.

'Aye! I do!' he vehemently responded.

Anne fiercely argued back telling him he didn't understand and that he knew nothing of the pain and hurt she'd suffered in her young life and that he knew nothing of James Bonny, her ex-husband. Jock admitted he didn't know him, nor Anne for that matter, when she was married, but he did know that everyone has a past that they'd rather forget, and that Anne was no different. He told her firmly that the only way she could move forward was to face the past, however painful it might be. Anne wasn't going to be lectured by McTavish, or anyone else come to that, and she told him bluntly to sod off! Jock just glared at her, as he knew Anne would always get defensive whenever she was questioned and especially when the person doing the questioning was right. The only way to get through to Anne was to stand up to her, not to give way at any point. Jock laughed and told her he wasn't that easy to get rid of, and he reminded her that she had forcefully expected them to face their past, but now that it was her turn, she couldn't do it. He urged her to face her past and he reminded her of how she had helped him, helped all of them, and now it was their turn to help her. He knew that it was not in her nature to accept help from others, but on this occasion she really needed to be pushed. Of course, he meant it metaphorically and not physically. Jock walked away, telling her not to bottle everything up and to think on what he'd said.

Anne turned back to gaze out across the ocean, and out of sight from everyone, as she wiped a tear that had begun trickling down her cheek. Perhaps she was a coward, she thought. Perhaps she didn't have as much courage as she believed. She knew the time would come when she had to face her memories as the voice in the wind had told her to. But now, the moment was here, she was frightened. She was more scared now than she could ever remember being. Raiding ships as a pirate, standing up to drunks in Taverns dressed as Andy Cormack, rebelling against the British army were all courageous actions, but to face her own memories, that was a different matter entirely.

Jock had barely reached the doorway, when something else crossed his mind and he turned to call to Anne, something about selfishness. It wasn't true, of course, but it might be enough to goad her into action. But Anne wasn't there. She couldn't have gone anywhere on deck, or else he would have seen her, he reasoned. A chilling thought crept into his mind, and he rushed to the taffrail where she had been standing only minutes before. Tightly clutching the rail, he leaned over the side of the ship, straining his eyes in the blackness to see if he could see what his brain was telling him. But it was too dark to make anything out in the jet-black water, two or three fathoms below. Then he heard it. Very quietly, he heard the sea water splashing far below. It wasn't the usual gentle lapping of the tide against the hull, this was the sound of something in the water.

'Jack!' he yelled as loudly as his lungs would allow. 'Jack! For God's sake, get up here NOW!'

Jack was in the captain's cabin so didn't have far to run when he heard Jock calling him urgently. Rushing out onto the deck, he called to Jock, asking him what was so wrong that warranted calling him at such a late hour. Jock just pointed over the side of the ship and shook his head. He had a startled look in his eyes and Jack knew at once what he meant.

'Anne?' he croaked, daring not to presume the obvious, but he was right, as Jock just nodded slowly.

Without a second's hesitation, Jack leapt up onto the taffrail, swayed momentarily while he gained his balance, then dived into the icy blackness of the ocean below.

Anne desperately tried to claw herself back up to the surface. She was drowning, but in the forefront of her mind was the lust for retaliation against the murderous devil that had pushed her over the side. She had been gazing out to sea and lost in her thoughts after the argument with Jock, when she felt the hands on her shoulders. The grip was so firm that she couldn't turn to face her attacker. The next minute she was plummeting down into the freezing water of the ocean. What with the shock of the assault and the quickness of everything, Anne had not been able to take a breath of air before hitting the water. Her lungs were on fire with the lack of oxygen, and she kicked hard, trying desperately to propel herself upwards and into the welcoming fresh air just above her. It was then she felt the hands around her waist, and she was ascending.

Her hand grabbed something heavy, and she tugged at it as hard as she could. There she was, under the water, desperately trying to breathe and at the same time she wouldn't let go of her prize! Finally, they broke the surface and James burst out laughing. Somehow they managed to haul the wooden chest out of the water and on to the sand of the little quiet cove. They both fell, exhausted, onto the beach and inadvertently, Anne fell into James' arms, and he playfully tightened them around her waist.

'Can't leave me now!' he giggled, and Anne slapped and pummelled his chest quite hard. The forceful blows made him release his grip, but he didn't stop laughing. In fact, he laughed even more.

'We did it! We did it Annie!' he managed to say between snorting.

They had been chatting on the quayside as the marines boarded Edward Teachs' ship, and they had seen his men dumping several chests overboard into the water of the harbour of Nassau. Obviously, they were trying to hide their ill-gotten gains from the Kings' men. It was the perfect hiding place, and easily retrievable later when the coast was clear. What Blackbeard and his men hadn't counted on, was they were seen by Anne Cormack and James Bonny as they stood in conversation. It wouldn't have mattered if it had been any other couple, as they would not have done anything about it. But Anne and James were not the people to let an opportunity like this slip through their fingers. They had waited until just before dark and then swam out to where the chests had been dumped, and diving down they readily found the crates strewn across the ocean floor. The water was reasonably shallow, just deep enough for the ships to enter the harbour, and so it was easy enough for them to reach the sunken treasure. Grabbing at one of the coffers, they struggled to get it to the surface due to its sheer weight, but somehow they managed to manhandle it, within feet of the shore. It was then that Anne lost her hold, and the box sank again to the seabed. She immediately dived after it again, as did James, and they play-wrestled under the water in a mock battle over the possession of the chest. When night fell, they dragged the chest into the undergrowth further up the beach, where they hid it with handfuls of sand and bracken. They would leave it there for a few days whilst Blackbeard and his crew retrieved the other boxes. They knew the pirates would miss one, so they had to wait until they'd given up looking for it. They assumed that Blackbeard's men wouldn't think to search on land as they had thrown all the chests into the sea, and so after a few days they reasoned, they could return and recover their treasure with the pirates being none the wiser. The acquired ill-gotten gains came in very useful. Anne gave some money to her father, as his plantation business was not doing particularly well and had lost some land, because he'd failed to keep up the rent payments. William Cormack needed some desperate capital investment which Anne was now able to provide. What gold remained, Anne and James divided between themselves. James spent most of his over the following few months in fine living, for which Anne chided him for. She, herself put most of her share away and buried it on her father's land, as insurance for the future.

Everything went black. Swimming through a blackness of the ocean, she spied a dim pool of light just ahead, and with her lungs burning through lack of oxygen, she desperately kicked her legs in an effort to reach whatever it was that lay ahead. As she glided into the blue, fluorescent light, she felt herself rising out of the water and she was standing in the familiar little chapel in the Province of Carolina. Next to her was James, who stood there grinning at her, and the priest was saying something about love, honour and obey. Annie Cormack was now Anne Bonny! Soon after their marriage, the couple moved to Nasau with the hope of indulging in profitable business. There were a lot of trade opportunities there, as it was a haven for shipping, including pirates. Anne was happy. She and James had been married for several months now. He was fun to be with and they'd had many adventures, some daring and some just decadent. It was James who had introduced her to the excitement of the Taverns and the drinking sessions, where fights had broken out and dodgy dealings were done with pirates. It had been rough and violent, but Anne had loved every minute of it. She would often cheat drunken sailors out of their hard-earned cash by betting them against some ploy she had invented where she could not loose. One of these scams that worked rather well, was wagering with those a little worse for drink, that they couldn't drink out of their own tankard without touching it. Many tried all sorts of ways to rise to the challenge, and at the same time gambling their money, in believing they could do it. Naturally, none of them could, and goaded Anne to prove it could be done before removing their hands from the pile of gold pieces on the table. Anne would simply say one word. 'James!' James would then pick up her tankard and place it to her lips, and she would take a large swig. Cries of 'cheat!' and 'scoundrel!' emitted from the mouths of the unfortunate victims of the scam, but Anne pointed out that she had not said they couldn't ask anyone else to help them! She would then scoop up her winnings, and they'd move on to another ale house to perform the routine all over again. It was during those times that she fell in love with life inside Taverns, but of course, as a woman, it was not a wise thing to do, but then, she had James Bonny who was a safeguard against any real harm coming to her. The memories of their raucous exploits ran through her mind, and she remembered how James gave her the life and freedom she had always craved. He wasn't pompous or possessive and he certainly didn't treat her as a second-class citizen because she was a woman! There was only one tinge of sadness, and that was her father no longer wanted anything to do with her, because of James.

William McCormack, or Cormack as he was now, having dropped the 'Mc' after they had arrived in the Americas, didn't attend the wedding ceremony because he was vehemently opposed to the marriage of his daughter to the rogue Bonny!

'He's a charlatan!' he would yell at Anne when she announced her engagement. 'He'll lead you into trouble, mark my words!' he would bellow.
But Anne wouldn't listen. All she knew was that James Bonny was exciting and made her feel alive. If her father didn't like it, then tough!

'I'm drowning!' her inner voice screeched through her brain and broke the dream about her wedding, her father and life with James. Was it a dream though? It all seemed so real. But whatever it was, it didn't matter as there was a more serious situation to deal with. Anne Bonny was dying! As her lungs yelled out for air, her mouth responded in sympathy and opened wide in a silent scream. She could feel his hands around her throat, and she couldn't breathe. She tried to scream but she had no air in her lungs, and besides, his hands restricted her vocal chords as they gripped her even more tightly. Suddenly the pressure on her neck subsided and she inhaled several gulps of air. Next, she felt herself hurtling across the room. James had forcefully lifted her up and thrown her, face down on the bed.

One night, they had gone to a local Inn as usual, James had said it was a special occasion as they had been married for six months. At first the atmosphere was pleasant, albeit rowdy, with people congratulating them on their anniversary. It would have been more appropriate to celebrate an anniversary after a year, but James often came up with lame excuses for an evening of drunken revelry. Jars of ale, glasses of whiskey, and rum flowed freely, and Anne felt giddy with excitement. As the hours passed, James began to change. He became moody and aggressive towards her. He told her to sit down when she wanted to dance as the minstrels struck up. He slapped her across the face when she spoke to an old sailor they had both known for some time. But none of that was as terrifying as the moment she was now living through. James had rented a room upstairs at the Inn and he had forcibly dragged her up there when he'd had enough of the celebrations. Anne wanted to stay and enjoy herself, but he had hit her across the back of the head and told her to get up those stairs. In the seedy little room, she had turned on him and told him what a spiteful dog he was and that he should learn to take his drink like a real man. Her words inflamed his temper further, and he reached out and grabbed her by the throat and tried to throttle her. Now he'd thrown her on the bed and was tugging at her clothes.

'NO, James!' she pleaded, not like this!'
But he didn't listen. All that was on James Bonnys' mind was satisfying his carnal thirst, and with that, he forced himself on her.

'He'll lead you into trouble, mark my words!'
Anne heard her father's remonstrations echo in her mind, as she fought for her own survival in the deep cold water of the north sea. Something had got hold of her and she felt trapped. She fought against whatever it was that was holding her fast beneath the waves, and she knew she hadn't got much time left, as her strength was rapidly declining.

The brute had fallen asleep in a drunken stupor, having had his pleasure. Anne slowly rolled over, sat up and considered her next move. From outside the window, she could hear some people singing and for some reason the song they were singing, seemed to encourage her. She had to get away from the monster and she had to get away now. Gently, so as not to wake him, although there was not much chance of that, given the amount of alcohol he'd consumed, she got off the bed. Her clothes were ripped and stained, and she couldn't possibly go out like this. It was not a wise thing for a woman to generally be out on the streets at this hour, for they were more than likely to be preyed upon by merciless pirates or other drunken louts, out for a good time. With the state she was in, being out on the streets would only invite trouble. James' clothes were strewn about the floor, and she picked up his breeches with an audacious plan running through her mind. She removed what was left of her skirts and pulled on the breeches. Next she donned his shirt and waistcoat and taking his coat and hat from the peg on the wall, she hurriedly made her escape. That night, after Anne Bonny nee Cormack, had been brutalised, a new chapter of her life began, and she became a different person. That night 'Andy Cormack' was born.

Finally, the air in Annes' lungs was spent and she blacked out. The last thought that flashed through her mind before the blackness overwhelmed her, was that, 'was it all worth it?'

Anne awoke, having fallen asleep across a table in a Tavern that she often frequented. It was late and she had to get home to her father. He had not been too well of late, probably due to all the upset over her failed marriage to James Bonny. Her father had forgiven her, and he'd comforted her after the brute had raped her, and he encouraged her to plan for the future and to live her life the way she wanted. He didn't even mind her dressing as "Andy" as he'd said, it would help her see and understand the harshness of the world, facts she would not see from the perspective of a woman. Her father told her of when James had recklessly spent all his share of the money from Blackbeard's chest, he had turned government informer to earn a living. He would befriend people in the Taverns and Inns of the town and elicit information from them, which he would then report to the Governor, for a small fee.

In her rush to get home to her father, she dashed out of the Tavern without really looking where she was going, and ran straight into a man who was innocently walking by. The stranger admonished her for her foolhardy actions and that he should look where he was going. The chap obviously thought Anne was a lad as he went to clip her round the back of the head. But before he could strike her, she recognised him and blurted out.

'Well, if it ain't Johnny Rackham as I live and breathe!'

Rackham was overjoyed to see her once she had removed her hat and coat to reveal her true self.

'Annie McCormack!' He exclaimed with elation, and grabbed her in an embrace that friends would often do when they meet again after several years.

The following few weeks were a whirlwind of activity. They were together most of the time and the seeds of love that had been sown five years previously, now came to fruition. It was difficult to say who led who on, especially with plans to take up piracy, but perhaps they were both responsible. Rackham had rescinded the pirate life and taken the Kings' pardon, but he was eager for adventure again, finding life pretty boring and unprofitable in Nassau. Anne, on the other hand, wanted shot of James Bonny and a new life at sea, and like Rackham, she had the thirst for adventure. The final decision was made to become pirates after Rackham tried to buy a divorce for Anne from James, and when he refused, Rackham landed him one, and vowed there and then, that if Bonny wouldn't divorce her legally, they would embark on a life of piracy where they could do exactly as they pleased. She remembered how James Bonny, had looked up from the floor with blood running from his nose, and shouted after them;

'I'll 'ave you for that, Calico Jack!'

That was the first time she had heard anyone call Rackham, the name he would become famous for.

Jack swam about in the cold darkness of the ocean, frantically searching for Anne and getting more desperate by the minute.

'Where is she?' he thought.

Anne was a good swimmer, and it was inconceivable that she had drowned so quickly, not unless she'd hit her head on something in the fall. Just then, he felt something under the surface brush against his leg. Taking a gulp of air, he dived under the water with his arms flaying about in the desperate search for his lover. Luckily his hands found her and with all his strength, he heaved her up to the surface.

'Jock!' he cried, 'lower a rope.'

Mary had rushed out onto the deck with all the noise of Jock and Jack shouting, and was alarmed to discover what the fuss was about. She helped Jock unravel a length of rope, tied a loop in one end, and threw it over the side of the ship. Holding Annes' lifeless body with one arm, he managed to get the loop of rope over Annes' shoulders with his free hand and tightened the knot, so it was secure under her armpits. Shouting at Jock and Mary to haul away, Jack watched as Annes' body was hoisted up onto the ship, wondering if she were still alive or not. Jack then grabbed the foot of a nearby rope ladder and sprung up and leapt onto the deck once again. Jock and Mary were kneeling by the prostrate form of Anne, but Jack knocked them out of the way in his attempt to get to her and see if she were alive. Taking her hand in his, all he could do was pat it and beg her to come back to him, but of course, she didn't. Mary suddenly pushed Jack out of the way saying;

'Let me.'

She started massaging Annes' nose and throat and told them how she'd seen a ship's surgeon do something like this when she was on a British naval ship. She explained the surgeon had said 'drowning was due to lack of air, and you must do what you can to get the air flowing in the body again.' Mary then bent down and put her mouth over Annes'.

'What the hell you doin?' Jack roared angrily.

'Blowin' air into her.' She casually replied.

The resuscitation of drowning victims was rare in their time as anatomy wasn't that advanced, but some ship's surgeons stumbled on mouth-to-mouth resuscitation quite accidentally, in the assumption that it was a good idea to get air into the victim. Mary attempted what she had learnt from the surgeon and after a few breaths, Anne spluttered and coughed up a mouthful of water, all over Jack, then she sat up.

'Who was the dog that pushed me overboard?' Anne roared with anger.

'Well, there's gratitude,' Jack sarcastically replied.

Anne accused everyone, and they all felt shaken by the unfounded accusations, because not only had none of them pushed Anne overboard, but none of them would have done such a thing in the first place.

Anne stormed off into the captain's cabin to look for a change of clothes, leaving the others to revel in the knowledge she was alive, but bemused at the same time.

'Who would have pushed her?' Mary asked, not to anyone in particular, but just to vent her thoughts.

Both Jack and Jock, confessed they had no idea and presumed she'd just slipped or lost her footing, but being Anne, she could never admit to her own fallibility. The mood was sombre because here was a situation that could have been fatal and none of them had the answers. Jock went and sat on one of the crates and Mary went across and sat on the floor next to him, while Jack perched himself on the raised platform the wheel stood upon. Everyone was silent and worried how Anne would treat them now, as she believed one of them had tried to murder her. It wasn't a pleasant prospect.

# CHAPTER 14

## A New Dawn

No one spoke. Jock got up and wandered around the deck collecting any old bits of wood he could find, and then placed them in the brazier. It was just before dawn, and the early morning air was chilly. Blowing on the last of the glowing embers, he managed to encourage the flames to take up the new wood. Before long, a small fire was blazing, and the others huddled round to get a bit of warmth. Still, no one spoke, they just stared into the dancing flames as they flickered and hopped about like little demons. The show of flames, was a nice distraction from the thought of what had happened to Anne. Had the three of them not built up a strong bond between themselves, it would have been likely that they would have all grown to suspect each other of the attempted murder of their crewmate. But they didn't think that, and that was a surprise, because three-hundred years ago, the opposite would have been the likely scenario.

A door banged and they all looked up in the direction it had come from. It was the captain's cabin door and Anne wandered back on deck, dressed in a pair of dark breeches and wearing one of Jacks' shirts, over which she sported a woollen waistcoat, and sat on the packing crate on the opposite side of the ship. Still, no one said anything. Anne looked out to sea and thought about recent events, she knew none of them could have pushed her really, because it didn't make any sense. Why would any of them push her? They certainly wouldn't have had any reservations in taking a life in the past, when their own was threatened. They could be ruthless and cunning, but they weren't cowards. Any one of them would have confronted her if they had a grievance, not sneak up behind her and commit the deed without showing themselves. No, something else had forced her over the side, but who or what? Anne considered that many strange things had happened since they returned, and it was more than conceivable that her accident was just another of these unfathomable incidents. What she knew, was that she had been forced to face her memories, or rather her memories took her over, whilst she struggled in the water. Perhaps that was it. Perhaps, something had knocked her overboard as a way to force her to face her memories, because she was too reticent to face them voluntarily. As the others warmed themselves by the fire and the water lapped gently against the side of the ship, Anne began to think about those times she had, for so long, refused to acknowledge. It wasn't so painful anymore to think of James Bonny and her father, because those memories were now part of her, they were who she was, and in a funny sort of way, she felt more complete as a person. A watery smile flickered across her lips as she thought about all the events that had happened so far, and how they had all been forced to relive times from their past. It had made all of them more human, she thought. In the past they just had to get on with living, and those sorts of situations made you just aware of what was necessary in your life, to survive. Any other semblance of humanity became buried beneath the persona one adopted, just to get through the rigors of life. Not unlike what she had seen with the people on the television. A part of those people had died, just as a part of them had died when they were pirates, yet here they all were, reconnected with their inner beings and being whole again, after a very long time. Anne realised that was why they all had to undergo these moments of experiencing their past lives again, so they could reunite the fragmented pieces of their souls. At this very moment, Anne, being the last to face the past in the unnatural manner they'd all been subjected to, understood that not only would the sun rise soon on a new day, but each of them was now entering a new dawn too. Casually she looked across at them huddled round the fire and whispered to herself.

'The dawn approaches and soon, the sun shall rise on a new day. The same may be said of us. The dark night of our past, is giving way to the light of a new dawn.' Had they really learned anything though, she wondered. Had their experiences taught them anything? Although a question without an answer at that point, one thing was clear to Anne, and that was; she had to guide her friends along a new path of life, where none of them had ever trodden before. The future was exciting, but daunting all at the same time.

Jack sat staring into the fire, warming his hands, and although he didn't speak, his mind was racing. He was appalled at what had happened to Anne, yet he had no answer for it. He knew Jock and Mary weren't responsible, and he also believed it was something to do with the strange events that had been happening. How would Anne react now she had faced her memories? She hadn't actually told any of them, what she had experienced under the water, but they could all guess. Yes, she had been aggressive in her words when she came round, but that was only to be expected. But when she came out of the cabin after changing, there was a slight change in her. Jack knew from the old days; Anne would often get agitated and snappy with everyone just before a raid, and he knew it was because she was nervous. Not nervous of battle, but of the uncertainty. Anne was always on edge when faced with situations she was not sure of, and didn't have total control over. Since coming out of the cabin however, she seemed more subdued, more relaxed, as if she no longer had the weight of the world on her shoulders. All Jacks' reasoning made sense, but was Anne really changed? Was she no longer the "quick to temper" girl he'd known before? Would she really not resort to violence when threatened? Would she seriously refrain from stealing and plundering, even when there was no other option? Only one way to find out, thought Jack. He got up and casually crept through the door into the captain's cabin, and returned after about a minute, clutching a small wooden box and a flintlock tucked in his belt. Jack had a secret, and a plan. Anne always persisted in fussing over him, or berating him for something or other, as if he was stupid or unemotional. Normally he would just put up with it because he knew she wasn't being vindictive; it was just her way. Other times, she was as loving and as sweet as any man could wish from their woman, and when he'd contrast the two sides of her personality, for him, the nice side of Anne always triumphed. Unfortunately, many others saw her negative side and they believed her to be a violent and nasty piece of work, but they didn't know her like Jack did.

Jack grinned to himself as he strolled across the deck towards where Anne was sitting. He had an idea. He stood about six feet from her, idly toying with the box. His actions were purely intentional. The idea was to present Anne with an image of a pirate with a gun, ready for action, and a treasure chest for the taking, but would she take the bait?

'You feelin' better?' he asked, but she just replied with a stubborn, no! Jack toyed with the box right in her line of vision, and he remarked that it wasn't easy looking back.

'What ye got there, Jack?' she then curiously asked him.

Jack smiled; it was working.

'Money!' he flippantly replied.

He noticed that quizzical look in her eyes, and he knew. That was a spark he recognised. When Anne got a passion in her mind for something, nothing would stop her until she succeeded in winning, or if it were an object, until she had possession of it. He knew this aspect of her personality would never leave her, however much she tried to pretend she was a changed woman. Anne then asked, where he got the money from, and Jack casually replied that he had stolen it. He wondered if she would flare up in a temper at the mention that he had committed burglary, like she did when she found the old drunk's bag amongst the others they'd got from the shop. If he knew Anne, he knew that she may well act differently, and he was right. She became all seductive, got up and started stroking his face.

'Oh, Jack. You wonderful man. I am sorry I've been so mean to you.'

Anne suggested they share the treasure, but Jack snatched the money box away, before she could get her hands on it, but she swiftly glided to his other side and made to reach for her prize. Jock glanced up from his position where he was relaxing by the fire and immediately recognised what was going on, and whispered to Mary that Anne was up to one of her tricks, trying to get one over on Jack. Both Mary and Jock knew that these occasions never ended well, and more often than not, ended up with Jack and Anne quarrelling, not a situation anyone in the right mind should be party to. Whilst Anne and Jack were engaged in the peculiar dance of seduction and resistance, Jock beckoned to Mary to follow him, as they both slipped quietly through one of the doors and into the interior of the ship, out of harm's way. Anne wrapped her arms around Jacks' neck, whilst he held the box out to the side, and whispered in his ear. Jack was no fool and knew very well when Anne was trying to butter him up with compliments so she could get what she wanted, namely the small treasure chest! Unfortunately, Jack was drawn in when she described being attracted to men who were rich, powerful, and with a huge.... It was when she paused that he fell right into her trap, because he stupidly asked her;

'A huge what?'

'Weapon!' replied Anne smugly, as she quickly drew the pistol from Jacks' belt and demanded he hand over the money box.

He reluctantly gave it to her, warning her that she would come to regret her actions. Anne just glared at him, and told him he had another think coming if he thought he would get the money back!

'Ah! Checkmate!' Jack cried, but Anne just stared at him with a look of bewilderment on her face.

She was puzzled as to what Jack meant, but she didn't have to wait long for the answer. Jack smarmily pointed out, that she was ever so righteous when she accused him of stealing from the old drunk in the tavern, but when it was something that had been taken from an unknown source, she was quite prepared to accept it. Anne knew he was right, and he had hit a nerve. She had tried to encourage all of them to be honest and trustworthy, yet here she was, doing exactly what she would have done three-hundred years ago. She was complicit in larceny. How could she save face? But she hit on an idea in an instant and declared that any ill-gotten gains on the ship would be hurled overboard, and with that, she ran to the side of the ship, holding the box aloft ready to hurl it into the ocean. Whilst she was distracted momentarily, Jack seized his chance and made a grab for the pistol still in her other hand. It wasn't loaded of course, but it was a symbol of authority and he brandished it in Annes' face as she spun round to look at him.

'Give me that treasure!' he snarled at her, like some crazed animal who was on the verge of losing its prey after it had taken the time and effort to kill it.

If he thought she would surrender with his ridiculous attempt at machoism, he was seriously mistaken, thought Anne. She had never capitulated to a man when they exerted their authority over her, and she wasn't going to start now, especially with Jack. Slamming the money box onto the wheel platform, she snatched her cutlas from her baldrick that hung on the broken newel, and wielded it in Jacks' face.

 'Ye want the treasure, then yer fight for it!' she spat at him.

Jack casually drew his sword from his frog that hung on the other newel, and raised the tip level with Annes'.

'Aye!' Jack snarled, and with that, he swung his sword high above his head, and brought it smashing down towards Annes' neck. She was too fast for him though, and she instantly parried the blow, and swung her sword down in anticipation of his next attack. Sure enough, he went for her legs, and she was ready. Blocking his aim, she swung her sword upwards and slid it along the shaft of his weapon to lock guards, and at the same time, she raised her knee and struck him hard in his manhood. Jack gasped as the searing pain shot through his body, and tears welled in his eyes. Stumbling backward, he composed himself as best as he could, given the discomfort he was now enduring, and after a few moments, whilst Anne stood there laughing at him, he lurched forward and lunged for her head. Again, she had the perfect defence and followed it through with an onslaught attack. She slashed to his right, then his left, and then to his head. Jack managed to see off the brutality of the assault, and with all his strength, he twisted her blade upwards, causing her to momentarily lose balance. That was enough time for Jack to strike out with his leg and kick her in the backside as he passed her. Rather than weaken her resolve, this action only served to inflame her aggression, and she flew at him again, swinging her sword in a fast and furious slashing motion. Jack defended himself well, and after deflecting one of the deadly blows rather successfully, or so he thought, he again went for her head. She didn't parry the blow this time however, instead she neatly side stepped him, and as he stumbled past her, she raised her knee once more and gave him another dose between his legs. This time Jack went down in agony. Anne just laughed and circled round him, taunting him as she went. Jack knelt there on the floor breathing deeply. He was getting tired, but he knew he had to come out on top or else he'd never live it down. He waited until Anne was satisfied she had won, and when she turned her back on him, he was at her. Yelling as he ran towards her with his sword above his head, he was ready to cleave her in two, but she simply side stepped him again and Jacks' sword came crashing down on the deck. Before he could recover, Annes' sword appeared between his legs.

'Do you yield?' she screamed at him.

'Yes.' Jack weakly responded, and the blade disappeared from its dangerous position in his groin.

As soon as she had withdrawn her sword, he turned and went to attack again, but the damned woman, blocked his move once more. They both tried to force each other backwards as their hilts locked for a second time. The more they both pushed, the harder they both resisted, until finally they both used up the last of their energy, and with one final effort, they both rammed at each other causing them both to fly backwards and fall over flat on the deck. For a few moments there was silence, as they were both shocked to find themselves staring up at the sky, but then Anne started to laugh.

'What's so funny?' Jack asked, as he himself started to chuckle.

'You!' Anne sniggered.

'What's so funny about me?' he responded.

Anne told him how she was amused at the idea that she had to get rid of the money, after he'd gone to the trouble of stealing it. She then asked him what he had found so amusing, and his answer was one she didn't expect. Sitting up to face her, Jack explained cheekily, that he had set a test for her, and that she had failed miserably! The look on her face made him chuckle even more as she had no idea what he was talking about. Jack had achieved a little victory over her; and he was delighted and revelled in the explanation that he gave. He described how he hadn't stolen the money; in fact, he had sold his ring to Mrs Macintyre in exchange for some modern coins, and with that money he'd paid the old drunk in the Tavern for the groceries. The only misdeed he had really done, was to deprive an old man of his shopping, in exchange for some coinage to buy more drink. When they got back on board after their excursion ashore, he had gone into his cabin and put the money he had exchanged, in the little wooden casket that she now wanted to throw over the side. Jack told her how he had seen the lust for treasure in her eyes, he had seen a glimpse of the true Anne Bonny, and not the false persona she was trying to hide behind. Yes, he pointed out, she was building a false façade around her personality. It was justified for them to be faced with their past, as it was teaching them things about themselves, they had forgotten about a long time ago. But although they should develop a new attitude, they must not change who they are or try to create new personalities for themselves. After all, that's exactly what Mary had done in the past. They were and should remain the people they had always been, but just develop better understanding of others.

'Don't try to be righteous, don't be a puritan, just be yourself, faults and all,' he impressed upon her.

He reminded her of when they used to go on raids, and he used to say they shouldn't cause death and destruction unless necessary. He pointed out that he never said they shouldn't go on raids, after all, they had to eat, but that he just wanted to minimise the suffering they caused, and that's exactly how they should be now. They would still have to be ruthless and cunning, and occasionally break with convention, and possibly even the law, but for the greater good. They can never change the way of things, and that they cannot change the attitude of all people, but they can try to influence by example.

'You see, Anne my love, it's called life!'

Anne was taken aback at Jacks' trickery, and his reasoning, and she had to concede that he had taught her a very valuable lesson. She had been totally blinkered in her vision that he, along with Mary and Jock, should all change their personalities, instead of just altering their attitude to seek out the path they were intended for. It also dawned upon her, that she had been so engrossed with changing the others, she had completely overlooked her own faults and misgivings. A few moments of silence past, as Anne absorbed everything Jack had said. Eventually she confessed that he was right, but what he said also triggered deep feelings that she had suppressed for so long. Just like she had suppressed the memories of James. She admitted that she had suppressed her true self, but then she saw something that freed her, and that something was Jack. She saw how much his outward attitude had changed, even though his true spirit remained, and that he was a true inspiration to her and because of that, she felt the surge of feelings for him she hadn't felt since those days back in Nassau, and she remembered how those feelings first began to grow inside her when she was a young girl in Ireland. She crawled across to Jack and put her arms around him, and he responded by stroking her hair gently.

'I remember how we used to be all those years

ago, when life was carefree,' Anne exclaimed. 'I remember the fields of Ireland, where we used to walk. I remember how I got you into trouble, and how my father sorted it all out. But I also remember how it all went wrong, and we ended up as selfish, violent individuals. I was never as happy, as I was when we were young. And that is when I was with you, Jack.'

Jack confessed how she, the "devil child," had influenced him, and made him more confident, and able to face the world with a more carefree attitude. It was true she had got him into trouble with the watch, but even that taught him; that however insurmountable a problem might appear, there are always ways to overcome such difficulties in life, if you have the conviction and courage to do so.

'I'm proud of you, Jack,' she declared. She was proud of the fact he had sold his ring, something he would never have done when they were pirates. By dreaming up the test with the money box, she had realised just how much he had actually become a "more rounded human being", much more than she had ever given him credit for. It had never occurred to Anne that it was possible to change their attitude, but keep their own personalities. She was convinced that for whatever purpose they had been resurrected for, they had to prove they've changed, but she now understood that changing didn't mean altering who they were. As pirates they had strengths, and retaining those strengths was necessary for what lay ahead, "the purpose" as she called it. Jack was puzzled by the so-called purpose as he couldn't understand that if there was some grand scheme for them, why wasn't it made clearer what was expected of them. But Anne suggested that was because they had to find that out for themselves, and just like his test for her with the money box, so what actions they took for themselves was also a test, but on a much larger scale. They both sat in silence for a while, holding each other and thinking about all the connotations of what was truly expected of them and where fate would ultimately lead them. Jack then asked her if she thought they were ghosts. She smiled, as she remembered she had asked the same question of the voice in the wind, and didn't get a straight answer. Another of those moments she was expected to discover the answer for herself.

'No, I don't believe we are,' she answered at length, but admitted she didn't truly know the answer, but she did feel it was not worth asking such questions. Instead, they should just accept and try to understand whatever situation they find themselves in, next.

'Besides,' she continued, 'I have a responsibility to the others, especially Mary.'

Jack just nodded and silence fell once more, whilst they both pondered on the meaning of everything.

'I don't know how she'll respond when she remembers about the baby....' Anne realised what she'd said.
She had voiced her thoughts out loud, and she shouldn't have done, but it was too late, Jack had heard. He pulled away from her and spun to face her, and demanded to know what baby she was talking about. He wasn't, or had ever been, aware of any baby, but Anne just put her fingers on his lips and told him all would be revealed in good time. It wasn't anything for him to worry about and that he should just let things follow their natural course. Jack seemed to accept what Anne said and relaxed again, as they both sat in silence listening to the lapping of the waves and the gentle flapping of the sails in the cold pre-dawn breeze.

Unbeknown to them, Jock and Mary had noticed that everything had gone quiet on the upper deck and presuming the tempest of Annes' and Jacks' fight had passed, Mary came up to see if everything was alright. As she reached the top of the narrow staircase, and just as she was about to come through the door, she heard Anne and Jack talking. They seemed to be in deep conversation and not wanting to disturb them in their private moment, she held back just out of sight. The unfortunate thing was Mary heard every word about the baby. Hastily she retreated down the steps and sat on the bottom tread, contemplating what Anne had said. This lost memory of hers about the baby was obviously significant, and she desperately tried to remember, but all that she succeeded in doing was triggering the agonising pain in her head again.

A silent peacefulness hung around the deck, and Jack was gazing up at the sky. The night was clear, and the stars twinkled in the heavens like little jewels winking at him. He turned to Anne who was deep in her own thoughts and nudged her.

'You see that star?' he asked.

She looked up and followed his gaze.

'Aye, the dog star!' We always used it to navigate.'

Jack said nothing, and continued to gaze at the small pinprick of light twinkling in the blackness. Jack then spoke with a voice that conveyed a deep emotion of sadness that she had never heard before. He told her; that he would always look up at that star, when the brain fever would come over him, and he would think on how it seemed so cold and lonely up there in the darkness, and how he thought it was much like himself, because he used to feel cold and lonely too. He felt, the star, somehow guided him through his own blackness as if it understood.

'Being called the dog star, seemed quite apt somehow.' He said forlornly.

For a moment, Anne absorbed what he had said, and was touched by it. He had never confessed anything like this before. This was the first time in all the years she had known him, that he had expressed a deep-rooted emotion. He hadn't even shown this depth of emotion when their baby had died. Her mind drifted back to the time six months before they'd been captured, when Jack had taken her to Cuba to have the child she was carrying. She remembered the pain and anguish she had felt when the infant had been born dead. She would have enjoyed bringing up a little one. It would have also cemented her and Jacks' relationship. But these things happen, and in her time, it was not uncommon for babies to be born dead. The irony was she did eventually have Jacks' child, but that was later, after he had been executed. Marys' situation though, was far more tragic, and she worried how it was going to affect her.

Jacks' thoughts slowly returned to the present, and he suddenly wondered what Mary and Jock were up to. He remembered the rumours that used to fly about, and a mischievous smirk crossed his face. But then he wondered how they were managing with everything that was happening, and he asked Anne if she thought they were coping well enough with the situation. Anne just reiterated her point that he should just let things develop at their own pace, and not question too much.

'Let us all just enjoy the voyage as best we can.' She said, and then turning to face Jack, she told him, in a rather seductive manner, that they could enjoy themselves too.

Her obvious hints for a romantic tryst went completely over his head, and instead of responding positively to her flirtations, he just got to his feet, stretched, and yawned, and said he was tired. Anne stood up and yelled;

'John Rackham!'

He spun round to face her, wondering what the hell he had done now, and expected a tongue lashing, but instead, she just sidled up to him, put her arms around his neck and kissed him passionately on the lips.

'Now,' she whispered in his ear, 'Shall we enjoy ourselves or not?' and with that, she skipped off towards the captain's cabin.

When she reached the door, she stopped, looked back and with a coquettish glance, she winked at him and then disappeared inside. Jack didn't need telling a second time, and he beamed, which then turned into a laugh. He punched the air and hissed;

'Yes!' and ran off to join his lover, just as the first flickers of the dawn danced on the horizon.

# CHAPTER 15

## <u>When the Bough Breaks</u>

The pain in Marys' head had subsided somewhat, although it hadn't gone altogether, and she still felt sick. Best thing was to get some fresh air she thought, and made her way back up to the top of the steps, out onto the deck, and went to the bow of the ship. Taking in large gulps of the rich morning air, she started to feel a little better when she heard a noise behind her. Turning round, she was confronted by the sight of Jock, staggering out of the doorway clutching his head.

'Och, I feel ill!' he moaned.

Mary had no sympathy, and told him he shouldn't drink so much. When Anne and Jack began their argument, he had taken Mary below and produced the bottle of whiskey he'd bought whilst on their jaunt ashore. Although he'd offered her a tot or two, she only had a couple of sips, as she was not very fond of alcohol. A flagon or two of ale was welcome sometimes, but anything stronger like whiskey, or rum, would turn her stomach. It was probably due to the fact that she had always had to keep her guard up against discovery of who she really was. By getting drunk, she ran the risk of letting her secret slip, and so, she'd never developed a drinking habit. It was more prudent to drink little and safeguard her secret. Jock on the other hand, was drawn to drink like a moth to a flame, but to give him credit, he only had binges now and again. He wasn't like some who craved the bottle constantly through waking hours. The trouble was though, when he did consume large amounts of alcohol, his system couldn't take it, and rather than getting drunk, it just made him feel ill. That was how he was now, feeling the effects of the whiskey. He sat himself down heavily on the treasure chest, and held his head in his hands, moaning about his throbbing cranium. Mary smiled, and turned to look out to sea again and watched the dark shadows form on the horizon as the sun began its slow ascent, heralding a new day.

Jack and Anne lay on the bunk in the captain's cabin huddled closely together, not through any sense of romanticism, but because the bunk was small, and only designed for one person. Jack was staring up at the ceiling and Anne snuggled up to him. She felt close to him, not just physically but emotionally too, because she had witnessed a new dimension to his personality, and she liked it, she liked it very much. Everything was peaceful on the ship. Whilst Anne and Jack were snug in their cabin, Mary was enjoying the tranquillity of the morning just before dawn, and Jock sat nursing his hangover. And that's when it happened.

The sea was calm, and the wind at a minimal breeze, so what caused it, no one could tell. The ship suddenly lurched, and the bow rose high into the air at an alarming rate, whilst at the same time, rocking violently from side to side. Anne and Jack fell out of their bunk, and Jock slid off the chest onto the floor, banging his already throbbing head on the side of the raised part of the deck. Mary stumbled, but steadied herself by grabbing hold of the taffrail. Then the explosion came. A tearing thunderbolt ripped apart the heavens above them. It wasn't like a normal storm, but then, what was normal for them?, then the clouds rumbled apart, revealing the first rays of the morning sun, that illuminated the front part of the ship, including Mary. Strangely, the rest of the deck remained in shadow. Whether it was the unknown forces that seemed to exist on the fringes of their existence, or whether it was just a result of the thunderclap disturbing the rigging high up the masts of the ship, but the end of a rope suddenly fell and snaked in the air as it tumbled from above. As it finally settled with one end remaining fixed overhead, the other end twisted into a frightening image. The disturbing feature was that the loose end curled back on the main body of the cable, creating a loop at the bottom, that had the startling appearance of the hangman's noose. At the sight of the noose hanging immediately in front of her, illuminated by the morning sun, and with a peculiar blue haze around it, Mary screamed, clutching at her temples, then fell to her knees. Visions in her mind swirled around in the fog inside her brain, and nightmare images presented themselves. Just like Jack previously, she was aware of being both on the ship, but at the same time, conscious she was in a prison cell. The walls were dark, damp, and claustrophobic and seemed to bear down on her. There was very little light coming from a small grill set high up in the wall, and rivulets of water ran down the oppressive brickwork of the tiny cell. Mary lay on a straw stuffed mattress that stunk of urine from the previous occupants, and this combined with the overall stench of human decay, made her want to vomit. Although it was chilly, globules of moisture formed on Marys' brow and her whole body was clammy with perspiration. Mary Read had the fever. As she lay there, she lapsed in and out of consciousness, and each time her mind withdrew from the waking world, she could hear the voice of the Magistrate, calling for her execution.

'No!...No!' Mary agonised in her sleep, partially bringing her round again, but she soon drifted back into the solitude of her mind, where she was pleading with the Judge to spare her life as she was with child. Her trial and sentencing had been over a week ago, and she'd been shoved in the tiny prison cell to await the birth. She was an inconvenience.

'This wretch deserves to be hanged! Not given a reprieve, because she's goin' to drop another bastard.'

'Should 'ang her, and kill the devil inside her at the same time!'

The taunts of the gaolers echoed through her mind, and she found them more disturbing than those of the Judge. As she dwindled on the edge of sleep and wakefulness, she heard the grating metallic sound of the grill in the door clank open, and a tray of slops was tossed in. Half the gooey mess that professed to be food, spilt on the floor, from where she could retrieve it if she were hungry enough, thought the guards, but somehow, gruel mixed with excrement was not something she could stomach. Mary drifted off again. How long she slept she couldn't tell, but when she came to, it was evidently night-time as the cell was in pitch darkness and no light spilled through the grill in the wall. She was awoken by a searing pain in her belly. The baby's coming! she thought, and tried to sit up and manoeuvre herself into a position where she could give birth as comfortably as possible. Finally, the baby arrived, and Mary scooped up the scrawny bundle of flesh into her arms and held it closely to her breast, trying desperately to feed it with her milk, but the little mite didn't respond. Holding the baby up in front of her face, she willed it to suckle. She stroked his red flaming hair and looked into his little eyes, as they darted around trying to make sense of the new world he had just arrived into, but as she watched hopelessly, the child gave off a soft slight moan and the light behind his eyes faded and went out. A tear ran down Marys' cheek and she again held the baby tightly to her breast. She knew the infant wouldn't suckle now. She fell backwards onto the bunk clutching the child in her arms and lay still. Both the child and Mary Read were dead.

As Mary fell to her knees in pain, forgetting his headache Jock scrambled to his feet, and rushed to her side. He put his arms around her and tried to comfort her, but he didn't know how.

He mumbled encouraging words like 'it'll be alright,' and 'I won't let anything happen to yer,' but although Jocks' attempts to reassure her were clumsy, it was partly because he was cautious not to make the situation worse.

Jock remembered everything now, but he was not sure how much Mary actually remembered the past, and as Anne had said, they should all face their memories as they returned, without any direct prompting from anyone else, for fear of distorting those memories.

Jack and Anne burst out of their cabin to find out what was going on and why the ship had suddenly lurched like it did. Jack was on the deck first, and seeing Mary writhing in pain, immediately started to rush to her aid, but Anne held him back.

'Wait!' she hissed at him.

Anne knew the moment had arrived and it was good she was there, but ultimately she knew Jock should be part of this moment, as he himself was indirectly involved. Jack and Anne just stood in silence and watched the drama of Mary unfold before their eyes. Mary embraced Jock, and he felt her body shaking violently as she sobbed.

'My baby, Jock. My baby died!'

Jock squeezed her hard in an attempt to reassure and comfort her, but she fought back with her own frustrations.

She yelled at the Scotsman, 'yer don't understand! The baby died 'cause of me!'

Jock tried to convince her it was just another of her waking nightmares and that it was not real, but again she pushed against him, and this time she freed herself from his embrace and collapsed on the floor sobbing her heart out.

'They weren't nightmares,' she yelled. 'They were memories, memories of real events that I'd blocked out and were trying to break through. You see, I had a baby, Jock, a baby, and because of me, it died!'

Jock put his arms around her again and she responded by holding on to him as if she never wanted to let him go, ever again. She sobbed about how she had been incarcerated in the filth and depravity of the cell, of how she had the fever, and how she'd let the baby die. The self-guilt was overwhelming her, and as Anne looked on, she willed Jock to understand, but he couldn't understand fully, because he didn't know. All Jock could do was try to reassure her and he tried to impress upon her that it wasn't her fault. Mary though was convinced that it was because she had been a pirate and done terrible things. She reasoned that had she not been a pirate, she would not have found herself in that inhuman place and the baby might have survived. Jock didn't say anything for several moments as the anger welled up inside him.

'Now you listen to me!' he said with an air of authority in his voice, and he reminded her of why she had become a pirate in the first place. She had not embarked on piracy because she had a thirst to kill people, she had done so out of the instinct to survive. It didn't make it right, he conceded, but he made it clear the choice she'd had wasn't so simple. He then spoke about the horrors of the gaol and how the baby was innocent and how the authorities, including the guards, should have taken more care over the baby.

'They did nothing! They didn't protect the life of an innocent baby by caring with human decency, for the mother. Because of their revulsion and inhumanity for you, they allowed that baby to die!'

Another few minutes of silence past, but then Jock whispered aloud;

'...and they called us the barbarians!'

Gradually Marys' sobbing subsided, and she buried her head in Jocks' shoulder. They both sat there for a little while, as Jock held her tight. After several minutes Mary looked up to Jock and whispered that she was sorry.

'Now, look!' he reprimanded her. 'I've told yer, you are not to blame.'

But Mary was insistent, she had a confession to make and that she was sorry for hurting him.

Jock was puzzled, 'how could you hurt me, lassie?'

Very quietly and slowly, Mary looked Jock in the eyes and said, 'because it was your baby too, Jock!'

It was Christmas 1719, and after a

successful raid, Rackhams' crew had secured plenty of fine provisions and they'd met up with another group of pirates from another ship, to enjoy the festive season. Rackhams' crew claimed it was to celebrate Christmas, but that was just an excuse for merry making. Jock and Mary, who were amongst that lot, became close that night. They had always been good companions, but whether it was the high spirits, or whether it was because feelings had been growing for some time, on this particular occasion they felt the bond between them become something more than fellowship. They kept their romance secret from the others because, they didn't want anyone to think they may be a liability; however, a secret like theirs couldn't remain a secret for long on a pirate's ship! Rumours flew about and naturally they denied them, but the rumours continued, nonetheless.

As the revelation spun around in Jocks' mind and he tried to make sense of it all, he reasoned the baby must have been conceived around mid-February when they'd all enjoyed a period of shore leave. Jock and Mary had decided to take off on their own for a little bit of tranquillity from the crew, and to enjoy each other's company in private.

Anne had stood there on deck without even daring to breathe in case she disturbed them. She knew this moment was important. She had always prayed she'd be with Mary when the truth finally dawned, but it was befitting that Jock was with her, after all, they had been connected for a very long time. She knew Jock would have remembered his affair with Mary after his memories returned, and it was commendable of him not to say anything, knowing Mary still had to remember hers for herself. Naturally, he didn't know anything about the baby, or that Mary had been pregnant before they were captured. It was shocking and upsetting for him, as up until this moment, he'd known nothing about the baby. But now it had happened, Mary had remembered, and everything was out in the open; the next step was to move on and learn from the meaning of it all.

Jack sat down on the chest with a blank expression on his face as he stared into the middle distance. Anne caught sight of him and following his gaze, a spark of understanding came into her mind. Mary had quietened down, but they both remained in their consoling embrace. Anne wandered over to them and put her arms around both of them.

'It's done now.'

They both looked up at her and smiled. Anne held the moment for several minutes until she broke the silence and told them she was sorry.

Sorry for both; the experience Mary had been through three-hundred years ago, and the trauma of living through it all again now. She was also sorry for having known about the baby all the time, and not saying anything, but Mary knew there was nothing to be sorry about.

'We have all had to go through some of the most harrowing times of our past life, but I understand this was for a reason. I just don't comprehend what those reasons are at the moment.'

Anne looked at them both, and then back at Jack, and finally she turned to face the rope that hung down in front of them, and she knew. Anne, walked around Mary and Jock and went to the rope, reaching aloft, she took hold of it as far up as she could reach, and with a forceful tug, dislodged it from its anchor point high up in the rigging. As the rope fell she coiled it up with the bottom loop still swinging beneath her arm.

'This,' she said, 'is the answer,' but everyone looked at her blankly.

Taking a deep breath, Anne explained that the rope represented the hangman's noose, which in itself represented death, death they had all experienced in the past. Jack, unfortunately was the only one of them to actually succumb to its fearful embrace. Anne and Jock, never had the privilege as he'd died in battle, and she died of old age. She paused briefly, as she knew this was the moment she had to reveal the circumstances of her own passing. Taking another deep breath, she continued and told them how her father had secured her release by paying a bond, and how shortly after, she too had given birth. Jack was about to speak, but she anticipated his question and answered it herself.

'Yes Jack, I had our son, your son, John.'

Jack just stared into the middle distance and Anne knew this was a shock to him. But at least their baby lived.

'I myself had several grandchildren, I remarried, and I believe I died around the age of 82. Don't remember much about it, mind. I vaguely remember sitting in my chair and feeling tired, and then I was here. Here is also a question for each of us,' Anne continued.

'The hangman's noose doesn't just represent death, it also represents justice, but whose justice? There is no decrying that what we all did when we were pirates was wrong,' she asserted, 'but was true justice really served?'

What Anne explained, was that she was just as guilty as Jack, yet she lived until old age, while he was executed. Here was a case of justice meted out to one unfortunate wretch, yet circumvented for another, because her family had money. Was what happened to Jack, justice or pure retaliation? Jock on the other hand had died in battle for a cause that he believed in. Was this natural justice? Who could say. To one side it was a deserved punishment, to the other, it was a tragic outcome of war. And here was the point. So-called justice appeared to favour one side without considering the circumstances of the other. Her point was reiterated by Marys' example. Jock had been right when he said that the authorities had done nothing to prevent the death of the baby. The baby was innocent, but was left to die; by the authorities, purely because of the actions of the mother, and to her mind that was not justice, but a revenge with abject cruelty. The question for everyone to consider, was how they should judge others in future. It was vital that they must always remember to try and understand a situation with empathy, rather than making spontaneous judgements, based on thoughtless reflexes. But above all else, they should try and see the whole situation, however uncomfortable, rather than only see the side they'd want to see.

The shadows of the dawn fell across everyone's face, as the sun's first rays pierced the clouds on the horizon, and it began its steady ascent bringing a new day. They absorbed Annes' words and knew that she spoke the truth, but it was late, or rather, it was early, and they were all extremely tired. Jack eventually spoke, and suggested they should all get some rest and talk about everything later when they were fresh. Anne agreed and ordered everyone to get below and get some rest. Jock helped Mary to her feet, and she drowsily allowed Jock to escort her back to the cabin below where they had first found their clothes, all those hours ago. A lot had happened since then, and although the occasion had been uncomfortable, especially when Jock had thrown off all his clothes, it now felt it was "their" space and contentedly, wandered off blissfully in each other's embrace, after such a long time.

'What happened to my son?' Jack asked, after Jock and Mary had gone. 'Did he live? Did he have a good life?'

Anne smiled sympathetically, as it was right he should ask about his son. He was showing more concern now than he had done when she had lost the baby in Cuba. It wasn't because he had been heartless then and changed now, it was because in the old days, he didn't know how to deal with his emotions, and he'd try to appear to be strong and tough by seemingly being unconcerned. Now though, in the few hours he had lived again; and because of what he had experienced, he was much more understanding of, not only his emotions, but of who he was, and his inner fears had now gone. Anne told him that the boy grew up and had a family of his own and that the son, led a good honest life. Naturally she didn't know what happened to him in the end, as she herself had died, but she presumed he had continued with a comfortable life and died, of old age. She paused for a moment as a thought occurred to her.

'Yer know what, Jack, we may very well have our descendants living out there, somewhere in this new world.'

Jack considered what she had said, and in a funny sort of way, he didn't feel they were totally on their own anymore. Anne then took his hand and remembered their night of passion had been interrupted by Marys' epiphany, and she reminded him that they had unfinished business in the cabin. He smiled and they wandered off to their quarters like two young innocent lovers, arm in arm, and to anyone watching, they'd never believe, these two were the infamous pirates Anne Bonny and John Rackham.

# CHAPTER 16

## Davy Jones

The autumnal sun shone weakly through the misty clouds and the ship rocked gently on its moorings. Everything was quiet on board the ship, as everyone was asleep below. The day before had been exhausting for everyone, but now they were finally resting, ready for whatever the day would bring forth.

It was mid-afternoon when Anne stormed on deck in a foul mood.

'After three-hundred years of celibacy and he's as limp and as a dead haddock!' She cursed.

She then marched to the bow of the ship and gazed out across the ocean as it gently swelled and dipped taking the ship with it. Jack came on deck soon after. He yawned, scratched himself and wandered over to Anne.

'I needed that,' he said, referring to the good sleep he'd had.

Anne just glanced at him with a reproachful look and said;

'Yes, I needed it too, but I didn't get it!'

Jack hadn't a clue what she meant, and just grinned stupidly.

Anne turned away to gaze at the panorama of the expanse of the ocean before them. She didn't say any more and they both just stood there for some time taking in the view. Anne soon recovered from her disappointment with Jack and her mind turned to other thoughts. After a while she asked him if he knew why she had been the only one to retain her memories of the past, but he couldn't find the reason. She answered her own question; by supposing it was because she was the only one of them, who actually lived out her life naturally. Perhaps it was because, as she got older she became wiser and able to reflect on her criminal past more objectively. If that was the reason for her retaining her memories, it would mean that she had a maturity about her, making her the perfect choice to lead and guide them. Jack had never really considered it up until now, but he turned to Anne and questioned that if she'd lived into her eighties, why did she look so much younger now? Yes, she looked older than he remembered her, as she had only been in her early twenty's when they'd been caught, but it was difficult to put an age to her now, maybe a few years older than himself, but certainly not in her eighty's.

'I wondered that meself,' she responded.

All of them, except Anne, had pretty much returned to the world at about the same age they left it. Why was it different for Anne? Jack offered his hypothesis and for once she believed he might actually be right. He suggested that whilst they'd been dead, time had stood still for all of them as they basically didn't exist and the spirits or whatever power was responsible for their reawakening could have taken each of them from any point in their history. It made sense to resurrect himself, Mary, and Jock from the point in time just following their deaths, a continuation if you like, he reasoned. But if Anne had lived through into old age, at her point of death she would have concluded her life and be very set in her ways. In other words, she had learned everything she was ever going to learn and experienced everything she was likely to experience. Unlike the others, her life had ended naturally, she had come to the full stop. Anne stared at him with wonder. This was an incredible, and a well thought out diagnostic of the situation and totally unlike him. As she thought about it, she saw that it did make a lot of sense and offered her opinion on the subject. It was clear that if she had been brought back moments after her initial death, she would not be so eager to accept new ideas and therefore unable to lead them. But by returning at an age that was chronologically about twenty years after their capture, she would have enough life experience to judge her past but not enough life experiences to dull her thirst for knowledge and adventure. At the end of her life, she had the wisdom of age and had already felt remorse for her past ways. Anne had always been one to try and find out as much as she could about virtually everything, as she believed this gave a person, powerful intellectual weapons for survival. At the point of death in old age though, she understood that one does not seek answers, just everlasting peace. The strange thing was that she still retained her memories of her old age, but they were more dreamlike than actual recollections.

As Anne and Jack stood conversing about the theories of all that had happened, they heard a noise behind them, and Mary and Jock walked out onto the deck. Mary looked so much more relaxed thought Jack, and although it had been a harrowing experience remembering her own death, it was better to get the poison of the past out of her, so she could begin to grow again in the new world. Jock had a spring in his step too, and it was rather comical to see the giant Scotsman holding the hand of the diminutive Mary in comparison.

'How yer feelin'?' Anne asked Mary.

'I'm alright,' she replied, and Anne decided nothing more was to be said on the subject of last night.

It was over and in the past. All Mary said was that she was pleased she had remembered and in a strange way she felt that it never really happed, although she knew it did. It was as if she was now her true self, and that the memory of her former self was only some distorted caricature. Jack thought that was an interesting remark and he questioned whether this was another reason why they were selected to return. Was it because in their first lives they had all undergone some traumatic and tragic episodes, that had warped their true sense of identity and that this was a way of redressing the balance and giving them the chance to prove they could be the people they ultimately should have been? An interesting theory, Jock agreed and went on with a revelation of his own.

'Yer know, I were thinkin' to meself aboot those skins we emerged from, an' I believe there was a reason for that too!'

Jack encouraged him to say more of what he thought, and Jock ventured the idea that the skins or 'ghouls' represented the evil that had consumed them in their past lives and that the people they were now represented the evolution from that evil into the embodiment of decency. Mary slapped his chest and told him not to be so modest and everyone burst out laughing.

'Identity!' Anne suddenly remarked.

'What?' Jack asked and Anne reminded him of what he had just said about losing their true identity in the past and that he'd inadvertently hit upon another very important point.

'We have all learned, that much of what happened to us was beyond our control and yet those events shaped us.'

She explained how they had failed to stand up for who they truly were and how they succumbed to the pressures of the time. But the question was why, and the answer was simple, fear! Jock was slightly puzzled by Annes' point and asked what she meant as they had all been brave much of the time, to do the things they had done.

'We may have been brave physically, but we were never brave when it came to our inner selves.' Anne responded.

Her point was that people tend to fear what they don't know or understand, and when something traumatic happens, they tend to try and absorb it in an attempt to cope. But in reality by absorbing it, one allows it to fester inside and in turn, it changes their personality. For example, a person who has been attacked at night, might then become afraid of the dark. But the dark didn't attack them so why fear the dark? Sometimes the dark can work in your favour if you don't want to be seen, for example, you can use the darkness to keep hidden. But, by being fearful of it you prevent yourself from utilising that issue you have become afraid of, and you therefore cannot operate with your true faculties as your judgement is clouded by fear. It is something we must always consider in future, others may act in a way we believe is wrong, but we must understand that they may act like they do, out of fear and if that is the case, then we tackle the reasons for their fear, and not judge purely on their actions.

'Yeh, yer right,' Jack said and talked about his own situation and how he'd acted in a certain way, because he was too afraid of the brain fog descending on him.

Anne then emphasised that his fear was not being in control and how he had to fight to dominate others, regardless of the outcome. She reminded him of the time when she got him into trouble with the watch and how that incident had built up a conflict within him. He wasn't in control of the situation and at the same time he was afraid of the consequences. Two sets of fear fighting for dominance, but the fear of consequences was drowned out by the more assertive fear of losing control. Had he just let things progress in their natural way and dealt with consequences as they arose, and had he not had this overpowering fear of not being in control, it was more than probable that he would never have become a pirate. She persuaded him that his strengths now were that he could have a deeper understanding of why others behave like they do, and because of that you realise others have weaknesses as well.

'Unlike in the past, you don't now capitalise on those weaknesses for your own advantage, you use that knowledge to gain the advantage for the greater good, which ultimately means you are in control but in much more subtle and healthier way.'

It was a lot to take in, but they understood the gist of what Anne meant.

It became clearer as she dissected the fear each of them had. Jocks' fear was making the wrong decision as to what side to fight with, in other words his conflicting fear was based on the fear of losing the battle between right and wrong. Even becoming a pirate was a symptom of this. Jock remembered his childhood and how the British failed to assist the Scottish colonials and consequently, many died unnecessarily, including his mother. He was also aware of the corruption within the British authorities with many government officials taking bribes and splitting the profits of illicit cargo from pirate ships. The pirates on the other hand, at least some of them, operated a fairer criminality. In other words, you knew where you stood with a pirate more than you did with the Governor of a particular area. For Jock, the choice was to either side with the corrupt British, or fight with the pirates and he chose the lesser of two evils. There was also the underlying fact in Jocks' subconscious, that neither the British nor the Spanish had helped his people when they first moved to the Americas. So, by becoming a pirate meant he could fight against the British and the Spanish! In fact, the best choice would have been to avoid both sides and find a better community that upheld stronger moral principles, but that was not always so easy. And let's not forget that Jock ultimately joined the Jacobites, a movement that he felt were right, in their principles. It wasn't about wanting to fight and kill others; the basic choice was who had the better ethics. All the while Jock just sat there and nodded in agreement and Anne then turned her attentions on Mary.

She pointed out that Mary had always operated under the guise of Mark Read as she was fearful of the treatment she would get as a woman, yet when she was married she had the confidence to be herself. When Louis tragically died, she reverted back to being Mark.

'That demonstrated how each and every one of us relies on the involvement with others in our lives.'

Humans only progress when they work together. The selfish individual never makes anything of themselves. The successful person has always been part of a team. But more importantly,

Marys' life shows us that it is not a sin to be different from others and she is an example to everyone who feels different, and her story encourages such people to have the courage to be who they really are and stand up to prejudice. That is not always easy, but it becomes easier when you understand prejudice is a type of fear in itself.

Anne believed her own fear was similar to Jack, in that she had a fear of not being in control because of how others had hurt her. The idea of being in control of others would make one less vulnerable, was irrational as one was liable to make more enemies, especially by one's unpleasant behaviour when fighting for dominance. Controlling others with understanding was far stronger than controlling others with violence and fear. Anne then made a poignant analogy when she described people as being like a treasure chest. '

'On the outside; we just see a wooden shell and we have no idea what lays inside, but when we open it we discover all sorts of treasures, and we must always remember this when dealing with people. Don't assume from the outward appearance but look inside to find who they really are.'

Jack smirked and retorted that although he agreed with the principle of her analogy it was all very well assuming the goodness of people, but one had to remember that when opening the treasure chest, one may find it empty. He also drew the assumption, that there were those who would utilise their inner contents as a way to influence others and in conclusion, he added that where Anne was right in not judging by outward appearances, they must still withhold judgement until the contents could be thoroughly analysed.

Anne was taken aback by Jacks' assertions because he was right; and never in her association with him had he ever reached such conclusions. From what he had said, she admired and loved him more than she had ever done. Jack was no longer her lover, he was becoming her soul mate. She felt a deep-rooted attraction for him and was not sure how to proceed with her theory after he had made such a strong assertion about her argument. She simply went on to declare that this philosophy was the doctrine they should adopt.

Jack yawned and said it was all very well theorising on human nature and that basically he agreed, but he went on to say that they were pirates, not some righteous band of do-gooders, and he didn't feel comfortable in adopting Annes' philosophy. He declared they were ruffians, with argumentative personalities, who had to fight for their own survival and as such, how on earth was anyone going to take them seriously.

Anne agreed and reaffirmed what Jack had said earlier in that they do not change personally but rather they just learn new skills to fight with and put simply, their greater understanding of humanity made them stronger. Anne fell silent and an expression of seriousness fell across her face, but after a few moments when everyone wondered what was coming next, she smiled and then began to laugh.

'Yes! We're pirates and we should be doing pirate things!' she announced.

'What the hell?' Jack responded with astonishment.

One minute she had been going on like the preacher on a Sunday, and the next she was advocating piracy!

' Who's hungry?' she yelled with excitement, and everyone responded.

'Aye!'

'And who's thirsty? she yelled with even more excitement than before.

Anne had ignited the fuse for an explosive celebration of their success.

An energised activity broke out on deck as they all prepared for merriment. Mary and Jock moved the crates together; to build a makeshift table and arranged a barrel, the treasure chest, and some other small boxes around the table for people to sit on. Anne raided the shopping bags and took out bread and fruit, and laid them on the table. Jack, meanwhile, unwrapped the fish from the newspaper and took some of the frozen meat, which had thawed out by this time, and tossed them on the burning coals of the brazier. Goblets and bottles of wine, ale and rum were accumulated on the crates and the pirates were ready for revelry.

For the next few hours, a raucous display of eating and drinking played out on the 18th Century ship sitting at anchor in the ocean, off the coast of Scotland. They chatted about the old days and Jock amused them with anecdotes of piracy and seamanship. They indulged in singing sea shanties and as the grog flowed, the melodies got more and more out of tune and each one tried to outdo everyone else. The shindig lasted well into the evening, but finally Jack declared that it was probably best that they call it a night and get some rest. Anne was already "at rest" as she had fallen face down across the table totally intoxicated. Jack decided to leave her there to sleep it off. Jock and Mary supported each other as they staggered in the direction of the door. Jock turned and slurred,

'You look after the lass, Jack, or you'll have me to deal with!'

He then, hiccupped and Mary led him towards the steps.

Jack replied saying that Anne would be alright

where she was, and besides he wasn't going to take her back to the cabin because when she was drunk she snored terribly. With that, both Mary and Jock laughed as they undertook the dangerous task of descending the narrow wooden steps totally plastered! Jack yelled after Jock and told him to relieve Anne at three bells, to which he received the reply of,

'Aye!' that echoed up from the bowels of the ship.

Jack turned to go to his cabin and muttered under his breath,

'Yeh, snores like a warthog she does!'

As he disappeared through the door, Anne stirred, snorted, lifted her head slightly and muttered to herself that;

'It was not her that snored, it was Jack! 'Pig!' she then shouted in her sleep, snored again, and collapsed back on the table.

Anne awoke in the early hours of the morning. It was still dark, and she was hazy and at first, not sure where she was. One thing was sure though, she was cold. Wearily, she got up and went and sat before the fire. Meat fat was making the glowing embers spit and smoke, which stung her eyes somewhat. It had been an enjoyable night and reminded her of the old days, when they would have such sessions in the balmy evenings of the Caribbean.

'I suppose we are real?' she questioned herself.

She dismissed the idea that they were ghosts because she could smell the salt in the air and feel the sea breeze on her face. She then had a worrying thought. It wasn't the question of who? or what? they were, that concerned her, it was what was waiting for them out there, in this new world. Her worries soon began to subside, as sleep took its comforting control over her once again. Sleepily she began to sing a song she herself had written for one of her grandchildren who had asked her one day, if pirates were real.

'Rest you now your sleepy head,
And dream of treasure, in your bed.
At night we come, on a sudden swell;
And send you on the road to hell.'

Anne was asleep again when a thick fog crept silently onto the deck and enveloped her. It was dark with the only light coming from the dying fire and the flickering oil lamps that hung on the walls as they cast a pale watery light around the deck. The atmosphere on board became oppressive and ominous as if danger lurked in the shadows. Over the left hand taffrail a hand suddenly appeared. Not an ordinary hand, but one that was skeletal with thin pale flesh hanging limply on the bones. Then another similar hand appeared and by levering itself, it pulled its putrid and foul body onto the ship. The creature, was not that dissimilar to the creatures that the pirates had emerged from some days earlier, but this one was larger and was more troll-like. Its dark, dead eyes scanned the deck, and fell upon the huddled form of the sleeping Anne. It moved towards her in a hideous stooping, dragging motion and the fiend, obviously from hell itself; began to speak. The Demon's voice was cracked and harsh but resonated with power and dominance as it alluded to the fact that these miserable seafaring villains had cheated death, and that there was no escape for the evil souls it had harvested. Encircling Anne as she slept, it sneered that the once feared pirate with her cunning and skills with a sword, was now reduced to a snivelling, righter of wrongs. The Demon, would return her to her rightful place though, beneath the sea and back to its Kingdom, the Kingdom of "Davy Jones," for the fiendish apparition, who was Davy Jones, started to sway, as its haggard frame became more distorted. Its gnarled hands clawed at its throat as if it were having difficulty breathing. That was precisely what was happening. The Demon was not used to an existence above the waves, it could only survive in the deep darkness at the bottom of the ocean, and oxygen was toxic to the creature. Under normal circumstances this might have thrown Anne a lifeline, but things weren't normal, in fact nothing that had occurred over the past three days, had any semblance of normality. The monster croaked that it needed to adopt human form to dwell above the waves and what better subject to host its evil soul, than the body of the infamous Anne Bonny! The Demon, placed its withered hands on Annes head, looked up and with a cry that would have tormented all the creatures of hell, it faded out of existence.

Everything fell deadly still. No noise and no movement. Then, Annes' hand twitched and she lifted her head. As she did so, the flesh on one side of her face became translucent, and the bones of her skull beneath became visible. The flesh shrivelled and fell away leaving the entire left side of her face, skeletal. Her eye floated and stared out from its bony cave, as it surveyed the scene. Her other eye clouded over, and the entire right side of her face became corpse like with the very essence of life sucked out of it. It was then she spoke, but it was not Annes' voice that echoed around the ship in the darkness, it was the hideous voice of Davy Jones!

'Ha! I Davy Jones; I Davy Jones live again!' the monster announced with a tone that would send a shiver down the spine of anyone that heard it.

Suddenly a bell rang out. It was the signal for "three bells," the time for the next watch. The beast stood motionless, waiting to see who would arrive. It didn't have to wait long, because after a few moments, Jock came through the door rubbing his eyes, due to not having had much sleep. Seeing the Scotsman, the creature that now inhabited Anne, glided into the shadows and out of sight and waited for the chance to snare another of its prey.

'Anne? Anne, yer there, lassie?' Jock called as he came to relieve her.

Of course, Anne was not there, she had been consumed by the devil that was Davy Jones. Jock didn't know this of course, and assumed she'd already gone to bed. Jock picked up a tankard that was still half full of ale and took a swig, then went and sat on the treasure chest still clutching the mug. As he sat there gazing out across the ocean, his mind drifted back to the old days, and he thought how Anne had helped him on many occasions, and how she had been there after the battle of Culloden, and had held him as he died. She had helped him in this new life too, and he was pleased that she had escaped execution, and that she had gone on to live out the rest of her natural life. He raised his tankard and saluted his old friend, then took a large gulp of the now flat ale. He went to take another swig but stopped, telling himself as he was on watch, he needed to keep a clear head. He placed the tankard on the floor and continued looking out towards the horizon, wondering what new adventures lay in store for them. As his mind drifted, to all the possibilities of what might lay in store, his eyelids began to droop, and it wasn't long before he was asleep.

The devilish creature that lurked in the shadows saw its chance, and in the body of Anne, it glided across the deck to where Jock sat sleeping. The thing lifted its arms, and the skeletal fingers of its hands became visible in the dim light from the lanterns. The process of turning Anne back into a ghoul was progressing. Davy Jones knew that possessing the woman was limited, and that soon, the body would be transformed back into a creature of the dead and just like the form it had used to get on board, it would soon succumb to the effects of fresh air above the waves. The creature knew it had little time to achieve this goal, to bring all of them back into its control. The demon placed its deathly hands, on Jocks' head and instantly both the creature and Jock became rigid, looked towards the heavens, and let out an unworldly howl. The monster released its grip on Jock who immediately collapsed forward for a moment. But then its eyes opened, and it looked up. The body of Jock McTavish got to its feet, but the spirit of the man was no longer in residence. The parasite had gained another soul, and it led its prey back into the confines of the darkness at the side of the ship.

Mary couldn't sleep. She didn't know why, but she had this uncomfortable feeling that all was not right. There was nothing tangible that concerned her, just this nagging feeling, that she should be on her guard. She had been lying on her bunk trying to put the disturbing thoughts out of her mind, when she was conscious of Jock getting up and going up on deck, to take the watch. After several minutes of tossing and turning she thought she'd go up, and keep him company.

'No point in lying in bed if you can't sleep,' she reasoned.

She got up and slipped on her breeches and a jacket, and headed up to the top deck. When she walked through the door, she was puzzled as Jock was nowhere to be seen. Probably walking around the back of the ship, she concluded and absent mindedly picked up a goblet from the table, but immediately put it down again, when she heard a noise behind her. Spinning round to see what was stalking her, she was relieved to find it was only Jack, who was also coming out on deck.

'Couldn't sleep?' she asked, and Jack just nodded.

He wandered aimlessly about for a moment, then asked her if she had seen Anne. Mary said she hadn't, and thought Anne had retired to her cabin when Jock came to relieve her at three bells. The funny thing was, Jock was missing too. Had they both gone off together somewhere? If so, why?

'Something's not right,' Jack then announced.

'You feel it too?' she asked, but Jack didn't

answer, he just stared blankly into space as if he was in a world of his own.

He then admitted he was concerned about everything, and wanted answers as to why? all this was happening. He could understand what had happened so far, and could theorise as to what certain things meant, but he didn't like the unknown. He described it, as being like sailing a ship into a thick fog and not knowing what lay ahead. What dangers lurked ahead of them now? And how did one find the answers? Normally one could make rational judgements about possible outcomes, but with what they had experienced so far, there were no indications of what to expect and as such, it was impossible to prepare for the future. Mary tried to alleviate his fears by suggesting that sometimes one must just sit back, and enjoy the journey, and simply wait for events to unfold. Dwelling on the ideas of what might, or might not happen, was illogical.

The beast that was Davy Jones which now inhabited the physical form of Anne Bonny, together with its henchman that was once known as Jock McTavish, stirred in the blackness behind them. Time was crucial for the monster, and here were the other two, ready to snatch. It was far easier to take control of its victims when they were unconscious, but as time was of the essence, the creature would have to strike now.

Jack sensed movement behind him and

instantly spun round. To his horror he came face to face with the ghoul of his lover and the decaying face of Jock, grinning at him with fleshless lips. Leaping to the newel, Jack snatched his sword from his baldrick, where it hung, and flourished it in the face of the hideous apparitions, that were now menacingly approaching him and Mary. Jack new immediately what was happing, and it came as no surprise to know Davy Jones wanted their souls back!

'Get back! Get back, you fiendish furies and return to whence you came!'

Jack knew he didn't stand a chance against the devils, armed with a mere sword and vocal admonishments, but he had to try something. At least he could play for time, whilst he thought of a better plan. The ghouls were too quick for him though, and as the Anne' ghoul came for him, Jocks' monster, flew at Mary. He heard her scream and he tried to encourage her to hold on. Suddenly, Annes' form was upon him and with little choice, he skipped backwards avoiding her grasps; and ran, doubling back on himself in a desperate bid to save Mary, but it was too late. There were three of them now, advancing towards him from different directions, each one desperate to claim his soul. Then Davy Jones spoke.

'It is foolish to resist me. Many have tried over the millennia, but they all come to me in the end; like all you miserable wretches, you will not escape me.'

The hideous thing about it, was not what it said, but the sound of the grotesque voice emanating from Annes' lips. It was inhuman and brutal, with a slight sense of desperation about it, and Jack leapt into the air with a determination to escape the beast. He landed on the platform next to the ship's wheel, but no sooner had he regained his balance, the fiend was on him, climbing up the steps with considerable speed. Backing away and down the other steps, he played right into the hands of Jocks' ghoul, that grabbed him from behind, and with a scream and a jerk, the fourth victim had been claimed.

A macabre stillness hung in the air, as Davy Jones stood at the ship's wheel and began to address its disciples. The body of Anne was starting to deteriorate fast, with bits of rotting flesh falling from her face, as the fiend prepared to speak. The other three, stood facing their demonic messiah, as the inhuman creature spouted its chilling sermon. The creature raved about how human life was weak and pathetically mortal, compared to the invincibility of its kind. It promised them greatness, and how the worship of the self, was the only path to salvation and true contentment. It spoke about having the power over all life, and that the ultimate goal was to destroy everything, enabling a new creation, a creation of hell on earth. The beast paused as if trying to collect its thoughts, but it suddenly looked upward and screamed;

'NO!'

The voice though, was not that of the devil, but Annes' own voice. Somehow she had reached into her pocket and felt the little wooden doll, the gypsies had given her all those years ago. As she gripped it harder, a rush of her own energy pulsated through her body, giving her strength to overcome the monster. Anne Bonnys' soul was fighting back!

The wind came without warning and howled around the deck; but unlike the previous occasions, when everything had unnaturally remained still, this time anything and everything was whipped up by the gale. Furniture was upended and sent crashing across the deck, the sails thrashed and buckled against their ropes, and the ship itself began to rock violently backwards and forwards. The wind was unrelenting in its violent protest and then it spoke.

'Fight him, Anne Bonny; all of you, fight him! Remember what you have learned. Remember who you are in your souls, not what you once were. Resist him. Davy Jones can only harness the souls of evil men. You four are not evil! FIGHT HIM!'

For the first time since its appearance, the creature that was Davy Jones showed its feebleness, as it staggered, desperately trying to reclaim control over Annes' fighting spirit and the force of the wind, which was obviously venomous to the creature. It desperately tried to shout back at the voice in the wind, but nothing came out of the withered fleshless mouth of Anne. The voice in the wind took up its condemnation of the beast, and forcefully rasped at the fiend, that the souls of the four pirates did not belong to it, and that the monster had wrongly stolen them many years ago. The voice continued that the four of them had suffered evils inflicted upon them, causing them to act wrongly, and that they were never given the chance to redeem themselves properly. Now, justice would finally be served, and they would finally be set free, to pursue their lives along the path that had been intended three-hundred years ago. The voice of the spirit then spoke to the soul of Anne and urged her to fight against the will of Davy Jones. The effect was astounding because the figure of Annes' physical body jolted upright with its arms outstretched and with her head tilted upward, her eyes staring skyward, her inner soul fought against the vile demon from hell. A blue electric haze developed around Anne, and just visible, behind the glowing bright light, it was possible to see the flesh regenerating, as her body repaired itself from the ravages of the demonic power of Davy Jones. The glare of the blue flames that Jack had previously called St Elmo's fire shot out from Anne and engulfed the other three. Their bodies jerked and they too, faced skyward as the energising power began its fantastical healing process. As the four of them stood transfixed in the glare, the voice of the wind rang out around them, enthusing them to go forward and be the people they should have been so long ago.

'You have proved you have humanity and empathy for others, so go now and use your skills to help those struggling against oppression. Anne Bonny, use your anger at the mistreatment of others, as your strength. John Rackham, use your cunning and deviousness to fight injustice. Mary Read, fill others with your compassion, so they too may find empathy and the courage to be themselves. Angus Jock McTavish, stand for honour, and be the comforter to those in distress. Go now, all of you, and live the lives stolen from you in the past.'

A deafening explosion suddenly erupted, and the flare of light formed into a glowing orb of energy that shot skyward. It was evident that this ball of light was not lightning, neither was it, St. Elmo's fire; this light was intelligent. But what was it? This question remained unanswered, for now. The four pirates collapsed onto the deck and lay motionless in the darkness.

It was still very early, and everything was calm and still on the ship as its four crewmembers laid unconscious. In all the uncertainty that had surrounded the events that had taken place over the past few days, from the arrival of the ship in the storm to the unworldly incident that had just occurred, one thing was certain, the lives of the four pirates were never to be the same again.

# CHAPTER 17

## The Buccaneers

The orange tinge of the early morning sun glowed faintly on the horizon. The sea was calm and there was a slight breeze but apart from that everything was still. Four bodies lay in deep slumber on the deck, and all the furniture was scattered about. One might have mistakenly thought that some wild party had taken place the night before, but they'd be wrong. Mary was the first to stir and as sleep left her, she sat bolt upright, as if she'd suddenly remembered something. Glancing at the others she knew they were alright because last night's merriments were still clear in her mind. It had been good-natured, and they had all drunk far too much. They had all passed out and slept it off, out on the deck. She smiled to herself as she remembered how they used to do this, all those years ago, and would spend most of the next day nursing hangovers.

Jack let out a long sigh as he regained consciousness and like Mary, he suddenly sat upright too.

'Mornin!' Jack yawned, just as Jock woke up.
The Scotsman didn't sit up quickly like Jack and Mary though, he took his time. He was used to waking up after a heavy night of drinking and he learnt long ago, that you never move quickly the morning after the night before a drinking session, in case it makes you sick. Jock felt alright though, but it was better to be safe than sorry, as he gradually raised himself up.

A loud snore, suddenly rang out from the direction of Anne. Jack took great delight in announcing to everyone that he had warned them, Anne snored! Mary, Jock, and Jack fell about laughing and they laughed even more, as Anne opened her eyes sleepily and asked what was going on.

'Nothing other than you gettin' drunk,' Jack scoffed.
Anne said nothing as everyone started laughing again. Still, Anne didn't speak. She got up and walked to the front of the ship, where she stood staring out without acknowledging any of them. It was that gloomy silence descending once again, that Anne often introduced, when

everyone was in jovial spirits, but this was not it. No one spoke, because it had become the custom when she was like this, nobody knew what she would do next. Would she rebuke them, or was she simply wrapped up in her own thoughts? The silence lasted for several minutes, and was finally broken by Mary.

'I had a peculiar dream, last night. I dreamt that Davy Jones came to collect our souls.'

The uncomfortable silence suddenly became ominous, as everyone turned to stare at her.

'I dreamt that too!' Jock replied.

'Me too!' Jack interjected.

The three of them just stared at each other. How could they all have the same dream?

'Memory is subjective!' Anne suddenly announced.

Turning to face them, she told them that all memories were different for each person. One may remember a sequence of events one way, and somebody else remembers them differently. Was Davy Jones real? She questioned herself; or was it just as real, as the visions they had all experienced when confronted with the times in their past. A person's memory is influenced by what they want to believe, and not necessarily as truthful as a particular event actually was.

'Another weapon in our armoury.' Jack ventured.

They had analysed every detail of the strange incidents they had all been subjected to, and it was true to say, they had learned a lot about human behaviour. The knowledge they have discovered, would help them in future, to understand situations better and allow them to control those situations for their own advantage. In the past, they had always strived to dominate, and that was usually with violence and force, but now they could it do it, by gentle persuasion and understanding. The only difference being that in the past, their aims had been selfish, but now they were far more in favour of positive manipulation for the benefit of all. This wasn't just a puerile selfless belief, but if society as a whole benefitted, then so would they.

Jock thought about what both Anne and Jack had said and offered his own suggestions and beliefs. He explained that, whether Davy Jones had been real or not, was not the issue. What was important was the temptation they had been presented with. They have been offered a choice, be selfish and evil and live forever, or live for a short while, but be remembered for one's kindness and compassion. Mary hugged him proudly and Jock, slightly embarrassed, went on with his theory;

'We've all been tested, haven't we? Like not remembering Mark was really Mary. Yon lass in the wind, wanted to see how we'd react, when we found out yer secret.' He said turning to her, and beaming like the cat who's got the cream.

'One thing's for sure,' Anne exclaimed, 'In the past we took so much and instilled a grotesque fear in others by what we stood for. But now, we know the time has come to give back. If you like, our kind now stand for forgiveness, for empathy, understanding and acceptance.' She continued.

'From now on we shall be ruthless in the struggle against oppression, as opposed to being ruthless because of greed,' Jack remarked.

Mary responded by saying that 'nothing had really changed.'

They had always fought against authority as more often than not, authority was biased, oppressive and corrupt. People were generally forced to live in ways that suited the oppressors. As pirates, they didn't just live outside the law, but outside of society too. They were free and freedom didn't necessarily mean being selfish, it meant one had a natural resistance to manipulation.

Anne agreed and said she believed that it was obvious there were many people in the modern world, who were happy to stoke division and encourage hate in their unsatiable thirst for power, by tapping into the most basic human instinct, the fear of the unknown. Anne remarked further that she believed;

'The politicians of today use these tactics, as it allows them to manipulate the population's prejudices, to achieve their goals and to gain selfish political supremacy.'

This was not unlike the strategies employed by the authorities in their day, and after three hundred years, it was shameful that such policies still existed. As Annes' words sunk in, they all realised the enormity of the challenge they now all faced. Their purpose was clear, it was up to them to fight against division and create unity; they, as pirates had achieved that, and the past few hours had proved by working together, they could achieve more positive outcomes. They should lead by example; and promote understanding and tolerance, and attempt to build bridges between different groups of people.

Jack, was deep in thought as he gazed up at the emblem high above their heads of the Jolly Roger. He pointed out, that if they were to fight injustice rather than terrorise their victims, wasn't their flag now redundant? Afterall, they wanted to champion rightfulness, not fear. But Anne explained that even the flag, now had a new purpose.

'Let the skull now stand for suffering and the two swords the fight for justice,' Anne proclaimed. She explained that 'it would continue to represent fear, but only in those who inflict pain and suffering.' It would be their sign and when seen by the oppressors, they shall know 'we are coming.'

It was a peculiar situation that had

occurred on the ship, because not more than three days previously, pirates were generally regarded as criminal murderous outlaws. But here they were, four of the most notorious pirates that ever lived, speaking of fighting for others. To many it would have been a preposterous idea, but in reality no one can truly say what the pirates of three-hundred years ago were really like as people. No one could say for certain what their true personalities were. But one thing was for sure, and that was, they were all people; some were evil, some were good, some were selfish whilst others were generous. Like with so much in history, the one remembered viewpoint has always been influenced by bias, and ultimately used as means to control the masses. There have always been, and there always will be questions unanswered; and those answers can only be found by exploring and dissecting every aspect of a situation. It is not enough to base belief and perspective on hearsay and rhetoric. In a world full of uncertainties, striving to discover the truth, should be the ultimate goal. When the never-ending journey, in search of the truth is abandoned, life stagnates and just like a stagnant pond, diseases fester. The disease of hate, of bitterness, of greed, and ultimately the disease of total destruction. Truth on the other hand leads to enlightenment and growth.

There are those that celebrate pirates, in the belief they represent a romanticism of freedom and adventure, of strength and chivalry, whilst others condemn them as thieves and rogues. But as they say, the real truth lies somewhere in the middle. For those that glorify the pirate life, they may consider that the reborn Anne Bonny and her crew, had become spineless. Others may accuse them of being too liberal and faint-hearted. But, in reality, they did not become weaker by their recent experiences; they had become stronger. It wasn't about them being reborn to atone for their past sins, everything that had happed, was for a far greater purpose. Mankind in the modern world has lost its way, has lost its empathy and tolerance of others, different from themselves; greed and power, fuelled by fear, has become the new religion, and the forces of nature have stirred to address the problem. By restoring those from a bygone age, it was almost like resetting the clock of existence and enabling the past to educate the future. Pirates have always been ruthless and aggressive, they had to be to survive, but because they stood outside of society, they were able to see more clearly, the injustices man inflicted on its own kind. They have always fought authority, not because of what it stood for, but because it was imperfect and always favoured one group over another. Subconsciously, they rebelled against the unfairness of the structure of society, rather than the concept of authority. Now, they could be those same pirates again, but this time with a stronger sense of purpose and strength to influence the course of humanity.

The tasks that lay ahead were daunting as they didn't really know what the modern world, was really like. They have had glimpses, and they formed an opinion, but that was no substitute for a lifetime of experience in the 21$^{st}$ Century. After all that had happened, the crew now felt a sense of anticlimax, as now they were on their own. All the events of the last fifty-two hours or so, had been thrust upon them, and nothing that occurred, had been of their doing. What happened now and in the future was up to them, and just like fledglings, fleeing the nest, they were unsure as to what they should do. Jack was concerned by the idea that if they just went out into the big wide world with no clue, as to what to expect or be prepared for, that they could face huge problems for themselves. They had no knowledge of the way of things, and they could easily run-foul of the modern man. Equally, the mere fact they were pirates, would invoke prejudice and condemnation, as they would be seen as mere criminals. No pirate would have walked into the Governor's office in Nassau and confessed to being a pirate, as that would certainly lead to the dance of death at the end of a rope. Why would it be so different now? Anne agreed and casually putting her hand in her pocket, she felt the shape of the rough wooden doll, the gypsies had given her all those years ago. It reminded her of the feeling, when the travellers would come to town, they would be bringing joy and excitement. She remembered how they brightened up the area, and how they made life exciting in an otherwise drab little town. They should be like the gypsies she thought, bringing joy and light to a gloomy and miserable world. Like the gypsies, not only would they be free, but they would be a powerful influence on the lives of so many. She knew they couldn't just announce their arrival with a fanfare, like the gypsies used to do, and that they must remain in the background. Their time was from a different era, and no matter how well they would adjust; they could never hope to be exactly like the people of today. They would have a purpose to fulfil, a purpose that was best accomplished, by being out of sight. Turning to the others, she told them that they could never fit into the modern world, and so they should hide behind the wind.

'We will lurk in the shadows, ready to act when called upon. We will be a force against injustice. We will fight for the oppressed, whether that may be an individual or nation.'

She then gave the order to splice the mainsail, weigh the anchor and set sail. Turning to her small crew, she announced with authority and determination that they would no longer be known as pirates; and that from that day forth, they shall forevermore be known as " The Buccaneers".

They didn't know it then, but as their new voyage of adventure began, so did the journey that would lead them to become part of their very own legend. And so it was on that cold early autumn morning, twenty miles north of the coast of Scotland, the unusual sight of an 18th Century galleon that leapt through time into the 21st Century, set sail with a crew of Buccaneers. Once again, three-hundred years after the Golden Age of Piracy, this crew were on a quest for adventure and riches, but this time, their mission wasn't in search of Spanish gold, pearls, and silver, their mission was to search for the most valuable treasure of all…..LIFE!'